IMPERSONAL ATTRACTIONS

IMPERSONAL ATTRACTIONS

Sarah Shankman

ST. MARTIN'S PRESS • NEW YORK

Library of Congress Cataloging in Publication Data
Shankman, Sarah.
    Impersonal attractions.
    I. Title.
PS3569.H3327I5   1985   813'.54   85-10905
ISBN 0-312-40997-4

First Edition

10 9 8 7 6 5 4 3 2 1

Grateful acknowledgment is made for permission to quote from the following:

"You Never Even Call Me By My Name" by Steve Goodman © 1971 Turnpike Tom Music
Rights Assigned by CBS Catalogue Partnership
All Rights Controlled & Administered by CBS U Catalog Inc.
All Rights Reserved. International Copyright Secured. Used by Permission.

"Over the Rainbow" Words by E. Y. Harburg, Music by Harold Arlen © 1938, Renewed 1966 Metro-Goldwyn-Mayer Inc. © 1939, Renewed 1967 Leo Feist Inc.
Rights Assigned to CBS Catalogue Partnership
All Rights Controlled & Administered by CBS Feist Catalog Inc.
All Rights Reserved. International Copyright Secured. Used by Permission.

"The Man I Love" by George and Ira Gershwin © 1924 (Renewed) New World Music Corp. All Rights Reserved. Used by Permission.

For my mother and father

with thanks to Rita Sitnick and Vin Gizzi
for their loving support
and to Allen Verne
for the advice

PART
ONE

ONE

As she fumbled for it, the silver-faced clock crashed to the floor. Annie Tannenbaum groaned and squinted at the time. Six A.M. Outside the Sunset Scavenger truck was chewing garbage.

Why, God, she asked, was her neighborhood first? Why couldn't they come at sunset as their sign advertised? Couldn't the garbage be allowed to age a little? Would that be asking too much?

She pulled the dusty-rose comforter over her head, but it didn't help. Light was already creeping in around the edges of the shades, through the white lace curtains. It was going to be another one of those flawless, bright blue San Francisco days.

Give me a break, guys. Sometimes a little gloom is good for the soul. The inside of her head felt foggy. Maybe today would be the day she stopped smoking. Maybe. But not likely.

At least she didn't have to get up this second. She snuggled down deeper under the creamy-white cotton sheets, reached for a mauve and pink flowered pillow that had fallen on the floor. She liked all four of the pillows tucked around her. Like a soft, snuggly cave.

There was a small black and brown bear wedged into one of the three white bookcases lining one wall. On another shelf sat a long-limbed doll with blonde hair and a blue satin dress. Her father had won it for her when she was a very little girl by tossing baseballs at the county fair. Next to iᵗ sat a red-bound book of fairy tales and fables. But the rest of the books weren't childish—Faulkner, Fitzgerald, Elmore Leonard among the thousands of volumes. Nor was the rest of the room.

But it was unquestionably a woman's bedroom: walls of palest pink, deepening in corners, flirting with the light; a Dresden-blue four-drawered bureau; a white wicker planter filled with various ferns; a rocking chair cushioned with cerise and violet cabbage roses, beside which a twenties wrought-iron lamp gilded golden through its elaborate jet-beaded silk shade. Old things. Comfortable.

Annie stretched and yawned. Nothing pressing until lunch with Sam. Maybe she'd just lie here for a while. Think about her book. Think about what she was going to have for lunch. She could always think about lunch.

Then her next-door neighbor turned over in bed. Christ! Annie sat up, holding the comforter to her chest against the cool San Francisco morning, and scowled at the wall behind her. Nothing like Bunny Dolan to ruin her day, not to mention the night before. She really had to do something about Bunny.

Not that she hadn't tried. She had complained to Tony, the super, but all he did was laugh. Bunny was pretty funny, Annie had to admit, but less funny if you shared a wall with her four-poster bed.

The infamous, elaborately carved, mahogany bed, inherited from one of Bunny's Irish-American ancestors (among the crème de la crème of San Francisco society, as Bunny managed to say at least once in every conversation) was separated from Annie's brass headboard by a wall that was thick, but not thick enough. The four-poster was large and wobbly, like an old wooden boat in a choppy sea, and it crashed into the wall every time Bunny moved.

And when Bunny had company in bed, she moved a lot. Luckily for Annie, Bunny had gained weight and lost suitors in the past year, so there had been relative quiet from the other side of the wall.

Last night, however, the swain Bunny referred to as the Italian Stallion had galloped into town. Aptly named, Annie thought. The man's staying power should be documented in the *Guinness Book of World Records.*

They were awake. Boom! A cannon shot would have been more discreet. Annie heard Bunny's murmur, then a sharp giggle, followed by the sound of the Stallion neighing.

Annie pulled the pink comforter over her head. It was no use. Once the concert began she was stuck with orchestra seats. It wasn't just Bunny's bed. Bunny herself could have gone on the Carson show doing animal imitations.

She was warming up now with the more frequently repeated bass line—a grunting that punctuated each breath.

Annie flopped over on her stomach, smashed her pillow over her head, and screamed into her mattress. It didn't help. Anything she could do, they could do louder.

At least this one was quick. Small favor, thank you, God. The Stallion sprinted to a finish. His neighs of pleasure, counterpointed with Bunny's shrieks, filled out the final chorus. It was a song one had to hear to believe. And lots of Bunny's neighbors were believers.

Including Jorge, the Colombian shipping clerk/drug dealer who lived on Bunny's other side. Once Bunny had had the gall to complain about the volume of Jorge's stereo.

"Hey, lady, you got some nerve!" he'd yelled. "I hear you, lady, I hear you fucking all night long!"

5

The battle lines had been drawn then, and Bunny averted her eyes whenever they passed in the hallway, as if Jorge would mind being cut dead by one from San Francisco society.

Jorge didn't give a damn. He was street smart and he played dirty. He taped her love wails one night and lay in wait for the perfect opportunity to replay them. It presented itself a few days later in the crowded elevator.

First there was stunned silence and embarrassed staring at the floor indicator. Then the tittering began, and in moments the elevator rocked with laughter. Bunny was reduced to tears.

This particular sunny morning Annie felt close to tears herself. Was a little jealousy nibbling at her soul?

Come on, Annie. Buck up, girl, she told herself. Give old Bunny a break. And give yourself a break too. But you'll just have to wait your turn. Right now, get out of this bed and face the day.

Annie hauled her long body toward the blue and white kitchen. Her stomach felt better already. She stood, naked, in front of the open fridge and stared at the possibilities.

Croissant. Blackberry preserves. Good strong coffee.

The day was looking sweeter already.

Besides, she was having lunch with Sam.

TWO

While Annie showered in her white-tiled bathroom in Pacific Heights, some thirty blocks south, on the other side of town, a young, curly-haired woman named Sondra Weinberg handed a man a dollar tip. He thanked her with a Buck knife in her chest.

"Oh God!" she gasped, staring down at the crimson stain that was her blood blossoming out across her white silk blouse. Red, like the paper poppies veterans handed out at shopping centers, blooming on her ample breast.

The dollar bill fluttered to her Oriental carpet and lay untouched as Sondra grasped at the pain with both hands.

The black-handled knife sat glowering, burning. Part of her mind detached and watched as the grinning man slowly pulled out the knife. His grin was wet. Spittle flashed obscenely. His tongue flicked at it. He pulled the knife slowly, sensually, as if he were detaching himself from her after a particularly lewd sex act.

A torrent of blood followed.

The pain will stop any minute, she thought. It's over now.

Of course it wasn't. The blond-haired man with the knife in his hand had just begun.

Before he was finished, Sondra's round belly, pillowy breasts, and soft thighs would be gulping with little mouths of blood. Crimson would stain his hands and lips and penis. And when she was quite still and quite dead he would dip one finger into the deep scarlet pool where her heart was beating just minutes before, before he cut it out, and draw four arms bent at right angles—the symbol for genocide—in the middle of her forehead.

Afterward he washed himself carefully in her silent, sunny bathroom and dried himself on her yellow towels. Then he trimmed the bottom of each stem of the twelve white roses he had brought her, trimmed them with his black-handled Buck knife and carefully placed them in a tall blue vase filled with cold water. They would live a long time.

Then he left, closing Sondra's door firmly behind him, checking to make sure it was safely latched.

THREE

Pacific Heights is one of San Francisco's oldest, most elegant neighborhoods. The great fire of 1906 stopped at the broad avenue called Van Ness, sparing the marble-stepped mansions and the colorfully painted gingerbread row houses. Annie's six-story apartment building, with the generous proportions of the late twenties, was creamy stucco with rococo cornices. Almost identical buildings were scattered throughout the neighborhood. Perched at the corner of Pierce and California, it was located on the last block going south that could still honestly claim the tony Pacific Heights name. Then there was a quick decline into the Western Addition, where poverty festered among gaping holes the city had torn out of the ghetto, meaning to reclaim them, someday.

Annie left her building and walked uphill northward, toward the neighborhood's prosperous heart. She passed the yellow Victorian that housed an exercise studio for the ladies who lunched. As classtime approached, the street's narrow parking spaces would fill with Mercedeses and BMWs. Passersby could watch the wealthy and trendy, waving their thin arms, clad in the very latest geranium, teal, and silver velour exercise gear.

Annie had tried the studio. After all, it was just across the street. But she found the distance much longer. It was like stepping into the society column of the morning paper, and frankly, she didn't care for it. She'd found her own class down at the Marina, filled with women who worked for their lunches—and their breakfasts and their dinners, as she did.

She was going to be late for this lunch with Sam if she didn't hurry. She could have taken her car, an old yellow Volkswagen convertible named Agatha, but parking in the city was such an ordeal that it was quicker to walk the fifteen or so blocks. Up the hill she climbed, skirting the edge of Alta Plaza Park, bracing her knees for the torturously steep downhill slope, passing one gorgeous house after another until she reached the flatlands and the glitzy, boutiqued commercial strip of Union Street.

Samantha was waiting for Annie at The Deli, sipping bottled water and holding down the best table in the restaurant. The best table, the whitest teeth, the shiniest black curls—all seemed to be Samantha Storey's birthright, along with her grandfather's money. She was the kind of woman

9

who entered a room and made you want to go home, lose five pounds, redo your hair, and get dressed all over again. You also might want to kill her, until, like Annie, you discovered that behind the *Vogue* cover was the best friend you could ever have.

Annie and Sam had met through a personal ad in the *Bay Guardian*. Annie had been "browsing," she said, when she found an ad by a gay man looking for a lover who sounded just right for her friend Hoyt. Hoyt answered and found his true love, Emmett—whose old high-school chum was Samantha.

As Hoyt and Emmett were becoming lovers, Annie and Sam became the best of friends. For the past three years they had seen each other at least once a week and talked on the phone almost daily.

Sam's sisters were in Southern California. Annie was an only child. They listened to one another through the little things ("Do you think I should shorten my gray skirt?") and the big ("I think I have a lump in my left breast"). They were family.

"Would you look at this place?" Sam waved her beautifully manicured hand.

Annie looked. The restaurant was done in standard California: redwood, ferns, a sliding greenhouse roof, a carved, Art Nouveau bar.

"So?"

"Couldn't you go blind from the glitter of gold chains?" Sam nodded in the direction of the stag line at the bar.

"I thought you meant interior decoration. I didn't know we were window shopping. Aren't we eating?" Annie reached for the menu.

"Since when can't we do both at the same time?"

"Since there's never anything here to choose from. Unless you've developed a sudden yen for coke dealers or twelve-year-olds." Annie looked past the gold chains to a handsome, very young man sipping a beer at the end of the bar. "I'd rather choose from the menu." She glanced down at it then closed it decisively. "I'll have the cheese blintzes. You have the pastrami. We'll share."

"Why, Annie Tannenbaum! Dairy and meat!" Sam clucked.

"God, what would I do without you, the guardian of my Jewish soul? My mother thanks you, my grandmother thanks you, my Aunt Essie thanks you."

It was an old joke. Samantha, with her dark curls, tawny complexion, and high cheekbones looked Sephardic—with a great nose job. She was as WASP as a Cabot. But in her soul sang the songs of the shtetl. She had always wanted to be Jewish and often talked about converting, which always made fair-haired, green-eyed Annie laugh.

"You want my guilt? My mother's chicken soup? I'll trade you even-steven for your grandfather."

Sam's mother's father. The wily one who had come to California without a dime in his jeans and had parlayed the sale of pickups to Okies into the largest truck dealership in the state. Who had invested his profits in thousands of acres of the San Fernando Valley before anybody else could see which way the wind was blowing. By the time others figured it out, several pretty millions were permanently ensconced in Sam's trust fund.

"No thanks. Why don't I just buy lunch instead?" Sam caught the waitress's eye and they ordered, including another Calistoga water for Sam.

Sam drank only coffee and water. On-again, off-again, a part-time Southern California rebel, part-time debutante, she had leap-frogged her way through Beverly Hills High, several medicine cabinets of recreational drugs, a society wedding to a stockbroker, with Alfred Hitchcock among

11

the guests, a divorce, Stanford Law School, a hard-driving junior partnership, and full-blown alcoholism by the time she was twenty-four. With the help of a good shrink and AA, she had left law, found herself, and had not touched liquor for the past twelve years.

Annie picked up the thread of their conversation. "What if you did meet somebody in a place like this? How could you ever tell anyone that you met in a singles bar?"

"This isn't a singles bar. This is a restaurant," Sam replied.

"It's a fine line, a very fine line," Annie muttered around a mouthful of blintze. "But I did talk with a woman the other day who met her husband next door."

Next door was Perry's, the original and most famous of the fern bars along Union Street, where beautiful bodies were a dime a dozen and the fine line among restaurants, boutiques, and pick-up bars was hazy. A nearby intersection with watering holes on three of its corners was so infamous for hearts and bodies colliding amid the tinkle of ice and crystal that it was nicknamed the "Bermuda Triangle."

Annie continued, "This woman had stopped in Perry's one night for a quick drink with a girl friend from out of town who wanted to see the six-deep ultimate singles bar. When this long, tall Texan walked in complete with ten-gallon hat and boots, she turned to her friend and laughed, 'Now there's the man I've been waiting for all my life.' Turned out he was. Also turned out he was an oil millionaire."

Sam groaned.

"I know. It's not fair, is it? Well, it's not fair to me. After all, Sam, you don't need a millionaire."

Complaining about the paucity of good men in their lives was a frequent theme of their conversations.

12

"Want to hear another one that'll make you sick?"

"Shoot."

"Okay, this one's a friend of a friend of a friend."

"Just tell it."

"Who's the writer here?"

"You're the writer, I'm the reporter. Who, what, where, when, why?"

Annie ignored her and went ahead in her own style. "Anyway, this Frenchwoman answered her phone in Paris. Wrong number. But a charming man. They started talking. One thing led to another and now they're married. He's Greek, a shipping tycoon, no less. In addition to lovely, sweet, handsome, gentle—"

Sam interrupted. "This could drive me back to booze."

"Wait. I have another one."

"One more and that's it."

"Okay. My friend Jane—you remember Jane—anyway, she has a friend, Estelle, who's lived over by Grace Cathedral for ten years. Knew practically no one in her building. Anyway, she got a home computer. One day there was a notice in the elevator. Seemed as though someone else in the building was getting her computer stuff on his TV screen."

"Just a minute," Sam protested.

"I don't understand the complexities of computers. This is a true story. You want to hear the end of it?"

"I think I know it."

"Of course you do. Estelle responded to the note in the elevator with an apology and an offer to meet with whoever it was to talk about the problem. Turned out to be the man who'd lived directly above her for five years, whom she'd never met. They worked out the crossed signals, and now they're a two-computer family."

"Is there a moral to these stories?"

"Sure. You want to meet a nice man? Hang out in Perry's, talk to wrong numbers, get a computer. What do I know? Am I married? Am I an expert?"

"No, but as they say, sweetheart, you're writing the book."

Annie laughed. She was indeed. It was called *Meeting Cute*. The book was a collection of anecdotes about how people met. It began as notes in her journal—her own adventures and tales people told her. As the notes grew, the idea for the book began to take shape.

Millie, the New York literary agent who had sold her collection of restaurant reviews, thought it was a great idea. Singles were a hot market, Millie thought. Tell me about it, said Annie.

She'd been single again for six years since her divorce from Bert. And though she hadn't run across Prince Charming, she'd sure met her share of frogs.

For example, the tall, Christlike young man playing Frisbee in Golden Gate Park. He'd asked her to hold his shopping bag, then treated her to garlic pizza. On their second date she'd held the same shopping bag while he played karate with strong, young Japanese men in white jackets belted in bright colors. On their third date she learned that the bag held five thousand Quaaludes.

But whether the meetings took or not, the possibilities of who might be around that next corner continued to fascinate her.

One of the things about being married was that when the phone rang she knew it was never going to be someone she had just met in a grocery checkout line asking her to a ball.

Which was always a possibility now. Especially with the Marina Safeway so close at hand.

The Safeway was just across the street from the Marina Green, where the city's most beautiful bodies ran against

14

the backdrop of Alcatraz, the Golden Gate, the hills of Marin County. Scenery and cruising just didn't get much better than that.

After running off a pound or two the pretty people in Adidas and running shorts would jam the Safeway. Cheeks flushed, bathed in a light glow of perspiration, they would cool down while wheeling their baskets around, picking up an artichoke here, a yogurt there, and, with any luck, another trim body to take home. Who knew how many of San Francisco's healthiest couples had met over a half gallon of chocolate chip wearing little more than their underwear?

It was as good a way as any. Better than some.

A woman she knew named Trudy swore by puppies. "It's simple," Trudy had said. "Who can resist a darling puppy? I just get one and walk it at six o'clock when everyone's coming home from work. You'd be amazed how many men I've met when they stopped to pet a cute little cocker."

Annie had never wanted to know what she did with the puppies when they got too big to help her meet cute.

"Meeting cute" was movie talk for the serendipitous coming together of couples like Tracy and Hepburn, Stewart and Kelly. A dropped glove, a mistaken room assignment—it was a phrase Annie had always liked, and so it became her title.

When dessert was suggested Sam and Annie both protested. The waitress just patted her rubber soled foot. She'd heard this a thousand times before. They looked like chocolate cheesecake to her.

She was right.

"Two forks," Annie said.

"You're going to have to take your fanny to exercise five times a week if you keep this up," said Sam, who never put an ounce on her curvy but slender 5′ 7″ frame. Not that

15

Annie was ever anything but thin. But to her mind, the whole point of exercise was cheesecake without guilt.

"Can't go any more often," said Annie, adding saccharin to her coffee. She was addicted to the stuff in the pink envelopes. "Three workouts a week is the limit. No time. My classes started again last week, remember?"

"Right. How're they going?"

"Okay." She shrugged. "It's too early to tell. But I hope I have some live wires. I want to use them as guinea pigs."

"What do you mean?" Sam asked through a mouthful of dessert.

"Not exactly guinea pigs. 'Contributors' would be more like it. More stories for the book. Their first writing assignment is a piece on the most interesting way they ever met anyone. Better than 'How I Spent My Summer Vacation,' don't you think?"

A couple of years earlier Annie had escaped from full-time teaching for almost full-time at her typewriter. A regular food and restaurant column in a city magazine plus free-lance assignments had brought in enough cash to keep her in a state of ecstatic poverty, delighted to be doing what she'd always wanted. She didn't mind supplementing her income with a couple of evening classes in creative writing. San Francisco State was a far cry from a high-school English classroom, and it was nice to keep her hand in.

Sam's writing was of a different sort. In the process of saving her life from the bottle she'd discovered that she'd gone to law school only to impress her father, the attorney. The things she really liked about law were the writing of briefs and murder. She was a real bloodhound when it came to gore.

So she put it all together and became Samantha Storey, Girl Reporter, Cops and Courts Beat, *San Francisco Chronicle*. It didn't hurt that one of her uncles owned a big chunk of the paper.

Not that Sam didn't earn both her stripes and her keep. She could live for weeks on coffee and adrenaline when a story was hot. And there had been a lot of opportunity for a reporter with a specialty in murder during the past few years in the Bay Area.

For a while, Santa Cruz County, fifty miles south of the city, had been dubbed the "U.S. Murder Capital." Three separate maniacs, John Linely Frazier, Herbert Mullin, and Edmund Kemper had been killing people wholesale. They were all behind bars, and the Santa Cruz Mountains were open to hikers and picnickers once again.

But now Mt. Diablo wasn't. In the past year three women hikers had been brutally murdered on its sunny slopes in the country just east of Oakland. Having proved her mettle as a cub in Santa Cruz, Sam was the *Chronicle*'s principal reporter on the story.

Annie shared Sam's fascination for murder, but she preferred hers in bed—on the pages of Agatha Christie, Raymond Chandler, Elmore Leonard. She loved to be terrified, but at home, where she could tuck herself under the covers with her book and a flashlight as she'd loved to do since childhood.

"What do you think a person has to do to get another cup of coffee in this place? Scream 'fire'?"

"Try 'murder,'" said Sam.

"Hey, that's not funny."

"I know. Sorry. I'm just preoccupied with this Diablo case. It's beginning to get to me."

"Anything you want to tell me about?" Annie hunkered forward in anticipation.

"I'm not supposed to, you know."

"I know. So tell me."

"Cross your heart."

"Cross my heart. Spill."

"Off the re—"

"I won't tell a soul, I promise. Anyway, you're a reporter. Aren't you supposed to be filling us all in? Or have I missed something here?"

"What you've missed is that sometimes we learn things that we're asked to sit on. Now, do you want to hear this or not?"

Annie nodded yes, her lips tightly sealed.

"The police found a pair of glasses on the trail where the last woman was shot. What's great is that they're an unusual prescription—should be traceable. Bulletins have gone out to all the optometrists and ophthalmologists in the area. It should be just a matter of time now. If they're not the killer's, at least maybe there's a witness."

Annie was pensive. She stirred her coffee quietly for a few minutes.

"Sam, what's with these guys? These psychopaths?"

"You mean why do they do it?" Sam pushed her black curls off her forehead. "I guess I'm supposed to be the expert." She sighed. "God knows I've met enough of them."

"Is it sex? Do they get off on it?"

"That's part of it. There's something pent up that seems to be released in the act of murder. But I don't think it's ever quite that simple. They're always complicated, lonely, screwed up. We could just say they're crazy, sociopaths, but what does that mean? Most of us are crazy, but we don't go around killing people.

"Revenge, a distorted revenge plays a role too. He blames everything that's wrong with his life on girls with long, dark hair because a girl like that turned him down when he was twelve. Or on women who look like his mother. Or blacks, people who whisper, whatever."

"I guess it doesn't matter what the motive is," said Annie, "except that the pattern helps to catch him."

"Sure. And meanwhile there are an awful lot of nervous

people out there who are afraid to go for a walk in their own neighborhoods, not to mention on Mt. Diablo."

"I wouldn't." Annie shivered. "Not even if Prince Charming were waiting for me at the top."

"Where *do* you think he's going to be waiting for you, in the ads?"

Sam's smirk made Annie want to reach over and pop her one, best friend or no.

"I think you're very cute, Sam, and if you don't stop giving me such a hard time, I'm never going to write those two ads."

"No, really, I think they're a great idea. You place a research query ad asking to talk with others who have already placed ads and then another ad as a personal of your own—and who knows what you'll get."

"Samantha, I've told you a hundred times, I'm just doing this for the book. Otherwise, I would never place an ad."

Sam stared at her guilelessly.

"Okay, okay," Annie said, "so I've answered a few thousand. But I've never placed one."

"And you never will, either, if you don't get it written. Or did you say you've done that?"

A quick look at Annie's face answered her question.

"Well, we'll do it later on the phone." She waved her credit card at the waitress. "I've got to get back to the office. You never can tell when a new loony may hit the streets with a story just for me."

"God, are you a ghoul. Don't worry, there'll always be someone waiting for you."

"Not so, my dear, not so. Sometimes you have to go out looking for a good murder, just like a good man."

Annie waved her away, dismissing Sam's last words as their very own brand of smart mouth.

But, on down the road, she would remember them.

FOUR

The bar where the blond man smiled at his reflection in the fly-specked mirror was on Folsom Street, in the gritty South-of-Market area. The streets were lined with big semis, tractor-trailer trucks bearing license plates from all over the country. Vagrants slept in bottle-littered empty lots, pulling blankets of old cardboard over them. Some of the bars attracted that segment of the gay world drawn to a little rough and tumble, the clink of chains, the smell of oiled black leather. But most of them were 6 A.M. to 2 A.M. joints, peopled with lonely men and women for whom the distinctions of desire had long been blurred by the bottle.

The blond man knocked back a shot of bar bourbon. He took a long pull on his beer chaser, set it down on the slightly sticky bar, and held his hands straight out in front of him. No shake, no tremble. He was relaxed.

Earlier he'd been nervous. It had been such a long time.

Looking in the mirror again, he flexed his biceps. He liked to watch his muscles move beneath his black T-shirt.

It was a fresh shirt. He'd been home to shower and change. He'd had to.

How surprised she'd looked when she realized that his present wasn't what she'd thought. He'd had something to give her, all right.

She'd smiled at first, right after she'd opened the door. So excited. They always were. Talked about how pretty the flowers were. How sweet they smelled.

The roses did smell good, but not good enough to cover up her smell.

He took a deep breath. Old whiskey, cigarette smoke, stale beer. Smells he was comfortable with.

She was so stupid to have let him in.

"Dumb bitch," he muttered to himself.

"I know what you mean, pal," said the man drinking next to him. "They're all alike."

The blond man wasn't looking for company or conversation. He liked to savor the time afterward, to roll it around in his mouth like the taste of a good steak.

"Women!" The man next to him spat on the already filthy floor. "They've ruined a lot more men than this." He gestured toward his half-empty glass of beer. "One of them break your heart, mister?"

"No," the blond man answered curtly as he stood up. He drained his beer and laughed. It wasn't a nice sound.

"That's good," he said. "Nope, not my heart. Her heart, that's more like it." He flipped onto the bar the dollar tip he'd picked off a red and blue carpet an hour earlier and walked out. On the street, he squinted into the bright afternoon.

FIVE

Leaving The Deli, Annie strolled west on Union Street, enjoying the shops and the warm afternoon. September was the time to enjoy San Francisco, during the Indian summer the poor August tourists had just missed.

She always felt so sorry for them, enshrouded in the bone-chilling, blowing fog that mischievously hid the Golden Gate Bridge from them day after gray day. Annie thought travel agents had a moral obligation to mother summer tourists into bringing plenty of warm clothing. Or to warn them to hold off their visits until September or October, when the fog went back out to sea and the crystalline blue days rivaled the postcards they all sent back home. Then the view from a thousand different spots could stop the heart of even a native.

But maybe this was better. The tourists were gone and San Franciscans could enjoy their city at its best, at the beginning of fall.

The beginning of the year would always be in September for Annie. She had been conditioned by so many sharpenings of pencils for school's opening both as a schoolgirl and, later, a schoolmarm. Nature seemed to be of the same mind here in California. The fall brought warmth and sunshine, and then the rains that would turn the hills from sere brown to luscious green.

Annie strolled and stretched, catlike, in the afternoon sun. It was so nice to be dressed in only a T-shirt and jeans—one of the rare days when she didn't need a sweater.

When she'd first arrived from Atlanta, her hometown, she hadn't believed the advice of her friends: always, and especially in summer, take a jacket. Now the wrap was a given, as was the phenomenon of San Francisco air conditioning—a confluence of ocean, bay, and inland heat that produced the city's clean, cool breath.

She reached the corner of Fillmore and turned to begin the steep climb up Fillmore Hill to her apartment over the crest of Pacific Heights. A young couple, out of control with downward momentum, almost crashed into her.

"Sorry, sorry," they apologized breathlessly. She watched their backs as they crossed the street. Clad in twin yellow sweat shirts and jeans, they were a couple out of a soft-drink commercial. Laughing, secure in their world. Annie felt a twinge of envy.

She knew that feeling. Us against the world. She'd had it before. And she'd have it again.

In the meantime, she had David.

David, her once-a-week lover. Like refined sugar, he was good for a quick surge, but always left her hungry for something substantial, something more. But as Samantha said, at least men like David kept women from gobbling up handsome young boys on the street.

Like the one who was smiling down the hill toward her. Blond, blue-eyed. The quintessential California kid. She was old enough to be his mother, if, of course, she'd been a child bride. She tried to control her puffing. She hoped she wasn't as noisy as her Volkswagen, Agatha, as she ground up the hill. San Francisco was not a city kind to old cars and old ladies with crunchy noises in their knees.

Shut up, she said to herself. You're beginning to sound like your mother, old before her time. At thirty-seven, you're not ready for the home yet, or worse, the endlessly boring flatlands of the South.

She picked up the pace and lengthened her stride, taking the steps up the hill two at a time. It was indeed a lovely day, a great day to be alive.

A *lucky* day to be alive. She could never walk up this hill without remembering what had once happened here to Sam, who almost hadn't been lucky or alive.

Sam, like Annie, tromped through cities whenever and however she pleased. With a sane person's healthy respect for dark, lonely streets, alleyways, and neighborhoods that everyone knew meant trouble, she was independent but not foolhardy.

One night, a year ago, having finally found a parking place in the neighborhood, a feat akin to winning the Bay to Breakers Race, Sam decided to pop in on Annie. She'd been with some friends six blocks away, a small party that had broken up at about nine.

Trudging up the Fillmore steps, thinking about a shopping trip she was planning to New York, mortality was hardly on her mind. Until a man jumped out of a dark driveway and grabbed her.

Time stopped. She'd seen plenty of self-defense maneuvers while hanging around with cops and had idly asked herself, *what if?* This was *if*.

In torturous slow motion, Sam learned what stuff she was made of.

With one long, reflexive move, she had stomped on his instep, smashed his nose with the side of a hand, and screamed at the top of her lungs. He let her go and she ran like hell. She didn't know if he was behind her or not. She just ran until she found a liquor store, where she'd caught her breath and stopped shaking long enough to call the police. Their response was quick, but they found nothing. Her attacker was long gone.

He'd been tall. He'd been black. He'd smelled of stale booze. And he ought to have a sore nose and a limp. That was all Sam could tell them.

Later, when she finally did arrive at Annie's, too rattled to go home though it was late, she was furious.

"Joe Kelly was one of the guys who answered the call. 'Sam,' he said, 'you know better than to be out on the streets of this city alone.' How the hell does he think I get around? With an armed guard, a Doberman?"

"He probably means you should be on the arm of a man."

"And he's right," Sam snorted, "for more reasons than one, but until that guy shows up, what do we all do? Double bolt our doors and stay inside?"

It was infuriating to live defensively. To concentrate on carefully locked doors, to be wary of where one walked, when, and with whom. They agreed that it meant that they'd given up, given up the night to the robbers and the rapists. They'd allowed the bad guys to circumscribe their world with fear.

"Not me," said Sam, "no way. Let them catch me if they can."

But bravado aside, for both of them the memory of that night was a bad taste that never quite went away.

At home, the red light on Annie's answering machine flashed four times.

David: "Hi, let's get together for a little R & R." His voice was low and insinuating.

Her mother in Atlanta: "Hello, darling. Just checking to

25

see if you're all right. We haven't heard from you in a while."

Sam: "I'm at the office. Nothing much happening here. Give me a call and we'll write that ad."

And a fourth from ten-year-old Quynh Nguyen.

"Hello, Auntie Annie. This is Quynh. I hope you're fine. Hudson and I are looking forward to seeing you. Give us a call soon."

Annie smiled at a photograph of the two of them in a silver frame on the bookcase. Quynh's beautiful, delicate-featured, Vietnamese face. She was very serious in the photograph—staring somberly into the camera. Hudson, on the other hand, wrapped around Quynh's neck, was wearing a Cheshire grin.

Hudson was the Abyssinian cat Annie had given Quynh as a kitten a year ago. If true to his breed, he would have grown cougarlike, but as elegant and delicate as Quynh. Instead, he was more like a linebacker. Annie kept threatening to buy him a baby 49ers jersey.

Quynh always ignored her jokes about Hudson. He was her blanket, her mantle. He was her family, lost in that once beautiful, napalmed country so far away. He was her heart.

Together they were the classiest twosome Annie knew. She couldn't wait to see them.

SIX

The narrow street, lined with small, brightly painted Victorians, ran downhill from the heights of Dolores Street to the Mission, the Chicano ghetto. It was a place in transition—gentrified row houses with restored beveled glass, tin ceilings, and lace parlor curtains slugging it out with the fried chicken stand on the corner.

This was a neighborhood of small, neat front lawns, wrought-iron fences, and pink and yellow rose bushes. It was difficult for the blond man, shivering in the darkness, lighting one cigarette after another, to find a place to hide. A large apartment house up on the corner of Guerrero provided him with a doorway. He could watch from here.

He shifted impatiently from one foot to the other. It was cold out here. Was she going to show or not?

He'd followed Cindy Dunbar from her office four days in a row. She'd stopped to run errands, pick up cleaning, and grocery shop, but was home most nights by six. When she went out again it was usually around seven or seven-thirty. Twice he'd seen her with the same man.

Someone turned the corner and walked toward her house. He had to wait, didn't want to attract attention, let her see him. That wasn't the click of her high heels.

Damn! It was that loony nigger he'd seen the night before, her nappy hair full of lint and grass from laying out in

Dolores Park, reeking of booze and piss, layers of rags, pink house slippers. Hard to tell how old she was, but her hair wasn't gray. Sucking up air, sucking up space. Shuffling around and around the city. Going nowhere. Talking to herself.

Across the street, a tall black man in his mid-thirties walked briskly to the gate of Cindy Dunbar's small house. He was dressed in a navy blazer, gray slacks, and a tan raincoat. A big man, he moved with the awkward roll of an ex-football player, proud but past his prime. In his hand he carried a cornucopia of green tissue paper.

The blond man started. Ah—there he was. He stepped on his cigarette and rubbed his hands together. Miss Dunbar's boyfriend. Carrying flowers. How sweet, he laughed. It wouldn't be long now.

He was right. Within moments Cindy and the man in the raincoat appeared, locking the front door, leaving.

He couldn't hear what they were saying. Their laughter floated in the air. Her voice was low for a woman, the man's even lower, rumbling like the low tones on an organ.

She was a tall, broad-shouldered, light-complexioned black woman. Her short, reddish, natural hair was carefully dressed. She had changed for the evening into an ivory flannel shirt with a narrow gray stripe, soft gray wool slacks, and darker gray flat-heeled shoes. A bright gold, short wool coat was tossed across her shoulders. In the streetlight, the coat echoed her tawny complexion and the flecks of gold in her green eyes.

Following half a block behind, the blond man watched Cindy Dunbar's back. Even through her coat, he could see her body move. Who did she think she was trying to fool? She couldn't hide that high Hottentot butt. Like they used to laugh about back home. Old fat nigger women walking. From behind they looked like two children fighting under a sheet. No matter about that fancy job in that fancy office in that fancy big building downtown. Strip all that and peel those pretty clothes off, underneath was a nigger. Putting on airs.

He realized that while he'd been daydreaming, they'd turned a corner and were gone. He raced to the intersection and frantically looked up and down the street. There were too many people here on Mission Street. They'd disappeared.

Shit! Why did they want to come over here anyway? Goddamned Mission. Nothing but spics. Spics made him nervous. Gangs of kids walking around with switchblades in their pockets.

Then he spotted Dunbar and her boyfriend entering a restaurant across the street. A red, yellow, and turquoise crepe paper donkey dangled in the window. As the door opened, he could hear the sound of mariachi music.

Made him want to puke, the thought of Mexican food. He'd forced down so many beans in Texas jails, years of beans and yellow rice, chilis, tomato sauce. It was eat it or go hungry. He'd sworn he'd never touch any of that slop again.

But what did spades know about food? It didn't matter. Let them eat crap. At least he knew where they'd be for the next hour. He could relax and wait.

He lit another Picayune cigarette, inhaling deeply the peculiar-smelling fumes. Picayunes were made in New Orleans and were hard to find elsewhere. Their funky smell was organic, like marsh mud, the Mississippi, the French Market, overripe fruit on a steamy afternoon.

Sometimes when he lit up, people thought he was smoking dope. That was stupid. But it was nice to be noticed. To be different and have people pay attention.

Like Missy Cartwright. He could see her, like it was yesterday, in that sweater, that short white skirt. Missy coming toward him in the moonlight. He could almost reach out and touch her.

But not tonight. That was years ago. That sweetness of Missy. And that pain.

He blinked rapidly, shook his head.

Why was he thinking of her tonight?

The memory edged back a bit. It was like a drug. So easy to give in to. He could feel himself drifting.

He stamped his feet. It was cold. It had been cold that night, too, so long ago, so far away, when he had brought Missy the roses.

"Hey, man, you got a light?"

His eyes made the leap back across miles and years from Missy to focus on the young Chicano smiling in front of him.

His body tightened. The muscles flexed involuntarily.

"No!" he barked. "No light."

"Come on, man. You smoking, you got a light."

The punk's voice was whiny, singsong Spanish. Look at him. What kind of man would dress like that? Shiny, pointed-toe black shoes, baggy black pants, white starched shirt outside his belt, red bandanna around his forehead. And, over his greasy black hair, a hairnet. They all looked like that—whiny beaner punks.

"What's the matter, man? You too good to give me a light?"

"Naw, sorry, here you go." He reached toward his back pocket as the young Chicano leaned forward with his cigarette in his mouth to receive the light.

The blond man wanted to grab the knife his pocket held. It burned there in his hand, as if it longed to be used. His hand twitched as he ran it across the smooth handle. It would only take a second.

But that was stupid. He had to be more careful than that. Don't blow it for yourself again, man. He pulled out his nickel-plated Zippo instead.

"Thanks, man." The young Chicano looked more closely into the Anglo's eyes and quickly walked away. He knew locos when he saw them, and he didn't need to be messing with that kind of trouble tonight.

Across the street, Cindy Dunbar and her boyfriend left the restaurant arm in arm. He held her tight. Goosed her. She yelped, both pleased and embarrassed. They stopped for a kiss. By the time they reached the next corner the blond man was twenty feet behind them.

It was close to nine o'clock as the threesome strolled up Mission, one tagging carefully behind.

The barrio, the Mission, its main drag a wide avenue bordered by towering old palms, was filled with music and mothers with bands of crying small children at all hours. South of downtown, separated from the business center of the city by lines of railroad tracks, it had its own businesses, sometimes tended secretly, but tended well. Here, behind curtained doors and beneath cellar entrances, were sweatshops, where needlework was stitched, clothes were assembled—and drugs were broken down into smaller and smaller packages late into the night.

There were also hardworking families in the three-and four-story buildings that housed thousands in warrenlike apartments. Churchgoing, respectable, they had too many children in too few rooms to ever really be comfortable.

But it was better here than where they had come from. Many of the residents of the Mission were illegal aliens working without green cards for whatever they could earn to support their families here and to send back home to Mexico, Chile, El Salvador, Nicaragua. Here there was al-

31

ways work, if a person was willing to do it, with shelter and plenty to eat. Here there was a chance.

And there was life and laughter in the streets, the young mustachioed Spanish men in their uniform black and white showing off their cars to one another and to the scores of young girls who gathered on street corners, the girls taking great care with their dead-white eye shadow, purple lipstick, and layer upon layer of thick black mascara.

A fleet of gaudy, chrome-covered cars popped and revved at the corner of Twenty-fourth and Mission as Cindy Dunbar and her boyfriend waited for the light.

The man following them let them cross ahead. He didn't want to crowd them.

He thought they were going back home, but a few doors up Twenty-fourth they turned into a coffeehouse.

He walked past, stopped, debated. It had been almost a week now that he'd been on her tail. Had she spotted him?

Screw it. He was cold. He'd been standing on the street a long time. A cup of coffee would taste good.

Once inside, he saw why they would pick the place. Full of their own kind. Blacks with long braids huddling over steaming mugs. A weird white girl with a star on her cheek snuggling up to a spic. Hippies, dykes, freaks.

He didn't see the oak tables, the French movie posters, the espresso machine, a marvel of chrome and copper tubing imported from Italy. He didn't appreciate the home-made brownies and blondies, the twenty-two kinds of coffees on the menu, the herbal teas. The overstuffed faded chintz sofa and chairs grouped as if in a living room didn't appeal to him. Nor did the camaraderie of the painters, sculptors, and dancers who lived in lofts on the fringes of the neighborhood in former industrial buildings and had designated this as their meeting place.

As he looked for a spot to sit, as far away from Dunbar

and her boyfriend as he could find, someone brushed his arm. Coffee slopped onto his jeans.

"Hey, man, I'm sorry. Here." A tall, young Chinese man with hair cropped half an inch long was offering him a couple of paper napkins. A spiral of red dye crawled around his short hair. Purple sunglasses shaded his eyes. In his left earlobe was a parade of ten rhinestone studs.

"Fuck you!" the blond man growled.

"Well, pardon me," the punker minced. "Creep," he added under his breath, and then he turned and ran to the back of the café.

The blond man rose to follow him, then sat back down.

This wasn't the time. He didn't want to attract attention now.

But he hated to let the freak get in his face like that. Nobody got away with that shit.

He gulped down what was left of his coffee. He had to get out of this place. It was getting on his nerves. Niggers, spics, Jews, gimps. Scum. The world was lousy with them.

But some of them weren't going to live too long.

He pushed up the sleeve of his black leather jacket and stared at the characters tattooed in blue on his forearm. They always calmed him down.

Then he stood, without even looking at Dunbar and her friend.

He didn't need to wait around any longer. He didn't need to walk them home.

He knew where she lived.

SEVEN

Annie returned Sam's call. It was now or never. The *Bay Guardian*'s deadline was tomorrow. She'd written the first ad, the query for volunteers to talk about their experiences with the personals. But now it was time for the second, her own looking-for-Mr.-Right personal.

"Okay," she could almost hear Samantha's pencil poised over the phone. "What *are* you looking for?"

"I'm telling you, I'm not really looking for anyone."

"God!" Sam was exasperated. They'd been over this before. "We know it's just an exercise, okay? We know it's just research. But you've got to pretend that it's real in order to write an ad that will get some kind of reasonable response. And you might as well. It's your fifty bucks."

"Okay, okay." Annie sighed. It was so much easier *answering* ads. She'd done that lots of times. It was like window shopping. This had the potential of being real life.

She pursed her lips.

"Well, you know I'm a sucker for a pretty face, but that's not number one. Tall. Healthy. Athletic, or at least not fat. Some hair, maybe curly. Reasonably good-looking. I'd settle for interesting-looking, if he's sexy, if the magic's there."

"You're too good-looking to settle, babe. There must be something else you want."

Annie smiled at Sam's compliment and thought about

her ex-husband Bert's warning when she had walked out the door six years before.

"It's going to be tough out there," he'd said. "You're no spring chicken anymore."

He was wrong. Her looks had more than held—she'd gotten better with age. Now, at thirty-seven, Annie was tall, lean, and small-breasted, with what lovers and men friends always called a great ass. She had her Grandmother Rose's wonderful green eyes and slender, almost perfect hands. Her long, thick, dark blonde hair glinted here and there with a touch of silver. Smile lines at the corners of her eyes and the crook of her mouth had just begun. But Annie felt secure that regardless of age, despite the fact that she was not, had never been, a classically pretty woman, she was a very handsome one.

"So he doesn't have to be Robert Redford," Sam was saying. "What else?"

Annie took a deep breath. "Well educated, intelligent, traveled, urbane, mad about me, and funny. Mostly funny."

"You don't want much, do you, lady?" Sam laughed.

"Why should I be looking for somebody whose idea of a good wine is Budweiser and lusts after football and Big Macs?"

"Come on, lighten up. I'm teasing." Sam cleared her throat. "More. I'm beginning to like this. What about," she paused, "values?" Her voice grew mock serious on the last word.

They laughed together. Annie knew that Sam was thinking of Mario.

Morose Mario, they'd nicknamed him, one of Annie's ex-lovers. He was a short, intense Marxist, who took all the fun out of everything except sex by worrying about the masses. Annie used to complain to Sam. "Every time we go out to dinner we have to feel guilty. I can always sense the hot breath of three imaginary starving Indians in the backseat."

"No, I don't want another Mario," she said, laughing.

35

"Not that I could ever sleep with anyone who voted for Nixon. But you know, even if old Moroseness's politics were a pain, he was great in bed. Though I'd like a lot more affection there if I could get it. A hell of a lot more. Some continuing romance would be real nice."

"Anything else?"

"Money wouldn't hurt."

"All in one package? We've got a real problem here."

"Well, hell, you asked. Besides, it's all just make-believe."

"No, it's not," Sam countered. "It's just a challenge. Not that you don't deserve him, my dear. I just think he's going to be hell to find." She read her notes back to Annie. "It's all here. Just boil it down so it won't cost you a fortune and get it in before deadline."

Annie could hear someone calling Sam's name in the background.

"Listen, something's happening here. I've got to go." And she hung up.

Five minutes later, she called back. Her voice was strained and tight. Annie knew that voice of Sam's, the one when the news was very bad.

"There has been a really ugly murder," she was saying, "in Noe Valley. Sondra Weinberg, Judge Weinberg's niece. They just found her, but it probably happened a couple of days ago."

"How did she . . ."

Sam interrupted. "Strangled. And a knife. You really don't want to know. And you won't read all the details in the paper."

"Rape too?"

"Yep, rape and torture and disfigurement—and I've got to go down to the morgue."

"Oh, Sam." Annie didn't know how she could do it. "Could this be the Mt. Diablo killer—come to town?"

"Don't think so. A different style. Maybe a burglary, but it's rare to see this kind of brutality. When you surprise a burglar he usually runs. Or if he kills, he just does it, grabs the stuff, and gets out. Maybe it was a lover."

Annie shuddered. The things people do in the name of love.

Sam's voice got even tighter. "I have a terrible feeling about this, A. It's so sick. It terrifies me that the man who did this is out there. He's going to do more."

"You don't know that."

"No, but I feel it in my bones."

There was a long silence on the line.

Finally Sam spoke again, and some of the tension was gone. "I know we're supposed to take Quynh to the park tomorrow. I think I can still make it. But if I can't, apologize to her for me and have a good time. Okay?"

"Right. We'll wait for you at the Conservatory. If you're not there by noon, we'll assume you're not coming."

"Good," said Sam. "I hope to see you then. You have a good night. Sweet dreams."

"You too."

"And Annie," she added softly, "make sure you double lock your door."

EIGHT

Quynh Nguyen lived in Outer Richmond, or the Avenues as the neighborhood was called, with numbered north-south streets running from the western edge of Pacific

Heights to the ocean. The real-estate values dropped as the street numbers grew larger and the intensity of the fog rolling in from the Pacific grew thicker. There were many days out in the Avenues that never saw the sun while downtown basked under blue skies.

Trees were scarce here, stucco houses close together. Old Plymouths and Dodges parked in driveways blocked the sidewalks. Large families, many of them Chinese, were crowded into floor-through flats.

One of the main east-west arteries was Clement, called Little Chinatown for the ever growing number and variety of Chinese restaurants. Mandarin, Szechuan, Hunan had been old hat in this neighborhood for a decade. Now San Francisco's foodies, ever in search of new taste sensations, were trekking to Clement to dine on Shanghai Strange Flavor Eggplant, Peking-style Capital Sauce Pork Ribbons, and to shop for peony blossoms, tea melon, and water chestnut powder for their own kitchens.

Annie had written a piece for *Gourmet* on the "new" Oriental food on Clement: Japanese, Thai, Vietnamese. Quynh's Uncle Quan owned one of the avenue's small Vietnamese restaurants she had reviewed. It was called Saigon.

Quan thought of his ownership as a miracle. That was also the word he used to describe his having escaped Vietnam when the last American forces pulled out. As miraculous as the simple fact of his being alive.

Quynh's parents hadn't been so lucky. Quynh didn't know how they had died. They simply never came home again. A week after they disappeared their house did, too, its bomb-blasted pieces flying in orange and red arcs through the air. Quynh watched it go up from a neighbor's house a block away while she was eating a bowl of fish and rice.

Suddenly there was nothing. She wandered, crying, a little girl in a once pink dress until, one day, an American soldier picked her up and took her to a Catholic orphanage. It was there that her Uncle Quan found her a year later.

She had cried on the plane all the way across the Pacific. The orphanage was the only refuge she had ever known from the horror of the world outside. To her, airplanes were instruments of death, poised at any moment to spit destruction. She sat braced through the endless hours, waiting for the bombing to start.

She had been told by the Red Cross worker holding her hand that her Uncle Quan would be waiting for her in San Francisco. But what was San Francisco?

It was the gorgeous white city on the hills where her uncle had found a new home, where he took her and fed her and tucked her in bed in her very own room.

It was where the bombs never fell.

Quynh already knew some English, in addition to her Vietnamese and French. Her language skills pyramided with the help of her American schoolmates and the staff of Uncle Quan's restaurant, where he insisted on English being used.

"You must practice," he said. "This is your country now. You must learn to speak its language if you want to get ahead." The rule went for Quynh, too, whether she was simply sitting on a stool chopping vegetables, running errands, or occasionally taking orders in the dining room when Uncle Quan was shorthanded.

It was there that Annie had first seen Quynh, serious and businesslike, and had fallen in love with her.

She wasn't a child to be approached with "Aren't you a cute little waitress?" Not that that would have been Annie's style. After all, she herself had been an only child born to older parents, and had stood on a stool behind the counter of their small neighborhood grocery store when she was six, ringing up cash sales on the register and writing up charges in little account books with customers' names penciled across the top.

She and Quynh discussed the menu seriously. Annie explained that she wrote about food for magazines. Quynh said matter-of-factly that she was a writer too. A poet. Annie asked if she might see some of her work the next time she came in and they made a date for dinner the following week.

Quynh's poetry was lovely, spare and lyrical. It was wise way beyond her ten years, but then, so was she. Soon Annie was dining with Quan and Quynh three and four times a week—with a good deal more frequency than her enthusiasm for Vietnamese food warranted.

One day she asked Quan if she might take Quynh to the zoo. He hesitated a moment, and she could see him battling demons in his mind.

"Only for a couple of hours, Quan," she reassured him. "I'll bring her back by three."

They fed peanuts to the monkeys, the elephants, and themselves. Quynh somberly considered her first chili dog and pronounced it terrific. She stood entranced before the cages of lions and tigers. Annie had to tear her away from the snow leopard to get her home on time as promised. But she knew that it was a very important promise and she was nervous as a boy on his first date about the 2 P.M. deadline. She knew that each second past that would be a horror for Quynh's uncle.

At ten minutes before three, they swept through the door of Saigon to meet Quan's broad smile, matched by one on Quynh's oval face, the first Annie had ever seen.

The little girl raced into Quan's arms and jumped headlong into a recital of her adventure. Annie couldn't understand a word.

"English, English, Quynh," Quan reminded her. He tousled her long, black ponytail with a gentleness that made Annie look away.

"The monkeys were so silly," Quynh was saying. "They were like the boys in my class at school." She made a face. "And the very best were the cats, the lions." Her eyes grew large. "The cougars, the panthers, but the very very best was the snow leopard. It was absolutely . . ." she searched for the word, "absolutely *mythical.*"

Quan and Annie laughed with one another over the little girl's head, but not aloud.

"Now I must go and write a poem about the leopard," she said, scampering down from Quan's lap.

She turned toward Annie and said with a slight bow of her head, "Thank you for the monkeys and the scrumptious chili dog and the absolutely, perfectly mythical snow leopard." Then she stepped forward a little. "Could you please lean down?" Annie did and Quynh threw her thin arms around her neck. "Thank you for an absolutely, perfectly mythical day, Tante Annie," she said, and kissed her on the cheek.

Annie barely had time to hug her back before Quynh disappeared through the kitchen door to tell the staff about her day.

That had settled it. Quan and Annie shared a pot of tea and he told her Quynh's history and she told him her own—her life as an only child in Atlanta, her marriage to Bert, and her feelings about his children from his first marriage, whom she no longer saw. She talked about the thoughts she'd entertained of having a child herself or adopting one, but how both those choices had seemed so hard, especially for a woman who also wanted to write.

41

How recently she'd been thinking of calling Big Sisters to find a child to whom she could be friend, godmother, aunt.

"I think you've found her," said Quan.

"I think you're right," she answered, then she leaned across the table and kissed him on the cheek.

A few days later Quynh presented Annie with a poem about the snow leopard artfully quilled on a piece of handmade paper. With Quan's permission, Annie had given Quynh the eight-week-old male Abyssinian kitten, whom she promptly named Hudson.

"Why Hudson?"

"After Henry Hudson," Quynh answered. "He was a great explorer, like cats are. We're studying him in school."

"Why not Henry?"

Quynh gave Annie the patient deadpan and shrug all kids use when adults say something unutterably stupid.

"They didn't name it the Henry River. Or the George Monument. Or the Abraham . . ."

"Okay, okay," Annie interrupted. "I get it. Do you like him?"

"I *love* him." Quynh squeezed the kitten's small body and he scrambled straight up her front and licked her nose. Obviously the feeling was mutual.

Quynh and Hudson had been waiting on the front step of the Saigon for fifteen minutes when Annie drove up to pick her up for their picnic in Golden Gate Park.

"She works too hard," Quynh said with disappointment when Annie told her that Sam might not be able to make it. Sam was among the child's absolutely favorite people, along with her Uncle Quan, Annie, Miss Teagarden, her teacher, the poet/novelist Shel Silverstein, and Michael Jackson.

She was holding a lacquered basket in her lap along with Hudson, who was sniffing the cracks mightily.

"Ham or eggs?" Annie asked. Hudson was mad for both. Ham sent him into ecstasies of drooling.

"I'm not sure," Quynh said innocently. As if she had had nothing to do with this picnic lunch, which Quan had prepared over Annie's protestations.

"You do too much. Always," he said. "You be American guide, auntie, teacher. I be restaurateur. I make picnic."

They entered the park from the north at Park Presidio and turned onto J. F. Kennedy Drive. Quynh, who was not only a great navigator but also had the magic touch when it came to finding parking places, spotted one right across the street from the Conservatory.

They locked the picnic basket and Hudson inside the car, carefully left the windows open a crack, and trooped up the steps to the gigantic Victorian greenhouse called the Conservatory. It was one of Quynh's prized places in the park, even if it didn't allow cats.

The center of the greenhouse was a tall, peaked dome, containing jungle plants with elephantlike trunks that seemed to reach out to the sky. The air inside was thick, heavy, almost green with the warm breath of exuberantly happy vegetation. The long arm branching off to the right ended in a pool filled with lily pads and trout-sized goldfish.

"Shel would love it here. Do you think he's ever been here?" Quynh tugged at Annie. Her hero, Shel Silverstein, had written a book called *Where the Sidewalk Ends,* whose animal characters fascinated Quynh. Silverstein had become a real presence in her life.

"Let's go see what's in the special room." She pulled Annie back toward the other wing, at the end of which, just past the orchids, was always a particular show. Here were gathered hundreds of varieties of one flower, once azaleas, once cyclamen, at Christmas, poinsettias. This time it was begonias. Fleshy, bulbous, with their waxy leaves in every color and variety imaginable. Whatever flower it was, it always knocked Quynh out.

"This one," she said, standing before a magnificent pale lilac variety, "this is it." Then she wavered. "Or *this* one," pointing at a bright orange and yellow beauty. "Or maybe . . ."

"Quynh, you don't *have* to choose. You can love them all," Annie told her.

"Oh, yes, you're right!" she exclaimed. Five minutes later, when they were ready to leave, she turned and waved to the roomful of blossoms, bidding them all adieu, equally.

Sam didn't meet them inside and they gave her another ten minutes while they inspected the handiwork of the Golden Gate gardeners, who that month had planted a perfect replica of the state seal of California in a circle before the Conservatory.

"I love your work," Quynh said seriously to an old man in green overalls who was snipping at the edge of the circle.

"Why, thank you," he said, a little taken aback.

"You're welcome." She nodded.

They finally gave up on Sam and walked back to Agatha to find Hudson glaring at them impatiently through the car's front window. He didn't give a fig about greenhouses, though he had been known to munch seriously on tulips. And he was more than frustrated at being locked up with a securely fastened picnic basket.

"Hudson, get in the back seat," Quynh ordered sternly. He obeyed.

Annie had had many cats over the years and had made the acquaintance of several hundred others. She had never known one who listened. Except Hudson, to whom Quynh's word was law. Whenever Annie made a request of him, he would look at her as if she were speaking Urdu.

44

Quynh considered all the possible picnicking spots and decided on the big recreation ground. They walked down Bowling Green past the tennis courts where the soft *thuck-thuck* of balls and groans of frustration echoed day and night, all year long. After serious deliberation Quynh chose a spot in the huge open field, where they could watch a soccer practice and a softball game simultaneously. They spread a red-and-blue tablecloth and settled down. Hudson sat at attention with his front paws on the edge of the cloth, never taking his eyes from the basket.

"Just wait." Quynh waggled a cautionary finger.

She opened the basket and carefully arranged a small banquet of Vietnamese and Chinese cold dishes of rice, fish, meat, each delicacy wrapped in seaweed or encased in tea leaves. When the repast met her definition of symmetry, she took out a small red bowl and lifted its cover to reveal a hard boiled egg, coarsely chopped and garnished with slivers of fresh tuna, which she placed before Hudson.

He lunged at his lunch, ignoring Quynh's reproving glare.

She passed chopsticks and vinegared dipping sauce to Annie, who laughed. "You didn't expect him to wait until we started, did you?"

Annie could tell from Quynh's expression that she had indeed. Poor Hudson. Annie thought that, for a cat with a basic linebacker's personality, he had a heavy load to shoulder in the etiquette department.

After finishing lunch they walked back up the hill and paused behind the aquarium, another one of Quynh's favorite haunts. She loved the circular walk inside, lined on both sides by thousands of fish at eye level. It was like walking on the floor of the ocean.

But there was Hudson, following at their heels. Cats were hardly welcome at the aquarium.

45

Annie scooped him up and hid him inside the almost empty picnic basket.

"We'll be quick. Now, you be good," Quynh cautioned him.

The woman in the blue uniform at the coat check smiled at the pretty little girl with the black ponytail who ever so seriously handed her a picnic basket and a tablecloth.

Skipping the snakes, which Quynh hated anyway, they were back to reclaim their belongings in half an hour flat. Hudson held his comments until the front steps.

The three of them ran most of the way back to the car, Quynh stopping a couple of times to demonstrate the back-flips she had learned in gymnastics class. Hudson didn't need a class to be a star in that department. Annie just tried to keep up.

Sam's morning had been no picnic.

She'd spent most of it interviewing Judge and Mrs. Weinberg about their niece Sondra, who had lived with them since her parents had been killed in a plane crash when she was eleven years old. They had invited Sam into their spacious apartment not far from her own on Russian Hill. The views out across the Bay were spectacular, but no one could see them today. The Weinbergs' eyes were red and blurred with tears, and Sam kept remembering the horror she had seen the night before in the morgue, their beautiful, beloved niece, disfigured beyond anyone's worst nightmares.

"She finished at the top of her med-school class," the kind-voiced, silver-haired judge was saying. "She was going to be a retinal surgeon."

"We are so proud of her." Mrs. Weinberg's hand shook as she poured coffee from a silver Queen Anne pot. "I mean, we were."

Sam got them through it as gently as she could, gathered her notes, once again expressed her sympathy, and left.

Threading her maroon BMW through the crowded streets toward her office, she thought about Sondra Weinberg. The face smiling out of all those happy photographs on the Weinbergs' piano was an intelligent one. She'd had wonderful eyes. Wise, perceptive, kindly eyes, like her uncle's. She was sure that, as Mrs. Weinberg said, she must have had a good heart.

But she didn't anymore. Her murderer had deprived her of her heart with a surgical skill that might have rivaled Sondra's own. The implications were terrifying. A crazed doctor at work? An amateur with lots of practice?

But she wouldn't write about that on her CRT. Nor about the swastika he'd painted with Sondra's blood on her forehead.

Her profile on Sondra Weinberg would be about her brave soul, her trained eyes, her steady hands, her kind deeds, her aspirations for the future, all gone.

NINE

Annie ran her finger down the column. There was her query ad—one of only four under the heading AUTHORS/ RESEARCHERS. Hers was the second, just under a request for interviewees to talk about the heartbreak of herpes.

Her personal ad was more difficult to find. She scanned

through hundreds with the dispatch born of practice. Annie had answered a few dozen herself and was a pro at ad language.

"Distinguished looks" meant gray hair and probably not much of it. "Entrepreneur" meant he owned his own business, could be a gas station, could be oil wells. "Humorous" was often a joke-a-minute. And there are no men 5' 10", a euphemism for 5' 8" and wishing. She'd found that ad copy was frequently what people wanted the truth to be, rather than the real thing.

But still, occasionally, struck by a burst of optimism or a particularly well-written string of adjectives, she would fire a letter into the void. Prince Charming could just as well be a *Bay Guardian* box number as a stranger on the street, she reasoned.

She remembered the last man she had met through the *Guardian*.

His ad had been very, very clever. However, as she waited for him in a bar in Berkeley, glancing up at each man who came in the door, she wondered about truth in advertising.

At least the bar was a pleasant place to wait. White plaster walls, leaded glass windows, a handsome old carved cherry bar. Ornate gold-framed mirrors mixed with blow-ups of Gold Rush working girls. It was on College Avenue, a strip of pricey boutique shopping for Berkeley and Oakland professionals, but more casual than its Union Street counterpart in the city. Everything in Berkeley was more casual. It was filled with men who proudly announced that they hadn't worn a suit since they'd moved out from New York six, eight, ten, twelve years ago.

Annie's date was late. She twiddled with the bowl of pretzels in front of her and ordered another Campari from the bartender, who at least wore a tie. But then, the bartender was a woman—probably.

48

Just as San Francisco was Nirvana for the country's gay males, the lesbians had claimed Berkeley as their own. There seemed to be a tacit agreement that the Bay, which separated the two geographically, was the sexual DMZ.

Her thoughts ended abruptly as her date walked in through the swinging doors. It was obvious he was the one from the way he scanned the bar. He was blond, as advertised. But this was no Robert Redford. He bore a stronger resemblance to Peter Rabbit.

His prominent, pink nose twitched. This man, as advertised, was a psychologist who specialized in stress-related physical disorders. She timed his nose at every seven seconds.

One went through the motions.

"What kind of music do you like?"

"What do you do on weekends?"

"Do you ski?"

After one drink, she mumbled something about an errand of mercy for a sick friend and shook his hand.

Don't call us, we'll call you.

That's how most of them went, though occasionally there was a happy surprise.

What were the possibilities today, she thought, still scanning the ads as she poured herself another cup of coffee and lit a cigarette.

The week's potpourri of wishes, dreams, and lies—20 cents per word, $2 minimum.

What was this?

Gentle, innocent, powerful, highly conscious, laughing, spiritual man embracing the child within himself and committed to truth more than to ego seeks similar, sweet, fine, natural, sensitive, shapely lady. I live in a secluded cabin, run a successful business part-time, and hope to build a wilderness home; 6', 150+, Harvard. Counselor, inventor, astrologer, poet, dancer. Send photo, birthdate, time, place.

49

What was the part-time business? Leather sandals, mac-
rame, or perhaps he was a marijuana grower. She read on.

SAN FRANCISCO COUPLE SEEKING high energy and sensual
meetings with other couples and women. Through Tai Chi,
education, and meditation, we are balancing our lives. We also
laugh and play through life. We are attractive, athletic, and
open-minded.

Not that she hadn't ever fantasized about a couple. But
Tai Chi? Meditation? She'd rather try her first threesie
without the granola.

Her friend Hoyt would love this one, Huck and Tom till-
ing the land. She clipped it for him.

GAY FARMER Long-hair-beard-Jewish-Aries-sensual needs
lover who is hirsute-tall-mellow-28–43.

Ads written by men seemed to outnumber the women's
by about ten to one. The ratio was backward, since San
Francisco women outnumbered straight men about five to
one. Maybe, like herself (until now), most women drew the
line at advertising.

Annie was growing impatient and her coffee cold. Where
was her ad? Then her eye fell upon a listing that almost
made her choke. She stubbed out her cigarette. Talk about
bad memories . . . she had met this one about six years
ago.

Tall, attractive, UC professor who likes sailing, great restaurants, and fine wines seeks Modiglianiesque woman for good
times and laughter. Late 30's, East Coast bkgrnd preferred.

It had been just after her divorce. She had run her mind
over what she remembered of Art History 101 and envi-

sioned a long, thin Modigliani lady done in blue. She dropped the professor a note.

He called and asked her to meet him at his place in Berkeley on Tuesday at seven.

She was a little apprehensive about the setup. She preferred meeting in a public place for coffee or a drink. Then she could make a quick getaway. But it would probably be okay. At seven, at least she'd get dinner.

Wrong. It was dinnertime for Bruce, but not for her. She had stumbled up the dark back steps of his apartment near the university campus on a miserable, cold, rainy night to find him frying a single pork chop. He was leaning over his grimy stove in an old, dark brown, wool bathrobe that did nothing to glamorize his thin, hairless chest.

He did ask if she'd eaten and he offered her something out of a crusty saucepan that looked like Chinese cabbage and tofu with snake sauce. No thank you.

They talked about books, degrees earned, credentials for ten long minutes. The desultory conversation hung around the kitchen like an old fart.

Whenever she was uncomfortable Annie would grow stiffer and stiffer, jaw locked. What little she said on this occasion plopped through clenched teeth like cold molasses.

She kept thinking, "Why are you asking me these dumb questions? What right do you have to know about my life, you cheap creep?"

But she didn't say it. She smiled as nicely as she could and said she really didn't think this was going anywhere. She wished him well, but thought that she would be on her way.

"Fine with me," Bruce said. "I don't know why you wasted my time. You're not a Modigliani, too skinny and flat-chested."

She didn't need to hear this from a man with greasy lips dressed in an ugly brown bathrobe.

"What exactly do you mean?" Her enunciation could have drilled a hole in his kitchen wall.

"You're not buxom, big, round." His hand drew circles in front of his chest. "You know, Rubenesque."

"Can't you keep your artists straight?" Her voice was low and soft, the way it got when she was very, very angry. "If you wanted Rubenesque, why the hell didn't you say Rubenesque, idiot?" And she slammed out the door.

Driving through the pouring rain, she decided she was still too mad to go straight home. She stopped in a neighborhood bar out on Clement, where the men tended to be young, bearded types in jeans. They drank beer, wore flannel shirts, and were more likely to be lumberjacks visiting from the northwest than professors.

She found a bar stool next to a tall curly-haired Idaho cowboy nicknamed Bugs. He didn't know Rubens or Modigliani from a hole in the ground, but he did know an awful lot about smiling and buying a lady a cognac while complimenting her pretty green eyes. She had ended the evening with Bugs, dancing to the jukebox and laughing.

She had read almost all the way to the end of the last column and was beginning to think they'd left it out when she spotted it, right there with the other Ws.

What I'd really like is a funny, tall, attractive, maybe Jewish, successful, articulate, sexy, 35–45, honest man, ready to consider life with me, a woman of similar description. 8 out of 10 will do. Photo appreciated/returned. Box 42S.

Well, there it was. Right out there for the whole world to see. What kind of doors was that going to open? She'd just have to wait for Box 42S to fill and she'd see.

TEN

Annie started poring through interview notes and kept at it for hours. Finally taking a break, she yawned and stretched, then rotated her neck in a circle. The popping and crunching sounded like gravel. Maybe she would see Sam's chiropractor after all. She decided it was time to read the morning paper, which she hadn't had time to look at since she'd picked it up outside her apartment door.

Where had she put it? She glanced around her living room, then paused to *really* look at it. She often thought how lucky she was to have found this place, this apartment she loved.

She adored the thick-walled twenties architecture, large rooms, tall ceilings, rich moldings, hardwood floors, and the bay windows in the living room. She had more closet space than friends of hers in New York City had apartment. French doors separated the small dining room from the living room. From the large entryway left to the living room was an arch, partially filled by a ceiling-sweeping broad-leaved corn plant that seemed to thrive on her rules.

She watered her plants once a week, fed them fertilizer once a month. If they wanted a new pot, they could go out and get one.

To the right off the entryway was the rose-colored bathroom with its original cabinetry, including a built-in

53

dressing table on top of which rested a gold-and-black cel-
luloid Deco vanity set: brush and comb, mirror, and a bevy
of little boxes for pins, powder, pretties. Silver beads, ribbons, and pearls draped the frame of a large, speckled mirror. The original tub stretched the width of the unusually
large room.

She had furnished the rose, white, and blue apartment
with the few good pieces of furniture that had survived her
marriage: a tapestried Jacobean Revival chair, a Queen
Anne dining table and chairs, a small golden-oak Mission
table. A stained-glass lampshade on a Deco base stood in
one corner. An antique rosewood clock perpetually
claimed it to be 4:10. Her home was feminine, comfortable,
eclectic.

Scattered about, tucked into the wall of white bookcases,
were a multitude of small objects—photographs, re-
membrances of good times past. Red leather boxes from a
trip long ago to Florence. A tiny metal alligator whose
head and tail had moved very slowly since her childhood.
Photos of Quynh and Hudson, her mother and father, herself in second grade, Sam wearing a beekeeper's hat, smiling through the green gauze.

Annie was a nester. And this fifth-floor corner aerie was
a most comfortable nest.

She finally found the newspaper under the coffee table.
Sam's byline jumped out at her from page one.

The story was about the Mt. Diablo killer.

Just after the third murder there an elderly couple had
been shot to death in Diablo Valley, a nearby hamlet.
Their son, the suspected murderer, had been on the run for
a week, writing letters to the police, the paper, and to Sam,
until he had finally turned himself in. The police found him
patiently waiting for them at a telephone booth with a small
arsenal in his blood-smeared trunk.

54

He was one of those crazy geniuses, frustrated by his inability to communicate his visions to others. No one understood what he was trying to say, including his parents. Sam's profile of him was masterful. But, she asked, was this the Mt. Diablo murderer? The proximity made one think so—but then, one wanted to think so. To think that the brutal killings that kept away the weekend hikers were now over.

Annie called to congratulate Sam on the piece, but got her answering machine.

"Nice going, Sherlock," she said after the beep.

Everybody she knew had a machine or a beeper or a service. Sometimes it was like a long tennis volley, messages left back and forth with no human contact. One of these days, she thought, the machines are going to start calling each other without us.

As if on cue, her phone rang. She started. It was David, her sometime lover. She pictured his wide mouth clenching a cigarette. He liked to pretend he was Humphrey Bogart, talking while smoke curled up through his fair hair.

"Hi, Annie, watcha doing?" he purred. No matter what time it was, David's voice always sounded as if it were 2 A.M. and he had just rolled over in bed.

"Working. What's on your mind?"

"A movie."

Annie's eyes narrowed. "*What* movie?" David had been trying to get her to go to a porno flick with him for months. She had seen a couple with Bert when they were married and found them unutterably boring and depressing.

"No, this isn't what you think. It's starring this really gorgeous girl, Marilyn Chambers."

"Don't you Marilyn Chambers me, David. I know exactly who she is. It's *Behind the Green Door,* isn't it?"

He laughed. "Loosen up, Annie, it'll do you good."

She didn't think so.

"Is that your best offer?"

"Of course not." His voice was low and insinuating. "We could always stay home and find something to do."

They made a date to do just that. After she hung up Annie went to the bathroom and took a long look at herself in the mirror.

You always think you can get by with that, don't you? she asked herself. Someone to fill in the gaps, to get you through until Rich Right shows up. But it never feels good enough, does it? That cold, in the meantime, in between time, comfort.

Later Sam returned her call.

"I loved the story, Sammie. Page one! Is this going to make you rich and famous?"

"Jealousy will get you nowhere, my dear." Annie could hear the happy excitement in her voice. They chatted for a few minutes about her scoop. Sam had received rare praise indeed, a complimentary call from the oak-paneled office of the publisher.

"You want to hear something really strange?" Sam continued. "Some man I never heard of called me at home this morning."

"And? Did he want to sell you a magazine subscription?"

"No, I'm serious, A. I mean, at first I thought I just couldn't place him. He was so friendly, so familiar."

"An old flame you'd forgotten?"

"Well, that's what I thought. But he wasn't. He knew my name, my number, where I lived. And I didn't know him from Adam. Turned out he was a guy driving a white Porsche I smiled at on the freeway coming from Mill Valley a couple of weeks ago. I just smiled, you know, the way you do when you realize someone's looking at you. Some-

how he found me, maybe through the Department of Motor Vehicles. Hell, I don't know. Jesus, he *must* be lonely. Or nuts. Probably both."

"What did he want?"

"To meet me for a drink."

"You hung up, I hope."

There was a long pause.

"No." Sam hesitated. "I agreed to one drink at the Square." The Washington Square Bar & Grill was the hangout of the newspaper crowd.

"Are you crazy? Why on earth did you do that?"

"I'm curious," she mumbled. "And it shows some ingenuity, you have to admit."

"Sammie." Annie's tone had a lot of schoolteacher in it.

"I don't know. He didn't look nuts."

"You could judge that on the freeway?"

"He *was* kind of cute. But I guess I just want to get it over with. He sounded very persistent. We'll be on my turf in a public place. What's he going to do? Pull out a gun and kill me over a glass of Perrier?"

"Don't even joke about it."

"Look, one drink, I'll tell him how charming he is, and isn't it too bad that I have a steady beau. Would that I did, but what's he to know?"

"For a hard-boiled reporter you are really naive, my friend."

"Are we still on for Woody Allen?" When Sam didn't want to be pushed on something, she had a way of simply changing the subject.

Annie allowed it to drop. "Couldn't keep me away. Want to grab a bite at the Chestnut first?"

"Sure. Maybe since I'm so rich and famous, I'll even treat. See you at the bar at five-thirty." She rang off.

Annie had meant to ask her how the other investigation

was going, the murder of Judge Weinberg's niece. But if Sam were going to be meeting a stranger from the freeway for drinks, she probably didn't want to be reminded.

A little business for Annie to take care of and she could get back to her work. First a call to the *Bay Guardian* to check on the responses to her ads. Then she needed to return a call to her friend Tom Albano.

The young man on the phone sounded like an 18-year-old Miss Lonely Hearts. Was he this enthusiastic over every call?

"Box Thirty-two-X, that's the one in the query column, has about ten letters. And Box Forty-two-S, that's the personal, wow! You hit the jackpot. Must have been a good ad. Looks like about fifty pieces. Do you want us to go ahead and mail them to you?"

Fifty responses to her personal! Mail them? Was he crazy? Tom could wait. She'd be right down.

When she did get around to calling Tom she couldn't resist telling him her news.

Tom was one of her oldest California friends. He and his wife Clara had lived and fought in the apartment next door when she'd first moved to the city. Clara was long gone and Tom had moved down the Peninsula to open his own architectural office in Palo Alto. As the electronics business boomed in the Silicon Valley, so did his practice. Tom was a good buddy, a supportive friend. He always loved hearing about her exploits, which he called "The Perils of Annie."

Something in his voice told her he wasn't so thrilled with the latest chapter.

"You're really going to meet all fifty of those guys?"

"I don't think so. What do I know? I haven't even opened all the letters yet."

"It just doesn't sound like a very safe idea to me."

58

He sounded like herself talking to Sam. The shoe wasn't so comfortable on the other foot.

She bristled. "What's the matter, Tom? You sound crabby. Did the Forty-niners lose you some money last week, or is Clara trying to garnishee your running shoes?" His ex-wife's demands for more were legendary.

"I'm sorry. I guess I'm letting this new Dynatrix project get to me. And Kim doesn't understand why I don't think it's a neat idea for a nine-year-old to go on a shopping trip to New York with her next-door neighbors. There's not going to be anything left for that kid to do by the time she's eighteen if Clara has her way."

Annie laughed. Tom became very Italian when it came to his daughter.

"Same old stuff," he continued. "But nothing that dinner and a movie with you next week couldn't straighten out."

"You got it. Thursday?"

"Great. Let's eat a duck at the Hunan and catch a western. And you can tell me about all those new men in your life."

Did she detect just a note of jealousy? What a nice man. How lucky she was to have him for a friend.

ELEVEN

Julia Child may define the tenderloin as the tenderest and most luxurious part of the animal, but many cities give the name to their centers of vice, naughtiness, and crime.

San Francisco's Tenderloin was downtown, bordered by Golden Gate Avenue, Larkin, O'Farrell, and Mason. Its residence hotels, middle-class apartments, and good Greek restaurants were obscured by sex shops with windows full of adult rubber novelties, barkers urging tourists into two-drink minimum, bump-and-grind shows, and theaters with names like the Pussycat.

The theaters catered to every nuance of sexual taste, featuring black women, white women, Oriental women, women in rubber, women with whips, women in chains, and in a couple of theaters that one has to know about to find—women in extremis: snuff films.

In a small theater a dozen or so men sat in the dark, scattered far apart. Cigarette and marijuana smoke climbed up through the projected light. There was the occasional pop of a beer can opening. This was not an atmosphere in which one had to bother with conventional rules. There was no talking, but that was because everyone's attention was riveted to the action taking place on the screen.

A Latina with large breasts was led into a room, blindfolded. Her frilly white blouse was cut low in the neck. Her short, black skirt was hiked well above her knees. There was a long run in her left stocking. Her hands were bound behind her with a leather thong.

The two men who directed her with rough pushes and shoves were also Latin. They were both dressed in black, with tight-fitting pants and a multitude of gold chains glinting on their open-shirted chests.

They tied the woman to a post in the room, furnished otherwise with only a bed. They beat her with short whips, then tortured her with wicked looking knives. Then they cut her down, raped her in a variety of sadistically imaginative ways, and finally garroted her with a length of barbed wire. It was a particularly hideous way to die.

60

Unless, of course, one was a connoisseur in such matters, as the blond man in the last row seemed to be. In the reflected light from the screen, he grinned as the woman struggled for breath, and then his body contorted as he and the woman on screen reached a climax of death and blood lust together.

He reached past the knife on his hip and tucked his soiled handkerchief and his $10 ticket stub into his back pocket as he left. He'd gotten his money's worth.

TWELVE

Sam had waved her way past several friends and acquaintances at the bar in the front room of the Washington Square Bar & Grill and asked the maître d' for a small table in the back. If the man in the white Porsche did show up, how could she introduce him? "I want you to meet a man who picked me up on the freeway." She didn't even know his name.

The down-and-out blues piano from the front room fought to be heard over the hubbub of conversation from the early-evening crowd. Friends called to one another, moved chairs, squeezed one more into large groups at circular tables. The Square was a favorite hangout of journalists and literati in the city. At a table nearby, Sam spied the novelist Alice Adams, her silver head bent toward her companion's, deep in conversation.

Sam's favorite waiter raised an eyebrow from across the room. Sam smiled and nodded, and within moments there was a large bottle of Perrier, a bucket of ice, and a small dish of limes in front of her. She glanced at her gold Cartier watch. She was right on time. Her date wasn't, or perhaps he just hadn't found her yet.

Well, she couldn't just twiddle her thumbs. She pulled out the black leather Filofax notebook that contained practically her entire life and thumbed to her notes on Sondra Weinberg. She had already filed her story, including the interview with the victim's aunt and uncle. It had run on page one and the next day she had received a call from Judge Weinberg, thanking her for the piece.

His call had brought tears to her eyes. Hardly anyone ever called to say positive things about the news and the circumstances of this story made it even more poignant. To think that the man could separate himself from his enormous grief to say thank you.

Sometimes she wondered about this job of hers. What was it that made her so fascinated with violence?

Was it her seemingly ever so safe upbringing, the elegant, spotlessly clean houses in Los Angeles and Santa Barbara that her parents and their decorator had filled with carefully chosen antiques? The years of her father at the head of the table, meticulously controlling and directing dinner conversation, with his three daughters and his wife nodding in the appropriate places, their hands folded in their laps? The pale, monochromatic platters of well-done beef, mashed potatoes, cauliflower served by a maid in white, antiseptically doling out the bland food as if she were a nurse? Everything so careful, so white.

It was all so clean, so proper, so calm, except for those occasional awful times when her father had had a particularly bad day augmented by one too many before-dinner drinks. He would badger them with questions, testing to see if they would slip up with an inappropriate opinion, a mistake of taste or decorum. Their mother would murmur, "Dear, dear," until he would turn and include her, too, in the verbal slaughter. Her face would grow paler, whiter. His would glow bright red as the booze and the blood would flush higher and higher.

Occasionally his anger would fly him out of the dining room and into a bedroom upstairs, where he would drag a small, sobbing daughter and bend her over a bed, pull her dress up and her underpants down and batter her with his belt until his passion had subsided.

Usually the daughter was Sam. She was the oldest. The prettiest. The smartest. And the most likely to talk back, coming to the defense of her opinions or of her younger sisters. She was the one of whom he was the fondest—and the most intolerant.

Later, in the therapy that had saved her, Sam would discover that there were years of her childhood she simply didn't remember. She had erased the rage that took her up those stairs and violated her bare bottom, just as if she were erasing notes from a tape.

Her mother always pretended that it never happened. She would smile vacantly, as she always had when Sam tried to enlist her help years later in piecing together her childhood.

"No, dear, I don't know what you mean. We were always happy, all of us. Don't you remember? The trips to the ranch to see Grandpa, the horses, the picnics. We always had such lovely times."

Her mother had smiled vacantly, too, when Sam had marched down the aisle on the arm of her beaming father to join in wedlock with Preston Mathews, the well-connected stockbroker. Her father thought he was a marvelous catch, one that would prove useful to the family. He had all the right qualities except kindness.

Sam hadn't noticed that until it was too late. She had met him at a deb party, and during the brief romance through which he danced her, high on champagne, vodka, mescaline, and a whole rainbow of red, yellow, green, and black capsules, she hadn't noticed anything about him, except that he was going to take her away from home.

It wasn't long, of course, before she discovered she had exchanged one fairy-tale castle with a rotten, secret room, clanking with chains and resounding with screams, for another.

Preston had thought the marriage was a good one. He had thought that all her millions, married to his financial acumen, would lead to a very quick pot of gold. He hadn't realized until too late that his rainbow girl's fortune would grow and grow and grow not in his hands, but from one generation to another, most of it carefully locked up in trust.

Then the sunshine in their house on the beach had faded. Preston had quickly grown cold and bitter, picking at the food she prepared for him, occasionally pillaging her body in a burst of savagery that always left her sore and unsatisfied. He railed against her slovenliness, demanding that she clean, on her hands and knees, the beach sand from the tracks of the sliding glass doors with Q-tips.

Sam, conditioned by her father, bore it for a year. Then one day, during a conversation with her younger sister Crista, she had burst into tears, and it had all spilled out. Within an hour, she was packed and gone.

She escaped northward, to Palo Alto and a favorite aunt, and then to Stanford, the law, the partnership, the pressure, easily slipping into the bottle to hide from her past and a self she didn't understand.

When she'd made it out on the other side she had found once again her sunny self, the one that was kind, laughed easily, was generous with her time and money. (But not so quick with her trust, if you please. One must tread lightly, achieve that slowly.) She wrote voluminous journals and read incessantly. But not fiction. Hardly ever fiction. It was real life, what made people tick, that held her fascination. People like Judge Weinberg, his poor dead niece Sondra, and the twisted, cold mind that had ended her life.

Sam looked down at her notebook and the page on Sondra. She had covered all the white space with doodles.

Her ice was melting. What time was it? She glanced at her watch. She'd been there for half an hour. Looked like the freeway cruiser wasn't going to show.

Then she felt the waiter's eyes on her. He hurried over with a menu.

"I didn't want to disturb you, Miss Samantha. You looked busy."

She brushed aside his apology as needless and began to scan the familiar list. Should she order? She hadn't made any plans for dinner, had thought she would just meet this man and then go home and snuggle into an old movie from the video store. She was beginning to feel a bit hungry, but she hesitated. It wasn't likely that he would appear if he were this late, but what if he did and she were committed to dinner. She didn't want to have to spend that kind of time with him.

She stared across the room blankly, considering the options, when she realized that her stare was being returned.

She started. Was it him? Was it the White Knight? No, it was that tall, handsome detective she'd passed a few times in her rounds downtown. The one who had moved out from New York not too long ago. Irish. Dark red hair. A

65

great smile. What was his name? Sean. Sean what? Sean O'Reilly.

He obviously had no trouble remembering her name as he strode over to her table.

"Hello, Samantha." He smiled down at her. "Are you alone? I mean, are you going to be alone?"

Sam hesitated. Well, was she or wasn't she? She didn't know.

"I'm sorry, I didn't mean to intrude. I saw you and thought what a lucky coincidence it was for me. I've been wanting to have a chance to talk with you for quite some time."

How could she refuse that?

"No, of course. I mean, you're not intruding. I was supposed to meet someone, but obviously my friend has been held up somewhere. Please sit down."

Besides, she thought, if he does show up, the hell with him.

"So," he said as he settled in, arranging his long legs under the table, "could I interest you in some oysters and champagne to start?"

Sam's response was a look he couldn't read.

"I mean, if you're interested in dining. If not, we could just have a drink and chat for a few minutes if you have somewhere else to be."

"No, that would be lovely. I'd like to. Dine, that is. The oysters would be grand."

"No champagne?"

"No."

"Some white wine, perhaps?"

"No."

He glanced at the bottle of Perrier and nodded in its direction.

"Another?"

66

"Yes, please."

"A dozen Belon, a dozen Apalachicola, another bottle of Perrier for the lady, and a glass of Chandon Brut for me," he reeled off to the waiter, who smiled at Sam. She smiled back, amused. The staff at the Square never missed a trick, knew who was seeing whom, pulled for their unattached regulars. She knew the waiter couldn't wait to get back to the service area to share the news that she had company. She wondered what they knew about Sean. Probably more than she did.

"Do you come here often?" she wondered aloud.

"More and more," he said. "What's your sign?"

She stared at him, taken aback. Then as the smile crinkled into his dimples, she got it. He was teasing her about her stereotypical California question.

"Burma Shave," she said, "with an ascendant in Pepperoni. And yours?"

"Staten Island Ferry. Very compatible."

"School?" she queried.

"P.S. One-o-six. And you?"

"Reform."

"Funny, I could have sworn you looked Orthodox. Hobbies?"

"Horse."

"You mean heroin?"

"No, my heroine is Superwoman."

"Hero?"

"Sandwich."

"Dagwood."

"Blondie."

"The singer."

"As in sewing machine?"

"As in jukebox."

Then they both lost it, dissolving into laughter just as the beaming waiter arrived with their oysters.

"Gosh, we have so much in common," Sean teased. He picked up a wedge of lemon and an oyster shell. "Help yourself," he invited.

Sam looked at the beautiful, frosty platter before them, the shells snuggled into a bed of ice. Could anyone ever eat an oyster in the presence of the opposite sex without thinking of that incredible, edible, slurpy, sexy scene in the movie *Tom Jones*?

She lifted her fork and raised her eyes to see Sean, across the table, grinning at her as one of the salty, coppery morsels slid down his throat. She knew that he knew what she was thinking. Well, her mind certainly wasn't going to be seduced *that* easily. All business, she lifted an oyster, hooked it out smartly, plopped it in her mouth, and chewed.

"Excellent," she said.

His mouth still held a grin. She hadn't fooled him for a second.

"So the mysterious Ms. Storey approves?"

"Indeed. But what's so mysterious?"

"You are. I've asked hundreds of questions about you and no one seems to know very much."

Sam didn't know whether to be flattered or insulted.

"What do you mean hundreds of questions?"

"I've asked around. 'Who is this beautiful woman? Where did she come from? Does she have a boyfriend? Where did she learn to be such a pro? Does she like cops?'"

"Her name is Samantha NMI ex-Mathews Storey. From Los Angeles. No. In law school and on the job. Not unequivocally; each one has to stand on his or her own merits. I'm surprised you didn't run me through the computer," she continued.

"I did," he said. "It didn't tell me what I wanted to know. Now, what would you like for dinner?"

Sam didn't know what struck her. This man was titillating in ways she wasn't used to. And he made her feel feisty.

"More oysters, please."

He raised an eyebrow. His eyes read and registered her challenge.

"Then more oysters it will be."

He signaled to the waiter, ordered two dozen more, which they polished off without much conversation but with a large number of sideways glances. Then another two dozen before Sam cried uncle.

"I give," she said, putting down her fork. "You're a better man than I."

"I should certainly hope so. Because I wouldn't want to ask you to go for a bit of dancing otherwise."

"Oh, I . . ."

"Couldn't? Why?"

Why indeed? Why should she deny herself this pleasure? She loved to dance. And it was so seldom she got the chance. Was she hesitating because she thought she was supposed to?

Sean watched her face carefully, as if he could see the conversation in her mind printed across her forehead.

"Good," he said, dropping cash on the table and taking her hand and leading her out of the restaurant. "We can walk from here. It's just up the street."

For someone who hadn't been in town long, he knew its secret places well. Unerringly, he led her to the small, grubby Italian bar with a few tables and a hardwood floor where the late-night cognoscenti went for a nightcap and a little tripping of the light fantastic.

He ordered a Martell cognac for himself and a Perrier with lime for Sam without even asking her. It was early.

Only the barman and two other couples were in the place. Sean got quarters from the bar and loaded up the jukebox.

He chose lots of Stones, some hot Ray Charles, Aretha, old stuff, all with a steady beat. He draped their jackets, bags, cases across a chair and bowed formally to her as "I Can't Get No Satisfaction" boomed through the room.

"May I have this dance?"

And then he swung her out and exploded into the most loose-hipped, long-legged, get-down dancing she'd ever seen. Whirl, twirl, twist, kick, clap, turn, bump. Again and again and again, in never ending variations of rhythm and motion that kept her twirling on her toes, shaking her behind, laughing with delight. Was this New York style, Staten Island, Irish cop? No, it couldn't be; what it looked like, felt like, was . . .

"Ghetto," Sean said to her as they stood side by side, bumping hips to the music, clapping hands, slide, slide, slide, as she followed him as if she'd done it all her life. "I grew up with a bunch of black friends who taught me how to dance. And you're not bad yourself."

"I love it," she said, almost out of breath with exhilaration.

"Good."

The last quarter dropped and Ray Charles crooned "Am I Blue?" Sean pulled her close and they danced slowly in small circles around the room. She felt hot and sweaty and wonderful. She could feel his heart beating against her shoulder.

Then it was over. He picked up their coats, waved good night to the barman, and led her out the door and into the night. She could hear the foghorns down by the Bay.

"Where's your car?" he asked.

"In a lot near the Square."

"I'll walk you there."

She took his arm. It seemed silly not to after all that dancing. This was the same thing without the music. Or was it? There was certainly something singing in her head. She couldn't quite make out the tune.

"We haven't talked shop all evening," she said to him.

"No, we haven't. It's nice to get away from it."

"I know. Especially with Diablo."

"And a new murder in the Mission."

"What?"

And before they knew it, they were into it. Sean was telling her things that a man and woman shouldn't be talking about at the end of such a lovely evening, about murder and gore, strangulation and a long, shiny knife.

Then they were at her car and she wished she'd never brought it up. Their magical bubble had been burst with the ugly reality of their particular workaday worlds.

"I'm sorry I asked," she said.

"And I'm sorry I answered. Here," he said and reached inside her BMW, switched on the radio, and flipped through the stations until he found some rock 'n' roll.

"Sean," she laughed, as he took her hand. "We can't dance here," she said, gesturing at the parking lot and the attendant, who grinned at them and shrugged his shoulders.

"Why?" Sean asked. "You think we're breaking a law? Leave that to me." And he twirled her out across the concrete floor. Flung her out. Pulled her back. Turned her round and round until all the ugliness had twirled right out of her head again and they had recaptured the evening.

Three songs later, he tucked her into the car, shut the door firmly, and watched while she locked it. He leaned in her window.

"Thanks. You're everything I'd hoped you'd be. I'll give you a call tomorrow."

Sam sat there with her motor running, watching him lope off into the night.

THIRTEEN

The sunset out behind the Golden Gate was, as usual, magnificent this evening, a symphony of vermilion, gold, and pink that even the most jaded San Franciscan couldn't ignore. In fact, it was the reason many of them had stayed on in the city so long or had never left.

At the Chestnut Bar & Grill, which named its sandwiches after its favorite hundred or so regulars, Annie waved as Sam walked in. How pretty she was, Annie thought, in her bottle-green silk blouse, perfect with her dark coloring.

They exchanged a quick hug.

"The usual?" asked Fred, the bartender. Sam nodded, and he handed her bottled water with lots of lime.

Annie couldn't wait. She reached into her big, purple leather tote and pulled out a large packet of letters tied with a ribbon. "Guess what I've got here?"

Sam's eyes widened. "The *Guardian* personal?"

Heads turned and a couple of people laughed.

"Shhhhh!" Annie was embarrassed. "Let's don't invite *everyone* to the party."

"I'm sorry." Sam giggled. She turned on her bar stool so they had as much privacy as possible, though Fred never took his eyes off them.

"I saved them for you. I only opened a few."

"God!" Sam waved her hands in excitement, then rubbed them together. "It's like Christmas! What if one of these is from someone standing right here?"

"Well, he won't know if you keep it down."

"I will too," said Fred, leaning over from behind the bar. "Mine's the one with all the dirty words."

"Scoot, Fred," Annie said, waving him away. "I'm sure there's much more creative filth here than you ever thought of."

"How do you want to do this?" Sam asked.

"Just take half of them and then we'll switch."

They were barely through the first letters when a man at Annie's elbow interrupted. He was wearing a stockbroker suit, a stockbroker belt, stockbroker shoes, and a stockbroker haircut. But at his neck was a blue-and-red polka-dot bow tie and on his head was a cowboy hat.

"Lemme buy you two pretty ladies a drink. I want to get to know you," he slurred, listing to the left. "I been here and there since eleven today, when I read the board, decided the day was fucked, and I might as well be too."

"You said it, not me." Sam laughed and they grabbed the letters and their drinks, and signaled to the hostess, who led them to a quiet table in the back. They both ordered Toots Burgers with jalapeños, cheese, and onions, and got serious about their reading.

"This man's married," Sam announced.

"Well, of course, some of them are going to be. It's a game, silly. You see what you can get away with."

They resumed sipping and reading.

"Two more married, Sam. Maybe they're all going to be. This certainly isn't what I was looking for."

"Who was just saying this was a game? Keep going."

Annie opened another one and laughed. "Listen to this.

'If you turn out to be my ex-wife, please never tell me about this.' Not bad-looking either."

Sam appraised his photograph as carefully as if she were buying mushrooms at $9.95 a pound.

"Okay," she ventured. "But I bet we'll do better."

"Who's this *we?*"

"Why, Annie, my dearest, my bosom, my heart, if you get more than any one woman can handle, don't tell me you're not going to share?"

"We'll see."

"Hmmmm." Sam was distracted. "What about this? Says he looks like Gene Wilder. And see, he does. But who's that woman with the boobs and the scarf? That's tacky, sending a photo of yourself with another woman. But he's tall enough. And forty-two."

"You know, I think we're forgetting something very important here. These men are not really *for me*. Remember? The point was to find more people for the book."

"Yes, but are you going to throw him away if you find a gem? Come on, Annie, don't spoil my fun."

"Okay . . . Listen to this. Is this Rich Right? One, two, three, no, four pages, single-spaced. Two of them are poetry. He's done lots of drugs, has a *heavy* interest in sex—does that mean he likes fat women—and says he's very good at it. Has a master's in counseling and works as a . . ."

"Therapist," Sam filled in the blank.

"You got it. He's also included a little list here of the things he craves: water, food, warmth, food, love, affection, food, recognition, more food, more love, warm love, warm food, desserts, bagels, and a pinch to grow an inch. And I quote. What do you think?"

"I think the man is hungry. And nuts."

There was a long silence from the other side of the table.

Finally Sam looked up. Annie was staring at a letter and shaking her head in disbelief.

"Let me guess," said Sam. "Jeff Bridges. Beau Bridges. That young Australian, whatsisname, Gibson, Mel Gibson."

"This letter's from Lloyd Andrews, the novelist."

"I'm giving you Jeff Bridges and you're giving me back a novelist?"

"Shut up. Remember, we were talking about him a couple of weeks ago, because I'd just finished his last book and you said you thought he lived in Bolinas. He lives here. On Telegraph Hill. And he answered my ad!" Annie gulped her Campari. "It's fate. I've read every word he ever wrote. I wonder if he makes love as well as he writes it?"

"Well, my dear, this is certainly your chance to find out. See, I told you you'd get into this."

"Oh, damn, he'll be out of town until next Thursday. Can I wait that long?"

"Why not? You've waited your whole life. Anyway, I thought you were complaining about how busy you are. Sure you've got time for Mr. Andrews?"

"Of course. I mean, I am busy. And I do have time. For *this*. Jeez, I almost forgot to tell you. I got some responses to the other ad too. Some good ones."

"Yes?"

"A black female lawyer, a lesbian transplanted from New York, a bisexual painter." She fanned a hand. "Could be some very kinky stuff there."

"Speaking of kinky, want to hear about my freeway cruiser?"

"God! Just talking about me, me, me. I'm sorry, I forgot."

"I guess he did too. Or maybe he just got cold feet. He never showed."

"After all that!"

"Takes all kinds. But I did run into Sean O'Reilly and we had dinner together."

"Well, that's not a bad trade-off. San Francisco's Finest's nomination for hunk of the year. He is that gorgeous detective, isn't he? The tall one, with the dark red hair, the flashing white teeth, the broad shoulders, the big gun. Did I miss anything?"

"No, that's him all right. But you left out the strawberry birthmark on his right shoulder."

"Sam! You devil. Did you?"

"No, silly. I'm teasing. We just ate dinner and talked shop. Murder shop. That guy who killed his parents on Mt. Diablo probably isn't the trail killer."

"Oh, no."

"And worse news. Sondra Weinberg?"

"Right! I meant to ask you about that the other day. Any leads?"

"Nothing. Except more of the same."

"What do you mean?"

"Afraid it looks like the first in a series. Sean said the body of a black woman was found yesterday in her apartment on the edge of the Mission. Looks like the same handiwork. Rape, strangulation, and a knife. Woman named Cindy Dunbar."

"Oh, Lord!"

"I know. Let's change the subject."

"Okay." But Annie was pensive as she stirred her coffee.

"What?"

"I don't know. They're making me nervous, all these murders. I'm beginning to imagine things."

"Like what?"

"Well . . . it was probably nothing. But the other night I

stayed late in my classroom at State to do some paperwork. It's always a little creepy out there with no one around."

"Just you and the sea gulls."

"Stop interrupting. I finished up and started walking toward my car and I heard footsteps behind me. I stopped and fished around in my bag for my keys—and the footsteps stopped too."

"Yikes."

"I know. That's when I got really nervous. So no fooling around, I was really moving, almost running, and so was he."

"He?"

"I didn't figure it was a woman. Sounded like a man. Anyway, just when I got to the car, I couldn't stand it any longer and I wheeled around."

"And?"

"Nobody there."

"What!"

"Just disappeared. I was so scared, I slammed my jacket in the door, but I wasn't opening it for anything."

"So what do you think?"

"I don't know. Maybe I just imagined the whole thing. Maybe it was the wind. Maybe your work"—she reached over and tweaked Sam on her lovely nose—"is getting to me."

"Well, let's go get some Woody Allen to aereate our brains." Sam snagged the passing waitress and paid the check.

Out on the sidewalk, Annie asked, "This isn't a funny one, is it?"

"No, the reviews said *real* serious."

They exchanged a look.

"Okay, okay," Sam agreed. "I know you're dying to see the Divine Miss M. Let's do it."

"You're so good to me, Missy Samantha," Annie said, fooling around. "I should be so lucky as to find a man like you."

"You should be, but your chances are slim to nothing. What is it Gloria Steinem said? 'We've become the men we were waiting for.'"

"Aw, come on, Sammie, let's don't get serious about that tonight."

"You're right. And you're probably going to find a perfectly wonderful man. Every bit as cute as me. Right here." She patted the letters in Annie's tote. "But while you're doing this thing, be careful, okay?"

"Sure. But if anything ever does happen to me, you promise me one thing."

"This is your last wish?"

"Right."

"What?"

"Promise me you'll sprinkle my ashes over Robert Redford."

FOURTEEN

The classroom Annie used at State two nights a week was standard: green chalkboard, rows of uncomfortable desks, a NO SMOKING sign that she sometimes chose to ignore posted prominently above the podium. But she hoped her classes in creative writing weren't standard. She really worked to make them good.

"Pass your papers around the circle to me, please," Annie said. "It's show-and-tell time."

The class groaned. Becky Beckwith stammered, "But you didn't tell us you were going to read them out loud. Mine is very personal."

"They're all personal, Ms. Beckwith. Everyone's story is about a personal experience of meeting someone."

"*Mine's* so personal, this chick's gonna blush if she reads it out loud," a tall, young, black man said to his friend.

How little he knew, Annie thought. She hoped some of them would be that good. Grist for her own mill.

She read through the first one quickly. Gladys Chiu, a meter maid, had met her husband Dennis while giving him a parking ticket. He had raised hell with her until he'd noticed the tears rolling down her cheeks. By way of apology, he had insisted on taking her to dinner, and eight months later Dennis was walking her down the aisle.

"Gladys, you one brave lady," commented the young, black man, whose name was Cornell. "You be giving me a ticket, I sure wouldn't be marrying you." Cornell winked at Gladys and flashed Annie a smile, testing the waters. Was banter cool in her class?

She read a few more stories—nothing out of the ordinary.

Cornell volunteered to read his own. He had met his current lady love on the #22 Fillmore bus, which, as it snaked its way from Pacific Heights down through the ghetto of the Western Addition, was better known for muggings and mayhem than romance.

"I was sitting there, reading my karate magazine, and I looked up and there was this chick that knocked me out, man. She was beautiful. She had this little kid in one arm and a bunch of packages in the other and she was trying to stand up on the bus in these skinny high heels. So naturally, being the gentleman that I am," Cornell's smile was a dazzler, "I gave her my seat, snowed her with my rap, carried her packages home for her, and man, I ain't hardly gone home since. Cynthia is one fine lady, for sure."

"You gonna marry her, blood?" asked Cornell's friend Mac.

"I don't know, my man, but if I do, it's gonna be on the Twenty-two Fillmore and we gonna dress you up like the MUNI man and let you collect the fares."

The class laughed. It was nice to see them relaxed, having a good time. Of course, the revisions weren't going to be so much fun.

Eve Gold, a blonde whose zoftig good looks were holding into her early sixties, reached across Annie's chair, gold bracelets ajingle, to take her paper. She too wanted to read it herself.

Eve had left Long Island years earlier, but her accent would always give her origins away. She patted her carefully coiffed hair and began.

"My daughter Linda is married to her stepbrother. My husband Al is married to his son's mother-in-law."

Eve smiled around the circle as people shook their heads, trying to get a handle on what she'd just said. It was a practiced line, one that Eve knew would get them every time.

She continued. "It happened like this. One, my daughter Linda married Richard Gold, who is now a doctor. Two, my husband Leonard died. Three, Richard's mother, Al's wife died. Four, I married Al, Richard's father, my daughter Linda's father-in-law. But," she hastened to add, "Al and I weren't involved before our spouses died. It was all after that."

Annie nodded, encouraging Eve to go on with the details of her romance with Al.

"And that's how I came to be my son-in-law's step-mother," Eve ended and settled back into her desk. Everyone smiled.

Or almost everyone.

The desk to Eve's left was pulled back from the circle. The man in it was sleeping, his face down on his folded arms.

Annie glanced at him and shrugged. You couldn't win 'em all, though she was always puzzled about why students who were bored would bother to sign up. After all, this wasn't compulsory education.

"This is for next week's assignment," Annie said as she passed out copies of the *Bay Guardian* personals column.

"In addition to the dialogue we talked about earlier, find one ad that you like and write a letter answering it. Then write an ad selling yourself. So that's three pieces of work for next meeting."

The class broke up with lots of chatter and several pats on the back to Eve Gold and Cornell. The sleeping student awoke and stretched, flopping his fair hair back out of his eyes. He yawned widely as he strolled out of the room. Annie noticed that he didn't bother to cover his mouth.

"Hey, Ms. Tannenbaum," Cornell called back from the doorway. "You said you were gonna do these assignments with us. You gonna let us read your personal ad?"

"Maybe you already did, Mr. Jones," she answered. "And maybe you already wrote me an answer."

"You wish." He winked at her and was gone.

Annie finished off her evening with a bit of high-stepping. She met Sam and Hoyt and Emmett at the I-Beam, their favorite dance bar on the edge of the Castro, the gay ghetto.

This was one of the many places where the city's pretty young men gathered to bump and sweat to a disco beat.

But being gay was not a requirement for admission. Every-one in the city knew that the best music was in the gay discos, and more than one gray-suited lawyer or Montgom-ery Street stockbroker had been seen with his bespangled wife mixing it up under the mirrored ball of the I-Beam.

They each grabbed a beer at the crowded bar in the front and then let 6' 5" Emmett blaze a trail through the crush.

"This way," he called, and they all fell into line.

Annie could never get over it. "Have you ever seen so many good-looking men?" she whispered to Sam.

"All 40 percent must be here tonight."

A recent survey had shown that to be the gays' cut of the city's single-male population. "And all smelling good." Sam sniffed. "Better than me."

It took them almost five minutes to work their way to the dance floor. A very handsome, black DJ was programming the sound in a plexiglass booth. He was dressed in a silver lamé cowboy shirt and pants, with gold and silver Lucchese boots to match. A virtuoso with the two spinning turntables before him, Sly held all the strings, winding the crowd up and letting the energy go. He nodded in recognition at An-nie. Women who loved to dance to his music were always welcome, and she and Hoyt came here often.

Hoyt grinned at her and wiped his brow. They had barely begun to move and he was sweating already. In ten minutes he would be soaking wet.

They began to rock with the ease of a long-married cou-ple who knew each others' every move. But then, they had been dancing together for twenty years. Annie and Hoyt had grown up in adjacent Atlanta neighborhoods, but didn't meet until a freshman English class at Emory. They quickly discovered they liked the same songs, the same movies, the same books and, sometimes, the same young men.

"Flip you," Hoyt said now, nodding at the model-perfect young man dancing beside them.

"You can have him," Annie replied. "I was just wondering who cuts his hair."

"You're not!" Hoyt exclaimed. He, like most men, loved her long, thick tresses.

"Someday, someday soon. Can't do Rapunzel forever."

"Why not?" asked Emmett, who had maneuvered himself and Sam next to them. They changed partners: boy/girl, boy/girl. Then swapped again, and Annie and Sam danced together.

"Just like in eighth grade," Annie gasped as she whirled Sam around.

"Get used to it, sweetheart. This is how it's going to be at the Storey Old Folks' Home." Sam ran a continuing gag about buying a multibedroomed Victorian when she turned sixty that all her single friends could come and live in. A spry older ladies' commune.

"We're going to dance all night long?"

"In my house, toots, we're gonna dance whenever we damn well please."

FIFTEEN

He sat alone in his room drinking a beer. The only light came from the television screen, where the faces from "Dallas" flickered.

He leaned over to switch the channel, then pushed his fair hair back out of his eyes. "Dallas"! What a joke. It sure wasn't any Texas he'd ever known. But then, his accommodations hadn't been private.

There was nothing else he wanted to watch. He flipped on a gooseneck lamp. The harsh direct light glared into his eyes, emphasizing lines that hadn't been etched by laughter.

He reached under his bed for a magazine. He'd read them all many times before. He went through the pictures quickly, looking for an old favorite, and then there she was: a tall, big-breasted black woman with wide hips.

Like Cindy's. He ran his mind over her body as he had his hands a couple of nights ago. It was too bad he had to wear the gloves. He never got to actually touch her body with his hands. As he thought about her face and the fear in her eyes, he grew hard. He could hear her begging and her screaming. See her body jerking with panic. And then it was over. With Cindy Dunbar in his mind, he didn't need dirty pictures.

He wondered how long it would be until next time. He could never tell. She had to be just right. He had a couple of prospects in mind. It was just a matter of choosing.

He realized the dull throbbing behind his eyes that had been bothering him all day was getting worse. The beer wasn't doing it any good. He slapped it down on top of the TV and went outside.

That was better. A walk would be better yet.

When he reached the park nearby he stopped and stretched out on a bench. The air smelled so good. It was a black night with stars blazing. If he were out in the country, he would be able to see all the constellations. But he could make out the Big Dipper now. He followed the Milky Way across the autumn sky.

He used to lie out in the grass when he was a kid and look up at the stars, trying to find the constellations that looked like pictures in his science book. He leaned over and grabbed a handful of the park's evening-damp grass and pressed it to his nose. The smell took him home.

Back to Louisiana and a night when he was a teenager, standing at the edge of a grassy field, smelling the damp cold earth, cow shit, and the odor of gasoline burning as torches lit the night.

Oh yes, he remembered that night.

He and his brother Lem had heard there was going to be some excitement over in Liggett's pasture. He'd brought it up at the supper table, and his mother shook her head while Pa growled, "You boys stay away from there. Don't go mixing in no nigger trouble."

They hadn't stayed away. When they could hear their pa snoring they'd crawled out from the midst of the four other kids asleep in the room and snuck out, their boots in their hands.

They'd scooted down the dirt roads as fast as they could go, jumping into bushes when a truck came up on them from behind. They didn't want to take the chance that somebody would tell Pa what they'd done. It never crossed their minds that someone at the meeting would snitch on them. They figured that once there, they were all in it to-gether.

They saw a glow in the sky and heard the low hum of male voices as they came out of the woods at the edge of Liggett's land.

There it was. A bonfire blazing orange, yellow, crimson in the middle of the pasture. Circling around, waving their torches and chanting something that he couldn't make out, were ten men robed in white, with the tall, pointed hoods he'd heard about but never seen before. Their faces were covered. But around the edges of the field he recognized the Ledbetter brothers from up a ways, Mr. Squires, who ran the little store down on Bottoms Road, and old Mr. Jackson, his friend Bobbie June's uncle.

Suddenly Lem gasped beside him and he jumped back, thinking that Lem had stepped on a snake. Then he followed where Lem's finger was pointing and he almost wet his pants.

Hanging from a big oak tree, off a low limb, was a rope, and from that rope, turning slowly like meat on a spit, was a colored man. As his body turned once again, he could see the man's tongue sticking out. A red stain spread across the front of the man's khaki work pants.

"Lem, do you think they . . ." he whispered to his brother.

Lem's eyes shimmied with excitement and fear as he nodded his head.

He stared from the dead man to the bonfire and back again. The circling of the robed men stopped and then it became very still. One of the men stepped out of the circle and began to talk as he uncovered his face.

Talked about the niggers getting uppity and the feds coming in and trying to tell people how to live.

"Niggers like this one here," he said as he waved his torch at the tree. "We got to show them they can't go around talking trash in the Quarters, organizing, without getting in trouble. Deep trouble. I reckon this here was one nigger who got himself in trouble right over his head."

The man laughed and the boy realized he'd heard that laugh and the singsong rhythm of the man's speech before. He focused on the man's face and knew that he was preaching the word now as he did three times a week in church: Sunday morning, Sunday night, and prayer meeting on Wednesdays. He was the minister of the Mt. Zion Primitive Baptist Church, Mr. Willard Lee Jones.

86

As he turned to share his astonishment with Lem, he felt someone approach from behind, and before he could see who it was, he felt the wind whistle and the sharp slap to his ear, and he knew. He didn't have to see to recognize the source of that kind of lick. It had to be Pa.

When they got back home, after he'd dragged them to the truck and kicked them into its open bed, Pa did what they knew he would do.

He never said a word. He bludgeoned them with the handle of an old broken ax that he kept just inside the shed door, first one, then the other, while they dodged and tried to cover their faces.

Finally their mother came to the back door and wailed, "Jesus, Jesse, that's enough." But it wasn't until Pa had grown tired and his rage had abated that he stopped. He walked back over to the shed, put the ax handle behind the door, and went into the house, letting the screen door slap shut slowly, as calmly and deliberately as if he'd just come home from a day of chopping cotton.

The next day, after church, the boy had waited around till practically everybody else had filed out, shaking hands with the preacher at the door. Offering Reverend Jones his left hand, because two fingers in his right one were broken, he whispered, "I want to talk with you about last night, sir."

Jones's eyebrows had shot up, and he'd hesitated for a moment, but then he'd said to come by his house that afternoon about three. That was the time after dinner and before evening service when most everybody else would be taking their naps, the principal Sunday afternoon activity in those parts for children, adults, and dogs alike.

They'd sat out talking on the preacher's front porch for a long spell, their rocking chairs pulled close together. When they finished the boy left with glowing eyes. He'd found something he could believe in, a home at last.

A dog barked and wakened him from his reverie. The man started up, rubbed his eyes, and walked back through the park toward his house.

He felt much better now. The night air had done him good. His headache was gone.

He stopped in front of his house for a moment and ran a hand along the roof of his car. It was wet with the damp air, but it was clean. He always kept it that way. But he'd forgotten to lower the radio antenna. That was asking for trouble. You couldn't be too careful these days.

SIXTEEN

Sam dropped her keys in the silver basket on the cherry sideboard just inside the door. She ran her hand along its polished surface. Her houseman, Jim, took such good care of her things, she thought.

She flipped through the pile of mail he had left neatly stacked for her, personal correspondence in one pile, bills in the other, so she could just add the latter to the collection on her desk in the study if she didn't want to deal with them now. Which she didn't.

There was a reminder from the benefit committee of the de Young Museum that she had to let them know how large a table she wanted to sponsor for the upcoming dance, a thank-you note from her mother for the flowers she had sent for her birthday, and a note on heavy, cream-colored vellum with Sean O'Reilly's name engraved at the top. It read, "What a lovely evening. Almost as lovely as you. Let's do it again soon. Very soon."

Indeed.

If she didn't believe it possible anymore, she'd think that the gentlemanly detective was courting her.

He'd called the day after they'd had dinner at the Square and had invited her for a sail the next weekend. It had been a lovely day. After fighting their way through the gales around the back side of Angel Island, they had tacked slowly over to Tiburon, where they'd sat out on the deck of a restaurant and devoured hamburgers and huge slabs of French fries. They'd exchanged a few stories about their pasts, but had talked mostly in the present, of their jobs, the people they knew in common. They'd kept it light, simple. When he'd dropped her off at her door, exhausted from the day of sunshine and sea spray, he leaned down and kissed her on the cheek and then was gone before she had time to decide if she wanted to invite him in or not.

Since then there'd been a movie, a lunch. They'd joked about going bowling sometime. He was warm, intelligent, caring. He made her laugh. But he didn't press her. He didn't ask about her drinking, or not drinking. He didn't pry. He was giving her so much rope, she knew she was going to hang herself.

Then one night, he asked her to join him and two old friends for dinner. They'd gone to a Russian restaurant off Union that had no sign outside—a well-kept secret with wonderful blini, and scrumptious caviar and borscht. Sam found herself holding Sean's hand under the table. She realized she suddenly wanted this man very much.

As they were leaving the restaurant, a few steps ahead of his friends, Sean swept her into the small entryway, where he enveloped her in kisses and whispered in a fake Eastern-European accent, "Katerina, Katerina, the soldiers, they are close behind. I do not think we can make it to the border, my love."

As his friends caught up to them, Sean and Samantha lost their footing and toppled to the floor, Sean landing on top of her.

"My darling Katerina, let me make wild passionate love to you, just one time, here in the drifting snow, before the soldiers take me away."

"Sean hasn't changed at all since high school," his friend Bob observed as he stepped over the snowbound lovers into the street.

When he'd pulled his car into her driveway that night and turned off the ignition she turned to him and simply said, "Yes."

"Good," he responded.

It had been. Very, very good. Better than she could remember in years. Maybe the all-time best.

The next morning he'd sent her a single stem of tiny orchids with a card on which he'd simply signed his name. It still lived in a crystal vase beside her bed.

She found herself stroking Sean's note. She tossed it aside and walked over to the expanse of windows that looked out toward the Golden Gate. The bridge lights twinkled like a Tiffany window in the dark. Below, the foghorns at the Presidio honked their familiar cry, which had kept her company through many a night.

Yes, Sean was great. She hadn't figured out what was wrong with him yet. But she was sure she would. She always did.

She kept herself very well protected in this elegant setting of glass, brass, and crystal. The walls of her apartment were thick and its doors secure. It was filled with her music and her books and her thoughts, and no one hurt her here. She wasn't so sure she wanted to give anyone the chance.

SEVENTEEN

Annie hummed as she carefully sprinkled parsley around the cold salmon. Next there was the mayonnaise to do in the processor and she was through. She checked to make sure the white wine was in the refrigerator, tidied up the kitchen, and put out ashtrays. She was ready to receive her guest.

Slim was a character she'd been told about by her good friends and neighbors across the hall, Angie and Frank. Frank had met Slim playing sandlot basketball.

"Slim has met everybody," Frank had said. "The man was a pro-ball player. He traveled with the Globetrotters for a while. Now he's a MUNI cop. There's nobody in this city he doesn't know. Even if you don't put him in your book, you ought to talk to my man Slim." Annie had let herself be persuaded. A cooking mood had struck her, so she'd invited him to lunch.

The radio was playing "Love the One You're With" as she opened the door to his buzz.

She had read once that people size one another up within seven seconds. Slim took her about two.

He was a moderately tall, well-built black man with a half-gray, shaggy Afro. Around his neck was a thick gold chain from which hung a wiggly Italian symbol that always reminded Annie of sperm. His pale blue shirt, with three buttons open, and his slightly soiled, light gray pants were made of the fabric she and Sam called Polly & Esther. But it was his slack-jawed smile, as he crooned, "Hello, baby," and his drugged-out eyes that made her feel creepy. Was she in trouble here? Could Frank have been mistaken?

Slim was barely coherent and had a single track playing in his head. While he didn't push himself on her, he kept invading Annie's space as she moved around the table and opened the wine.

The kitchen seemed smaller than it ever had before. She was aware of his breath, watchful of his body. As she sighed over the wasted effort of the mayonnaise, she ran a quick eye over her countertop. She knew she wouldn't need it, but there it was, a ten-inch French chef's knife close at hand.

Slim didn't want to talk about playing basketball, pro players he had met, or basketball groupies. He didn't want to talk about being a MUNI cop, weird passengers he had known and loved, fun and games on the #22 Fillmore line, nothing.

Slim wanted to mutter, "Thass cool, momma. Do you have a boyfriend, a lover? What do you do for fun?" She made a mental note for the future that an interview lunch was not necessarily a good idea.

He wanted to peer soulfully into her eyes, his own heavy-lidded ones weighed down with whatever drug he had snorted, swallowed, inhaled, injected. He wanted to hold her hand with his dry, cold one across her dining table. And as she edged him toward the door, excusing herself with an imaginary midafternoon appointment a bare hour after his arrival, he wanted to lay on a big, juicy kiss. Annie turned her head and got it in the ear.

92

She double-locked the door behind him and bolted into the bathroom, where she scrubbed her ear and her face, and brushed her teeth. She laughed as she caught a glimpse of herself in the mirror.

Miss Anne, you look like you've just seen the Big Bad Wolf.

EIGHTEEN

Lola Davis, the black lawyer who had answered Annie's query ad, had called and agreed to see her later that night. Annie set off for her five o'clock exercise class filled with anticipation.

She'd been working out for a little over a year. The class combined aerobic running and jumping with slow stretches, lifts, and bends, all set to music.

The repetition and the oxygen coursing through her system both energized and relaxed her. For those three hours every week she thought about nothing. Exercise was a form of meditation. Body on, mind off.

And it worked. Finding new muscles every week, challenging herself to new heights, her body had grown strong. Some mornings, she'd told Sam, she looked at herself naked in the mirror and could hardly bear to put her clothes on.

Thinking about it made her laugh. Growing up as her mother's southern flower, warned not to go out into the sun for fear of ruining her complexion, Annie had never learned to ski, play tennis, or hit any kind of ball. When she'd first moved to California she took one look at all the physical activity around her and decided she'd moved into a gym.

At first she resisted, and then she gave it a try. But her tennis instructor made her cry. And, at a picnic, she'd embarrassed her jock date by striking out nine consecutive times at bat. When she passed thirty, and the holiday goodies seemed to hang around her tummy long into January, she'd begun to jog. She could soon do two miles, but she thought she'd die of boredom.

Finally she'd found her exercise class, with its sweet, smiling instructor, Mimi Trask, who regaled them with tales of her life as a beautiful divorcée in Sausalito while she worked their buns off.

Most of her classmates were female—of every size, race, and age. She'd become friendly with a few, had an occasional cup of coffee at Greens, the restaurant next door to class, and she had a nodding acquaintanceship with the other regulars. She was forever seeing women on the street, at the ballet, in a restaurant whom she couldn't quite place until she realized she'd never seen them before with their clothes on.

Tonight Brian, one of the lone males in class, was there. Annie called him Byron, after the womanizing English poet.

Brian used the class like an ongoing Happy Hour. The policy was that any paying member could bring a guest once for free. So every time Brian picked up another woman, which seemed to be daily, he brought her to class for a no-expense date and also got a free look at her body gyrating in a leotard.

Or if he had had no luck out in the world that day, he

94

would simply come to class alone and hope to find a fresh victim.

"You in the pink tights, be careful, Brian's behind you," a regular would call out.

And he almost always scored. Why wouldn't he? He was tall, thin, well built, with classic mustachioed California good looks and a BMW. Granted, he hadn't earned the red and white Stanford sweat suit he always wore, but in these times that didn't seem like much of a flaw.

Her workout class was at Fort Mason, a jumble of reclaimed military warehouses on the Bay, across the street from the Marina Safeway. It took Annie about four minutes to get from there to her appointment with Lola Davis.

Like many San Francisco dwellings that look deceptively small from the street, Lola's white-stuccoed, red-tiled building hid surprises. As did Lola herself.

A petite, slinky lady of about thirty-five, she was dressed in a white cashmere pullover and matching slacks, which offered a creamy contrast to her café au lait complexion. There was a wiry sensuality in her movement that reminded Annie of Eartha Kitt, as did the quality of her voice. There was also a hint of the south in her throaty "Welcome, come right in" at the door.

The apartment was huge, with heavily waxed, dark wood floors, elegant cornices, a blue-tiled fireplace in the long living room, and, off the formal dining room, a large, glass-roofed deck. Exotic flowering plants flourished there with the help of lots of Marina sunshine. They were bright spots of color around the sleek, white, Brown Jordan outdoor furniture. Lola Davis not only had taste but a law practice that must have been doing quite well. Annie wondered why a woman like this was looking for love in the personals.

Of course, she thought, so am I.

And then she decided to stop talking to herself and talk to Lola instead.

From the depths of a huge, overstuffed, blue tweed chair, Lola purred, "Before we start, there's something I wanted to ask you. I almost did it on the phone, but thought I'd wait."

"Shoot," Annie replied, thinking oh hell, she's going to chicken out on me.

The hint of a drawl that Annie had picked up earlier in Lola's speech thickened, deepened in richness like a good gumbo after hours on the stove as she asked, "Honey, where in the South are you from?"

Annie looked her straight in the eye. "Hotlanta. Georgia, sugah, and wheah did you grow up?"

"Why, I was raised in Valdosta, Miss Anne."

It wasn't until Annie had left the South that she had learned that Miss Anne is the name blacks use for all white women. It conjures up crinolines, parasols, helplessness, and airs.

The two women threw back their heads and hooted long and loud, finally wiping tears from their eyes. They slapped their knees and laughed in the way that southerners do, born out of a tradition of storytelling and enjoying a good joke.

They got up from their chairs and hugged. It was a hug of recognition, of a knowing that exists between southern blacks and whites transplanted from home, grown out of shared roots, shared territory, and a mixture of love and hate for the land that spawned them and for what they represent to one another.

That settled, Lola began to tell Annie her story.

Her father had been that exceptional character, a black doctor in a small south Georgia town. His clientele had been his own people, of course, except for an occasional redneck who, having driven off drunk into a ditch, would allow the staunching of his life's blood by a black. Lola's mother had been a schoolteacher. They had tutored her at home, stuffing her shelves and mind with books to augment her education at the local colored schoolhouse.

Lola had easily gained admittance to Atlanta University and then had won a scholarship to Georgetown, where she made Law Review. For graduation, her parents had given her a trip to Hawaii. On her way she stopped over in San Francisco and, like so many others before her, couldn't wait to get back. Passing the California boards had been no problem, nor was finding a job. San Francisco liberalism, Affirmative Action, the quota system all stood in her favor. She was brilliant and beautiful and black. Everything was going her way—until her workday ended and playtime began.

"If you think you have problems in this town, try putting yourself in my shoes," snorted Lola. "How many attractive, successful, intelligent, sophisticated *single* black men do you know, right off hand?"

Annie frowned, thinking. "None, but," she hesitated, "do you date only blacks?"

"No, but I want to marry black. I'll go to dinner, parties, dancing with anybody who's fun, but when it comes to serious romance, the children I want to have, it's different. And it's tough."

Annie agreed and encouraged Lola to go on.

"Oh, Lawsy mercy, honey," Lola joked as she settled back into her chair. "There are tales I could tell.

"Some friends fixed me up with a blind date. A doctor. A rarity, a black gynecologist. My friends had given Howard a great build up. Fantastic credentials, tennis player, divorced, no children, anxious to settle down again.

But I thought to myself, 'Lola, a doctor who's available for a blind date, there is something wrong here.'

"When I opened the door, I knew what it was." She drew herself up to her full height. "How tall would you say I am?"

"Five three?"

"Close. Try five two. I was wearing sandals that were maybe two inches. But when I opened the door, I looked *down* into his eyes. I have never looked down at a full-grown man in my life.

"Hell, he doesn't even have to bend over at the end of the examining table."

Annie rocked with laughter.

"Oh, Lola! But was he nice?"

"Sure, he was nice, but what did I care? I know it's silly, but I made him take me to a little French place way out in the Avenues where I knew we wouldn't see anyone I knew. I just felt dumb. When he called again I'd suddenly become engaged. My friends will never forgive me and certainly never fix me up again."

"How else do you meet men? Bars? Business contacts?"

"I used to do bars. Perry's, MacArthur Park, you know. But something happened to a friend in Henry Africa's and I got spooked with that whole scene."

"Tell me about it."

"My friend Lillie hadn't been in town very long and didn't know many people. One night she stopped for a drink and began talking with a man who said he was a computer engineer in Palo Alto. The next thing she knew was when she woke up the next day in a hotel room, alone, with a body like a used car. He had definitely run up some miles on her engine and put a few dents in her too. No broken bones, but lots of big purple bruises and belt marks across her back. She didn't remember a thing. Sounds trite, but it must have been the classic Mickey Finn in her drink."

"Jesus. What did she do?"

"First she had herself a good cry. Then she pulled herself together, called a taxi and went home. Filled her tub with bubble bath and soaked. The next day she went to her doctor and had herself checked for about forty-two kinds of VD and decided to try and forget about it."

"She didn't report it?"

"Why? What are the cops going to do? She didn't know his real name, where he lived or worked. And she was a black woman who allowed herself to be picked up. You pays your money and you takes your chances, you know. Most folks think a woman in a bar is Goodbarring, looking for trouble, anyway."

"And you think the personals are safer? You can ask for photos, but you really don't even know what the guys look like until they show up."

"Yes, but you can screen them. If you place the ad, you have their letters, photos, and you decide whether to call them. You can tell an awful lot on the phone. You don't have to give them your name unless you feel good about them. And then you always set up the meeting in a café— for a cup of coffee—no booze, and you can get away quick."

"How many responses did you get?"

"An even dozen. And some of those weren't even in the ballpark. Four prisoners. Ha! I work the other side of that street.

"One's a dentist who sounds nice, if a bit stuffy. And a salesman I'm meeting next weekend."

"I wish you luck. And me too."

"I'll drink to that." Lola raised her glass. "We'll keep each other posted. Okay?"

The time had slipped by. It was getting late.

They walked down the stairs together. At the bottom

99

Lola turned, gave her a quick hug, and said, "Ya'll come back, y'hear?"

It was the standard southern parting line, often a pleasantry, signifying nothing, but Annie knew that in Lola she had a newfound friend. She would be coming back, soon.

NINETEEN

The steps of the Jewish Community Center were humming. Small boys in short pants scampered up and down, yelling. Several gray-haired ladies waited for the bus. A friendly black Labrador was searching for a tossed ball.

He leaned against the building, watching the scene on the steps while keeping one eye on the door.

He had only recently discovered the center at the corner of California and Presidio in Pacific Heights, far from his home. In the past few days he had spent several hours here, watching.

A class let out. Ten or fifteen women exited, cheeks glowing, talking in twos and threes. A few were alone. He noted the time, six-thirty. They were right on schedule, chattering, gold earrings flashing, bursts of red and purple dresses. Their perfume and conversation filled the air.

A short woman with masses of dark curls caught his eye. She carried a large sketch pad in one hand, a straw tote slung over a shoulder. Her free hand smoothed her full black cotton skirt over her hips.

She had nice legs, pretty ankles. She turned to see who

100

was calling her. Behind her a woman waved. "Marcia, Marcia."

Her glance crossed his. She smiled. Pretty, strong, white teeth. Hints of a full bosom billowed beneath a loose pink blouse. A gold six-pointed star twinkled in the hollow of her throat.

Marcia. He said the name to himself. Rolled it around in his mouth.

She was it.

She didn't wait for the bus, but walked a half-block to her old orange and gray Volkswagen van. An ancient sticker that read BRANDEIS UNIVERSITY was peeling across the rear window. It was easy to follow the slow-moving vehicle south across town, Masonic to Clayton, along the tops of the hills, intersecting Market, into the Castro area. She parked the van in front of a pink and purple Victorian, and scrambled up the steps with her arms full. She never saw him behind her.

In the next few days he would follow Marcia to the laundry, the art supply store, her studio on Arkansas Street. Her thoughts were filled with a new sculpture she was doing for a group show.

His thoughts were filled with her.

TWENTY

Like most of her students, Annie usually dressed for class in casual slacks or jeans, a sweater, and a comfortable old blazer. But tonight, this last class before Halloween, the quintessential San Francisco holiday, she was putting on her Halloween costume. Annie was going to class as Dolly Parton.

She had borrowed the basic components from Sam, who had worn them to a party the year before: a bubbly, bouffant platinum wig and a 40DD bra. Annie provided her own polyester pillow stuffing, heavy makeup, gold hoop earrings, and too tight jeans. The southern accent she already had.

As she walked down the hall to her classroom, the overhead lamps casting highlights in her silvery hair, a transformation began. She felt herself getting into it: a giggle in her throat, a new wiggle in her walk, a proud, chest-out arch in her back.

She had planned to be just a couple of minutes late for a dramatic entrance. When she opened the classroom door and sauntered in there were looks of shock, surprise, leers of admiration, but no recognition in the eyes of her students. She had pulled it off.

"Howdy. How'ya doing this evening?" she drawled.

"Fine." "Okay," a couple of students answered.

"Ms. Tannenbaum couldn't be with ya'll tonight, so she asked me to fill in for her." She sat on the edge of the desk.

"Awwwwwright," cheered Cornell.

"Why you must be Cornell." She batted her false eyelashes at him. "Ms. Tannenbaum warned me about you."

A few students in the front of the room began to titter. Eve Gold nudged the woman next to her. "Ms. Parton, we're delighted to make your acquaintance."

"Mrs. Gold, that's not Dolly Parton. She just looks like her," corrected Cornell.

"That's right," Eve flashed back, "and who do you think she is, if you're so smart, young man?"

Laughter erupted in the room and Annie could see the light dawning on Cornell's handsome brown face.

"Holy shit, Ms. Tannenbaum, is that you in there?"

The class broke up.

Annie waggled over to his desk and leaned down. "Why sure, sugar, who'd you think it was?"

Eventually the class was able to settle down to the business at hand, which this week was the reading of their horror stories, written in honor of the season. Mayhem, gore, ghosts, dismembered bodies marched up and down the creaky stairs of their minds. There were some real beauts.

It was all in good fun until Annie called on Eddie Simms, the student who usually slept through class. He smirked as he read his story, the first assignment he had ever completed. Annie wished he hadn't. His wasn't just a horror story; it was a loathsome journey into a country she never wanted to visit.

"That is *sick*, man," Cornell finally said in the silence that followed.

"Yuk," Gladys Chiu agreed, and they moved on to old Mr. Garfield's whimsical tale about a little boy who was afraid of his image in the mirror when his back was turned.

After class there was some close-up inspection of Annie's costume and talk of what everyone was going to wear on the big night. Cornell volunteered that he was going as either Colonel Sanders or a chicken.

At home Annie pulled Agatha up into the driveway of her building's large communal garage. As she got out to unlock and pull up the heavy door, a couple walking their dog across the street whistled. She was startled; San Franciscans are usually a bit more reserved. Then she remembered her costume and waved at them.

She flipped the light switch at the door, got back into Agatha, and drove to her parking space toward the back of the garage. Her high-heeled steps echoed on the concrete floor. This walk made her especially nervous since neighbors told her a tenant had once been raped here.

The safest procedure was to drive the car through, stop just inside, pull the exterior door down, and lock it. But no one ever did. It was too much trouble.

So too was making sure the connecting door to the lobby was locked from the garage side.

But the security of that door was problematic. If both the lobby door and the exterior garage doors were locked, the building was secure, but you could be locked in a box with an intruder. The alternative was to make the building more vulnerable to a burglar, who could open any glass-paned apartment door in the building with a glass cutter.

Was it better to roll down a mountain with one's seat belt tightly fastened after a picnic and a bottle of wine, or to take one's chances in jumping? Annie could never decide.

She kept meaning to speak to Tony, the super, about it.

Across the hall, Angie was practicing "Für Elise" on her piano. She was getting a lot better. In front of her door was a note from Angie inviting her over for a piece of chocolate cake.

Frank and Angie were the best neighbors she'd ever had, with the exception of Tom Albano long ago. Sometimes, when Frank was out, she and Angie would leave their doors open and traipse back and forth in their nightgowns with their respective phones pulled near the doors as they drank coffee and chatted.

A little blonde brick from the Bronx, Angie had a kind of solid common sense that Angie had come to lean on. A bonus was her mother's spaghetti gravy, calamari, and other Italian recipes that had given Annie a whole new way of looking at North Beach Italian restaurants and had even resulted in a couple of articles.

Frank was another kind of joy, a horse of a different color. Whereas Angie barely cleared five feet with a chrysanthemum burst of blonde hair and energy, Frank loomed up at 6' 5" and was a slow-talking, slow-moving black man from Tennessee. He was enthusiastic about computer programming, which he did for a living, the basketball he played in his spare time, both reading and writing poetry, and Angie. He was most often a quiet man, though he loved to laugh and, even more, to tickle Angie.

There was a time when he goosed her so loudly in the bathroom ventilated by an airshaft that conducted sound up and down the six stories that a note had suddenly appeared in the elevator exhorting Frank's lady to hold down her early morning passion or to keep her business to herself.

Frank's response concerned itself with those who ain't getting any. Both signs were decorated with graffiti and neighbors' votes of confidence for a day or two and then disappeared, the tempest fading away.

In addition to being the building's tallest tenant, Frank was also its only black. Several times, little old ladies had visibly jumped at opening the elevator door to find Frank's lanky dark form standing there. He always smiled.

Annie rang their buzzer. "Okay," yelled Angie, "I'm coming.

"Oh, my God," she shrieked when she saw Annie's Dolly Parton drag.

Frank sat down on the carpet and rolled with laughter.

Then they got down to the serious business of stuffing half a dark chocolate cake with chocolate filling and whipped cream down their faces.

They were licking their fingers when Annie's downstairs buzzer rang. It was Sam, on her way home from work.

"Great!" said Frank. They liked Sam, but didn't see her very often.

Angie got another plate and fork, and began to make a fresh pot of coffee.

Sam was looking beautiful in a gray wool suit and purple silk blouse.

Settled at the kitchen table, she twitted Annie. "Do you think this is proper schoolmarm behavior?" she asked Frank.

"Well, I sure never had any teachers who looked like that in Memphis," he drawled. "If I had, I'd probably have gone to school more often."

Angie poured coffee all around and asked Sam, "You're working on the Mt. Diablo story, aren't you? Didn't I see your by-line?"

"Yes. Thanks for noticing it. Boy, it's really a killer."

They all groaned.

"Sorry. This guy Murphy who killed his parents has got me going. Very spooky. Very cool, very brilliant, and so controlled. But with enough screws loose to make a tool kit."

"So is he the one who killed all the hikers?"

"Doesn't look like it. No, I don't think so."

"Oh, shit," said Angie.

"I know. No closer than they were a month ago."

The conversation moved on to something much more pleasant, Angie and Frank's upcoming wedding. With her relatives and his, it was going to require the skills of a UN protocol chief, but Angie was determined it was going to go smoothly.

"We'll just keep shoveling food and booze down them," she said. "They won't even notice what's happening. After that, the baby will be easy."

"Baby!" Annie cried.

"No, no, not yet. First the wedding. But soon." She grinned. "Frank can't wait to see what an Afro-Italian named Spike is going to look like."

"And if it's a girl?" asked Sam.

"No difference," Frank said, serious-faced. "And she still has to play basketball."

"Get out of here." Angie slapped at him.

Then they all kissed good night, and Sam and Annie went across the hall.

"The man in the Porsche called again." Sam couldn't wait to share her news.

"He said he didn't show up that time at the Square because he was too shy. He felt unworthy. Seems as though I'm a shining star he should worship from a distance. Tomorrow he's going to send me a token of his affection."

"Did you tell him to buzz off?"

"I told him he was making me very uncomfortable and that I didn't want him to carry on like this. I swear, I think he was breathing heavy at the discouragement."

"The next thing you know, he'll send you a whip from that freak shop, Hard-On Leather."

"I wouldn't doubt it." She paused. "I wonder what it's going to be?"

"Don't ask me, dearie. You're the one with the weird taste in playmates."

"Ha! Who's talking? David the Deviant isn't exactly Laurence Olivier."

"And how do you know what Olivier's *really* like?"

"I bet he never took Vivien Leigh to dinner at the Doggie Diner."

Annie poked at her.

The ringing phone interrupted their play.

"If it's David, tell him the ferry leaves for Alcatraz in ten minutes."

"Very funny."

It was Slim. In a semistupor. He wanted to have a drink soon. Annie was evasive.

"Why didn't you just tell him to buzz off?"

107

"Because my mother raised me to be a southern lady."
Sam guffawed. "If you think about that a minute, you'll
get the joke."

Before turning out her bedside light Annie made a list of
what she had to do the next day, the day before Halloween: Talk with Quan about taking Quynh trick or treat-
ing. Costume consultation with Quynh. Finish the piece on
southwestern food. Stop by for a drink with David. Answer
her parents' letter. Pick up cleaning. Call Lola Davis about
lunch soon.

TWENTY-ONE

As she pulled on her favorite orchid sweats and rolled up
her blue exercise mat, Annie remembered what Sam's very
active, silver-haired Aunt Catherine had said to her recently.

"You know, dear, I watch other women in my exercise
class, and what fascinates me is the expression on their
faces. Their eyes are all glazed, their gazes turned inward,
totally absorbed with their bodies. I'm reminded of the
eyes of dogs I've seen copulating."

She and Sam had exploded with laughter, but the
thought kept coming to mind. Is that what she looked like?

And, if so, is that the same way she looked when she did
have sex? Totally absorbed with her body? That pretty

much described how she felt with David. There certainly wasn't much else happening between them.

She was headed toward him now.

"Why don't you drop by for a drink, Annie?"

Or a "pop."

Or a "bite."

It all meant the same thing. Their bodies were going to spend an hour, or two, or sometimes even three together, and then one of them was going to get dressed and go home.

It certainly wasn't unpleasant. It just wasn't enough.

Today it certainly wasn't. Because, as sometimes happened, he wasn't home.

He didn't stand her up too often. He wasn't entirely foolhardy or mean. But occasionally something came up or their date seemed to slip his mind.

Maybe today he was just late. He had said something about some errands to run. She let herself in. They'd exchanged keys for convenience's sake.

A stale smell hit her in the face. She flipped on the light. No wonder. Food sat on the dining table.

"Dammit!" She'd kicked over a cold cup of coffee on the floor, greasy with old cream.

How could David, a photographer who did very fine work, live like such a pig? He seemed to be getting worse. She eyed his water bed over in the corner, unmade, with rumpled sheets askew. She wondered how long they had been on the bed. And under whom? It didn't do to think about.

But he was clean about his person. She always pushed him in the shower first and made sure of that.

She was thirsty. A soda or tonic would be nice. She wondered if she dared to look in the refrigerator.

She steeled herself and opened it.

109

Not so bad. Nothing green growing. Mostly empty, in fact. Except for film and two six-packs of beer. She opened one can and settled down in his easy chair. Might as well make herself comfortable.

She looked around for something to read.

Shuffling through a pile of papers on the floor, she found an old copy of the *Bay Guardian* opened to the classifieds, the personals. Some were circled in red with the china marker he used on contact sheets. She looked around the room, shifted in her chair. Was this like reading someone's mail?

Maybe. But that certainly wasn't going to stop her.

"Zoftig brown-eyed beauty seeks mensch," began one.

"Asian lady looking for man of any race to celebrate fall as well as cherry blossoms."

"Is there anyone out there who's man enough to appreciate a petite black female lawyer?"

Was that Lola's ad? She slapped her forehead and laughed.

So David was playing the ads too. It was just too funny.

She looked back at Lola's ad. He certainly hadn't read it through. As she thought, Lola specified a black man. Maybe David couldn't read.

Uh, oh. Bitchy, bitchy, she reprimanded herself. He's entitled. Or was he?

There were several other papers in the pile. All *Guardian*s. She started through them and suddenly the thought hit her. She riffled through them quickly, looking for the right date. There it was. *Her* issue of the paper.

She flipped quickly to the back, to the end, the last column. There it was, circled.

"What I'd really like is a funny, tall . . ." It was her ad!

Had he written to her? She didn't think so. But maybe she hadn't read closely enough and had skipped over it. She couldn't wait to get home and see.

As a matter of fact, since he was so late, she was leaving right now.

TWENTY-TWO

After a fruitless search through her pile of letters for one from David, Annie made a quick dinner of pasta with mushrooms and tucked herself into bed with a Dick Francis novel she hadn't read. The young jockey hero had just begun to suspect who was fixing his races when Annie called it a night.

She dreamed that she was romping through a meadow in a billowy, yellow organdy dress with a ribboned straw hat in one hand. Her other hand was holding that of a tall, big-shouldered man. He picked her up and swung her around as if she were a child. They tripped and rolled down a grassy hill together, tumbling over and over, landing in a tangled mass of laughter and kisses.

She awakened with a cry. She wanted to go back to the dream. She didn't want to leave the meadow and the man whose face she had never seen, whose name she didn't know. But she knew that she had been his beloved.

No matter how much she wanted to pretend, however, it was her alarm clock that had awakened her, not Prince Charming. Snow White would just have to keep on dreaming. In the meantime, the reality was that it was Halloween and she still had a million things to do and had better get cracking.

She looked at her list. Mission Street for typewriter ribbons. The costume shop for masks. Quynh was dressing as a cat tonight and she wanted to get her something really special—maybe she'd pick up masks for Sam and herself too. While she was in the neighborhood she might as well swing by the flower market. It would be nice to take something, maybe some calla lilies, to Quan.

She threw on a pair of jeans, and a purple-and-blue sweater Sam had given her and started out the door when she noticed the blinking red light on her answering machine. She had switched off its ring the night before.

Three calls. People had been up very late or very early. Slim's call she would ignore. A limp apology from David. Well, he'd have to do a hell of a lot better than that, if and when she spoke with him again. Sam's early morning not-quite-awake-but-all-business voice. What time were they picking up Quynh? Had she made a decision yet about going to Sam's annual charity ball? Sean O'Reilly had her really worried. She still couldn't figure out what was wrong with him. A final mysterioso P.S. about the White Knight in the charging Porsche that made Annie put her bag down and call Sam right back.

"He was waiting for me when I got home. Sitting on my doorstep with a rose in his hand. A symbol, he said, of my purity."

Annie snorted. "I think he has you confused with some other fairy-tale princess."

Sam ignored the comment. "He looks normal enough. Dressed like anybody else: jeans, yellow shirt. He's rather nice looking, good body, blond hair. His name is Jack Sharder and I think he's bonkers."

"Yeah?"

"I thanked him nicely and said 'Okay, now this is it, I appreciate the posy, but I have a boyfriend and you have to go away now.' He didn't get the message. Said he doesn't want to be a bother, but it's his job to worship and protect me."

"Oh, great. A regular knight. I thought those guys went out with armor and sword fighting."

"Well, this one is still alive and kicking in San Francisco. I think I'm going to ask Sean to run a check on Sharder. Oh, crap, that reminds me."

"What?"

"More bad news, Annie."

It was definitely bad news. Another young woman's body had been found—in her studio South of Market.

"Rape, strangulation, a knife. Same pattern as the other two. A sculptor. Her name was Marcia Cohen."

TWENTY-THREE

After that Sunday afternoon meeting with Reverend Lee the boy had met once a week with the men as they sat around on their haunches smoking cigarettes, chewing, spitting, and plotting.

They weren't as exciting squatting in their work clothes as they had been on that first night. Now they were just neighbors, young and old, he'd known forever.

But when they circled and burned in the nighttime, with the flames flickering up and down their white robes, they became strange and wonderful, powerful, magical, grand.

113

They were the most marvelous things the boy had ever known. They made him tingle with dreams of possibilities.

If he could be one of them, he would be somebody. He wouldn't be just one of his pa's boys riding the bus to school, town girls like Missy Cartwright laughing at him. It wouldn't matter that when he played basketball he didn't wear a number and satin shorts. The chicken shit on his boots and the mended holes in his jeans wouldn't be important when he covered them with a white robe. He would be special. He would have power.

But the power didn't come free.

He had to earn it.

Brother Jones had spelled it out for him simple and slow one night.

"You've got to prove it to us, that you're man enough to belong. You got to want it like you never wanted anything in your life. Bad enough to taste it. Bad enough to die for it."

I do, I can, the boy thought. I'll do anything. Just tell me what you want.

"It won't be easy," the Reverend had said.

Neither was jumping off the top of the barn when he was four because Lem had dared him to. Neither was walking home six miles with a broken arm after he'd fallen off a railroad trestle. Neither was picking up a rattlesnake at a healing meeting and watching it crawl across his chest, its tongue licking at his cheeks, and feeling it wrap itself around his ears. But he'd done it and it had worked. His headaches had gone away for a while.

Neither was living with his pa all his life, for that matter, but he'd done that too.

"And afterward, you have to bring back something to prove that you did it," Reverend Jones was saying.

Eddie had rolled back his head and laughed.

Was that all they wanted?
Easy as falling off a log.

He'd followed Lucinda Washington for a couple of days, and he could see why they wanted her. She was one uppity little nigger girl.

She'd won some scholarship that the Yankees gave to smart little niggers who wanted to better themselves. Now she was getting ready to go off to college.

She'd be the first one anybody ever heard of who'd gone up north to school. Then, she said, she planned to come back home and help her people.

That's what it looked like Lucinda Washington thought she was going to do as she sashayed her tight little butt to town with her momma, buying yards of material to make her some pretty dresses to take off to Yankeeland.

It wouldn't take him long to put a stop to that.

When she stepped out her back door that night, like she always did, at about ten o'clock to put the trash in the burn barrel, he was waiting for her.

After the first soft "Uunh" when he grabbed her from behind she hadn't made a sound. Her eyes had rolled, shining white in her black face in the dark night, and then they had bulged bigger and bigger as he had choked all the breath out of her. The knife had made a little *splllt* as it slipped through her skirt into her belly, and Lucinda was one still little nigger girl. Dying. Her legs had moved then, flopped apart as he dropped her beside the trash barrel. It was then that he realized the blood pounding in his ears was also pumping in his groin and he was hard.

Why not? he thought. First piece might as well be her. Sure as hell was easier than wrestling some little piece of white trash out of her drawers.

It was just as good as they'd told him it would be.

He almost forgot what Reverend Jones had said and was halfway out of the yard and her momma was yelling out the back door. "Lucinda, what's taking you so long, girl?"

Then he remembered. He scrambled back into the yard, his heart pounding like crazy, his breath short and loud. Mrs. Washington must be able to hear him from the back porch. It was so dark he almost stumbled over Lucinda's body. He grabbed the first thing he came to.

Walking on home, he felt it in his jacket pocket, squeezed it and laughed.

Niggertoes. That's what everybody around here called Brazil nuts, and he had a real one in his pocket.

It was his ticket of admission into the club.

TWENTY-FOUR

New York has its Thanksgiving Day Parade and the Christmas windows on Fifth Avenue. New Orleans has Mardi Gras. But Halloween is San Francisco at its most essential: indulger of fantasies, home of aberrants, encourager of dreams, playground for many a flashy loser whose private parade has not yet led him to nose dive off the Golden Gate Bridge.

The holiday, like the city, wears more than one face.

Doors opened with alacrity at Quynh's excited ringing, and a bounty of goodies came her way. But careful, careful, Annie and Sam had to warn her. Put nothing in your mouth until we get home. And then they had to explain to the little girl that generosity was not always what it seemed as they discarded anything that was not presealed or wrapped. Hudson watched solemnly as the fudge, apples, and candied corn balls went into the trash.

"But why would anyone want to hurt children with razor blades or glass, Auntie Annie?"

Why indeed?

Why would anyone want to turn a masquerade ball into a brawl? That was the question Annie and Sam had asked themselves a few years earlier when they had dressed up and traipsed off to the Hookers' Ball.

Founded as a semiprivate affair by Margo St. James, an ex-madam, the ball was a benefit for COYOTE, Call Off Your Old Tired Ethics. COYOTE was a support group for prostitutes, and the affair was one of those events that gave the outlanders a reason to pour into the city to watch the crazies and the naughty ladies. And then it had grown too large. The ball Annie and Sam attended had five thousand costumed drunks stumbling around the Civic Auditorium.

Some partygoers were completely naked; many others wore strategically placed G-strings, body paint, feathers, sequins, and tassels. Men paraded as Cleopatra, Brigitte Bardot, French maids, nurses, and sex slaves from *The Story of O,* with gold chains and long dresses. They saw women dressed as Charlie Chaplin, Little Bo Peep, and Joan of Arc. Team efforts included Tarzan and Jane, Laurel and Hardy, and Little Miss Muffet and her Tuffet. Mass efforts were the Marx Brothers and the Dionne Quintuplets. Their favorite was a group of five: a bacon, lettuce, and tomato sandwich on rye.

But there were too many people, too much dope, too much booze. The outlanders included groups of young

117

toughs who thought the Ball's title guaranteed that all the women present were hookers or wanted to be. Women were molested in corridors and ladies' rooms. The escalating ugliness reached a peak at about midnight as Annie and Sam pushed through an upstairs hall trying to find their way out.

They were holding hands, Annie in her Boy Scout uniform, Sam dressed as a Brownie, when suddenly they were stuck.

In front of them was a Hooker's Helper, a supplementary security guard in a red T-shirt who looked like his colors usually read "Hell's Angels." He was talking with a small gang of young toughs. They had surrounded a terrified young blonde and were giving her a bad time. The spokesman of the group stepped up in a nose-to-nose confrontation with the Helper. Words became shouts, fist-shaking escalated to the crack of a flashlight against an arm bone, and then a switchblade glinted in the overhead light.

Sam and Annie were on the inside of the circle of fascinated spectators that had quickly formed. They were trying to get out. The ringside action was threatening to spill over onto their bodies.

Sam had seen enough blood in her career to know that this was going to get very ugly very fast. Annie, like most people, had almost always had the cushion of a 19-inch color TV screen between her and real blood and guts. An occasional fight between kids when she was teaching had been stopped quickly with a loud, "Okay, let's break it up here." Most kids just wanted to get in a few licks to prove their manhood and were grateful to back away.

This, however, was hardball.

The flash of the knife made Annie feel sick to her stomach. Before she and Sam could push their way out the knife had found a home in the Helper's belly. A darker red quickly began to flood onto his crimson T-shirt.

Annie felt the corridor start spinning. Waves of nausea were crashing, threatening to overflow. Her mouth tasted yellow.

Finally they broke loose from the crowd and escaped into the street. They ran through the great open space that is the Civic Plaza, ringed by white-marbled, mansard-roofed public buildings.

That night the plaza was quiet, dark, cold, still—its emptiness a welcome surcease from the claustrophobic madness. It was a couple of years yet until Dan White would murder George Moscone and Harvey Milk in cold blood in one of those cool, white buildings, and protestors would turn the plaza into a burning stage.

That had done it for them. The next few Halloweens they had stayed home, but seeing the evening through Quynh's eyes this year made them brave again. When she was a child Annie had loved Halloween best of all. Roaming the streets of Atlanta in a bed sheet, being fed hot chocolate, bobbing for apples, surveying her haul when she got back home was better than Christmas and Hanukkah.

So, after they had left Quynh and Hudson stuffed and groggy with sugar, they decided to give the Castro Street celebration a chance. Five minutes. If they didn't like it, they could always go home.

The gay community had long since claimed the holiday as well as the city for their own. It was dress-up time for even the most staid and closeted drag queens. And as the center of homosexual activity had moved from Polk Street to Castro, so had the main Halloween promenade route. Two blocks from the epicenter at Castro and Market, almost right in front of Hoyt's building, they found a parking spot. Perhaps it was a good omen.

Quynh had insisted that Annie take her cat mask and

Sam was wearing the face of Frankenstein. They double-checked that Agatha was all locked up and, before they knew it, they were swept away by the crowd.

"Yowhee," Sam shouted. "This is great."

Teetering beside them on the sidewalk were two men in tall, pink, rubbery contraptions that ended just above their heads. Their bodies were garbed in pink leotards and tights. Gold rings encircled their chests.

"They're dicks," Sam cried.

"Samantha, hush!"

"No, look. That's what they are. Penises—with cock rings."

The two pink phalli bobbed at them and disappeared into the crush.

Next was a flurry of drag queens with excessive bosoms, wobbly high heels, and yards of lace and brocade. With their broad shoulders they resembled Eastern European matrons on their way to a garage sale, but they were obviously giddy on their illusions.

As Annie and Sam turned the corner onto Castro Street, they gasped at the size of the crowd. Both sidewalks were jammed, the mob undulating like snakes. The center of the street was open to traffic by order of the police.

Scores of street marshals recruited from the gay community wore white T-shirts with red lettering proclaiming THERE IS NO STREET PARTY. They politely encouraged people to stay on the sidewalks and keep cool. Real cops were in their regular dark blues, though a few here and there sported Groucho glasses and big smiles. So far, so good. Everything was under control.

Halfway up the block, an open convertible cruised slowly. Perched in the back seat was a pretty young red-haired man, blue-eyed, lithe of body, wearing a shimmering, golden, woman's bathing suit and high heels. Atop his curls was a rhinestone tiara. He waved majestically to the cheering crowed. His lifelong dream of being homecoming queen had come true.

A man in head-to-toe Frankenstein garb bumped into Sam and they became embroiled in a good-natured argument about who was the real Frankenstein. He won hands down, and Sam defaulted by removing her mask. As she leaned over to give him a congratulatory kiss, he grabbed her and lifted her high above the crowd. Sam screamed in perfect imitation of Elsa Lanchester. Annie wished she'd brought her camera.

She could have tucked it into her bag along with her cat mask. Its eye holes had been fine for Quynh, but she found she couldn't see very well through it and she didn't want to miss a thing.

Now, both bare-faced, they waded on toward Eighteenth Street. From somewhere in the crowd, a voice yelled, "Samantha, Samantha, over here."

They both turned. But there were too many faces.

"Over here, Samantha. I love you!"

"What the hell," Sam sputtered. Then Annie grabbed her arm and turned her around.

"Look," she pointed to the middle of the street. "There."

"Oh, my God, it's Jack Sharder."

"Who?"

"Sharder. The White Knight."

Annie finally focused on the white sports car he was driving. The Porsche.

He had stopped his car in traffic and was getting out, brandishing a large bouquet of flowers. However, a very large policeman was pushing him back in.

"Where do you think you're going, buddy? This isn't a parking lot."

121

"Samantha!" he cried again, tossing the bouquet toward her as if she were a bridesmaid.

"Oh, Jesus," Sam said. "I don't believe this."

"Yaaaaaa!" the crowd yelled, and a man in a long purple robe and full makeup caught the bouquet, which he turned and gallantly presented to Sam.

"No, thank you, Princess," she said. "They're all yours."

The policeman was insisting and the Porsche scooted off with Sharder, half-turned, blowing good-bye kisses.

"You think he carries flowers with him all the time, on the off chance he's going to run into you?"

"That, or more likely he's tailing me."

"Not so funny."

"No, not funny at all." Sam was not smiling.

But it was hard to stay somber in the carnival atmosphere. They were pushed along into the middle of a drag-queen beauty contest in front of the Castro Theater. Most of the participants were overdressed, blowsy, camping it up for the crowd. Then onto the imaginary runway stepped a gorgeous brunette, sylphlike in a black satin sheath. A gamin face with huge brown eyes peeped shyly from behind long, long lashes. He was Audrey Hepburn, a shy young faun.

Even the silly queens knew class when they saw it, and there was a tiny island of stillness around him for just a moment. Then respectful applause began, swelling into an ovation.

Annie found a lump growing in her throat.

It was silly and sentimental, and more than a little twisted, but then, she even cried at touching television commercials. She was a pushover.

Annie scanned the crowd. There was so much going on it was difficult to focus. Then she caught a glimpse of a familiar profile beneath a black cowboy hat. The crush shifted for a moment and she saw a black shirt, black pants, sparks of silver. Was it David?

How many people could they run into in one night whom they knew? But San Francisco really was a small town, so small that one saw people who were strangers over and over again in the same restaurants, bars, in movie lines, until they became familiar.

The man in black turned. She was right, it was David. But those weren't gay drag leathers. He was in costume as her all-time favorite cowboy, Lash LaRue. She couldn't see the long black whip, but she was sure it was there on his hip.

"David, David," she called. Why did she want him to see her?

He turned and seemed to look her full in the face. She was positive there was eye contact, that she was not just a face in the crowd. But he looked away and, like quicksilver, disappeared into a crack in the wall of flesh.

It was getting late, and fighting to stay vertical in the crowd was exhausting.

"How about a Just Desserts run before we go home?" Sam asked. The dessert shop was only a couple of blocks away.

Annie grinned. She never had to be asked twice.

As usual, the pecan pie and chocolate brownies washed down with good, strong coffee were wonderful. They were wiping the last crumbs off their plates with their fingers when a young man dressed as Count Dracula came in, excitedly announcing a fire a few blocks away.

Annie and Sam exchanged a look. The combination of danger, dark blue uniforms, athletic bodies, and those shiny, long, red trucks spelled a fascination they shared.

They followed the sirens and the glow in the dark sky.

Street traffic was hopelessly snarled as one piece of fire equipment after another raced toward the exploding, three-story Victorian house. They couldn't have moved Agatha if they'd wanted to.

It was a spectacular blaze. Flames shot out the top of the building, completely engulfing a utility shed on the roof. It stood out in black relief against the orange inferno.

The crowd buzzed with admiration for the firemen. How quickly they'd responded. How daring they were. Three of them scaled an impossibly tall ladder to the roof, with cheers and applause from the crowd below.

Two mustachioed young gays stood next to Sam and Annie.

"God, would you look at that!" said the one in the yellow sweater.

"I know. Isn't it frightening," said his friend in blue. "I'm terrified of heights."

"No," his friend pointed, "I mean *that*. Isn't he a hunk?"

It was, after all, the Castro.

Of course, Annie and Sam were thinking the same thoughts.

"What do you think caused it?" someone asked.

"A torch job probably, for the insurance."

"No," piped up a short young man in Levis and a purple T-shirt proclaiming SEX IS LIKE SNOW. YOU NEVER KNOW HOW MANY INCHES YOU'RE GOING TO GET OR HOW LONG IT'S GOING TO LAST. "I live over there," he pointed a couple of houses down, "and this building was just being renovated. It was almost finished, a real beauty. I can't imagine why anyone would *want* to burn it down."

"Unless it was some nut," volunteered a woman in a ladybug costume.

After half an hour Annie and Sam had had enough, and the crowd had begun to break up. They left the stragglers to their speculations, rescued Agatha from among the engines and hoses, and headed home.

"That really was fun," Sam said on the drive crosstown. "Best Halloween I can remember in a long time."

"Me too." The Volkswagen protested the ski slope climb up Lombard to Sam's house. "And here's your front door, madam. Shall I see you in to check for tributes from your White Knight? Or ghosties or goblins?"

"No, thank you. I can handle them all by myself."

Annie waited until Sam had unlocked her downstairs door and was waving good night from inside. It was a small courtesy they always paid one another at night. Not just door to door, but inside and safe.

The next morning Annie sat on the steps of her apartment building waiting for a ride from her friend Jacqui to exercise class. The door behind her opened and Rick, a young tenant she had seen several times on the elevator, brushed past her. She smiled and said hello. He smiled back sheepishly.

Then she understood. A few feet behind him was the young man he had obviously picked up the night before. His friend was dressed in a golden, gauzy fairy costume with a tulle tutu skirt, shimmery tights, and a golden wand. For whatever reason, probably because he might never see him again, Rick hadn't lent him clothes to get home in.

Annie couldn't stop the giggle that followed them across the street to Rick's car. He waved at her with an embarrassed flip of a hand as he loaded his trick-or-treat favor into the car for the ride back to morning-after reality and home. She waved good-bye to the ghost of Halloween Past.

TWENTY-FIVE

Lola and Annie had concurred that the best burger in town was at the Balboa Café, and a burger was the perfect antidote to Thanksgiving turkey. The restaurant was part of that great singles swamp at Fillmore and Filbert they called the Bermuda Triangle, but the hamburger on baguette with grilled onions was worth it. Lola ordered a bottle of Mirassou champagne to wash it down. "Why not?" she said. "We deserve it. To *Meeting Cute.*" She toasted Annie with her tulip-shaped glass.

"So," Lola continued, "tell me how it's going. Met anybody interesting? How about that writer you were so enthusiastic about?"

Annie groaned. "Lloyd Andrews. I was slapping on wrinkle cream for a week before I met him. Needn't have bothered."

"Wasn't he interested in your long, white body?"

"He's not interested in much of anything that doesn't relate directly to the life and times of Lloyd Andrews."

"From what you said about his letter, he certainly seemed interested. How did that line go?"

"I wanted to tell you about this, so I brought it along." Annie held up the letter she'd found in her bag.

"'I read your ad and wanted you, wishing I could transport you here immediately, naked and hot and curious. I would open a bottle of champagne and we would make love until hunger drove us out at some mad hour of the night in search of food, feeling wonderful, a little crazy, and very pleasantly close.'"

Lola poured Annie another glass of champagne. "So which part didn't you get? The bubbly, the feeling wonderful, or the pleasantly close?"

"The champagne I got. The a little crazy, too, from just being there. Great apartment in Telegraph Landing, those new co-ops down by the Embarcadero, all multileveled, lots of thick carpet and views over to the East Bay. That was nice. But I also got two nonstop hours of the Lloyd Andrews Story. With no breaks for audience participation.

"He never asked. 'And what do you do? Or think? Or are you alive?'

"It wouldn't have been so bad, but as I told you, I'd read all his work and it's very autobiographical, so I already knew the stories. It was like going to the movie after you've read the book. Except the book was better."

Lola laughed, and signaled the waiter to clear, ordering some coffee for both of them. "Was he at least nice looking?"

"A little like Kenny Rogers, which certainly isn't bad. But with a few more pounds in the gut. That was okay, if he just hadn't been so God-awful egocentric."

"We can hope that when you become a rich and famous author you don't also become fat, pompous, and boring, or does it come with the territory?"

"God, I hope not. I plan to remain svelte and humble and fascinating, my own self."

"I'll drink to that." Lola sipped her coffee.

"And how about you? How's *your* love life? Met any more midget gynecologists?"

"Nope. No blind dates. No ads."

"Why?"

"I've pretty much run through the possibilities of the letters I got."

"Oh, God, that reminds me." Annie told her about David and the ads he had circled in the *Guardian,* including Lola's.

"I'll look back and see if there's anybody who sounds like him. It's possible. I just skimmed over the ones from white boys. If I find him, should I give him a call?"

Annie laughed. "Wouldn't that be funny? Up to you, my friend. Depends on what you're looking for."

"Worth an hour or two?" Lola arched her eyebrows suggestively.

"Definitely."

"I was just teasing. I'll look and let you know."

They both ordered raspberries with *crème fraîche* and another cup of espresso.

"So you've written off Lloyd Andrews and David. Anybody else on the horizon?"

"Not really. Except this man Harry that my friend Sam introduced me to a few weeks ago at a party. But he's never called. Maybe I should give him a jingle."

The party had been in a mansion perched high on a hill in Pacific Heights. The twinkling lights of Sausalito and Tiburon across the Bay had been reflected in three mammoth mirrors on the living-room wall. The room was done in Art Deco plum, blue, white, and silver. Acres of cloud gray carpet billowed, threatening as quicksand to her high-heeled black sandals. Calla lilies and purple irises bloomed out of season in Baccarat vases. Tuxedoed waiters circulated with oysters Rockefeller, shrimp *rémoulade,* crayfish bisque in minuscule pastry cups.

Their hostess greeted Sam and Annie with a hug, handed them long-stemmed glasses of Lillet, and introduced them

128

to a small group of bejeweled older women and dark-suited men.

Annie had wandered over to the baby Steinway to give a closer listen to the Cole Porter. She chatted a bit with the pianist, Tim Belk. He was very good. He was playing Frank Sinatra's "Emily" for her when Sam approached with Harry.

Sam had mentioned Harry on the way over, a friend of an old boyfriend. She had often thought that Annie might like him, but he wasn't an easy one. He could be a little off-putting at first.

Annie could see what she meant. It wasn't that he wasn't attractive. He was 6' 2", about 200 pounds, with football shoulders but a little softness around the middle. His face was round, his teeth even and white, his eyes that kind of chameleon hazel that changed with the color of his shirt. What was left of his hair was about the color of hers. But she didn't mind balding men.

The oddness was in his manner. After Sam introduced them and tactfully disappeared they exchanged the usual pleasantries about the house, the view, the food, and were just about to move to a second more personal plateau when he lurched off. He evaporated, with a sudden flash of shoulders and elbows that seemed to be the first part of him to go.

So he didn't find me fascinating, she thought. But I won't take this personally. I'm appropriately dressed. My hair is clean. She checked herself quickly in a mirror. I do not have spinach in my teeth. I did not say anything stupid. This is his problem, not mine.

Then he reappeared at her elbow. He steered her into the dining room to show her a painting. He was a collector. He would have loved to own this piece, a magnificent Frankenthaler, but hadn't had the cash at the time. Their hostess obviously never had any kind of cash flow problem.

His style of conversation was thrust-parry. He talked

129

very rapidly. His sentences seemed to come out of the middle of paragraphs that were running in his mind. Once he had spoken, he disappeared—either he walked away a few steps with that strange leading of shoulders and elbows or his attention seemed to take flight.

After about ten minutes he muttered something about a head stop and flew out altogether.

Odd, very odd, Annie thought. Yet there was a lot that interested her. He was witty. He had a certain presence. He was a mover and shaker in the city. He was sophisticated. He was cute. But he was also gone.

She sighed and mingled with a group chatting about sailing and then another speculating on how the 49ers were going to finish the season.

Finally she found Sam in the living room, gave her the high sign, and they got their coats.

When they were almost out the door Harry appeared again slightly behind her. "I'll give you a jingle soon," he said, "and we'll have dinner." He squeezed her upper arm and was off.

"And you haven't heard from him since?" Lola asked. "Nope."

"Nice thing about phones is that they work both ways. I'd give him a call."

When she got home from lunch Annie had had just enough champagne in her to take Lola's advice. Harry's secretary said he was in a meeting. She was sure he'd get back to her as soon as possible. Easy for her to say.

Later that evening Annie and her friend Tom Albano walked back to her place after catching a revival of *Bonnie and Clyde*.

"What's the matter, pal?" He threw an arm around her shoulder. "You seem a little down tonight."

130

"Not really. Maybe just working too hard."

"Those forty-five men from the *Bay Guardian* keeping you up too late?" He never forgot a thing.

"That's research, my friend."

"Uh-huh. No keepers then?" Tom was a fisherman who often spoke the lingo.

"Nope, I threw them all back."

"Well, that's their problem, not yours. You just haven't found the right one yet—the lucky guy who deserves you."

"I thought you didn't believe in Prince Charming."

"I don't. That's your problem. No one's perfect, you know." He chucked her under the chin.

"And what about you?"

"What about me?"

"When are you getting married again?"

"I'm not in any rush. This has been good for me. I've learned to cook. To do my laundry without everything turning pink."

"Really? What's your secret?"

"I take it to the Chinese laundry."

Annie laughed. "I guess being married to Clara would make you cautious about getting hooked up again. But what's your fantasy? When you do start looking what are you going to be looking for?"

He grinned down at her as he took her key. "I want a tall blonde woman with long legs and popcorn in her teeth."

Annie shoved him through the door ahead of her. She shook her head at his rear end. Tom had always worn the worst pants she'd ever seen on a human being. Underneath that bagginess might be a nice body, but who would ever know?

As usual, they played a few hands of gin rummy. Tom was a real shark. Over the years she had amassed a debt of several thousand dollars to him on paper. This time she stayed even. He had a nightcap and went home, giving her a big hug at the door.

Then there was a blank space. She didn't come up against it often, kept very busy so she wouldn't. But sometimes it crept in anyway.

Loneliness sat and looked at her from the other end of her rose-colored sofa.

Sometimes she thought that her chances of finding love in this town were about as good as finding a unicorn on her fire escape.

Brushing her teeth, she remembered that there had been a call on her answering machine. She'd thought it would be rude to check her messages while Tom was there. She flipped it on. There was Harry's voice. She clutched the neck of her nightgown in excitement.

Oh, crap. She and Sam had been fooling around and she'd left that stupid request on her tape. "Leave your name and number and any other personal statistics you feel comfortable saying aloud, and I will get back to you as soon as possible." He was going to think she was a fool.

"Hello? This is the author? I want to leave my personal statistics.

"My name is Harry.

"I have a cold.

"I am leaving town on business, but I'd like to take you to dinner next Tuesday night. I'll pick you up at eight.

"I wear a size twelve shoe.

"I wear a tie.

"I like collar pins.

"I like to drink wine, particularly red wine.

"And I like fish. What do you like?"

TWENTY-SIX

After he'd proved himself with Lucinda Washington he'd had to wait a couple of months for his official initiation at a state gathering in a little town near Baton Rouge. But the smiles and the slaps on the back were enough. He knew he belonged.

The feeling grew after the midnight swearing in that took place in the middle of a field, about two hundred men, their voices rolling like thunder, welcoming him. For the first time in his life he was part of something big, something important, and his life had purpose.

Now he had two lives. The old one, going to school, doing his chores, staying out of Pa's reach. And the new one, the secret one, where men older than he was admired him as he proved himself to be the most deadly of the night riders.

He didn't mind the meetings, the planning, the organizing, the sitting around on his haunches on cold barn floors. It all led to the bloody bursts of midnight glory.

After Lucinda there had been a nigger preacher from a small community nearby, New Blessings. He had been stirring up trouble among his congregation.

The boy had never made a bomb before, but once he got the hang of it, it was easy. The blasts had gone off like clockwork, right in the middle of choir practice.

133

Three of them had died and a couple more were blown up pretty good. They had learned their lesson. There were no more meetings in the A.M.E. Baptist Church, and the doors in the Quarter were locked shut to the knockings of Yankees in the night. They'd have to find a town other than New Blessings wherein to do their good deeds.

But the bombing didn't have the thrill of contact with women like Lucinda Washington. And that kind of opportunity didn't present itself very often. Most of the nigger women stayed home and minded their kids while their menfolk took the chances, spoke out, and got themselves killed. So, occasionally, he had to do a little something on his own.

Sometimes he rode at night with his friend T.J., a sheriff's deputy. Patrolling the back roads could be boring, T.J. had told him, unless you knew what you were looking for: dark nights, parked cars with steamed windshields, a makeshift lovers' lane at the edge of a cotton field.

The trick was to spot them and drive up real slow with the lights doused. Then zap them with the big lights and what you had was a tangled mess of arms and legs and titties and underwear and sweat.

If they were white, you stood and lectured them while they put their clothes back on, listening to them stutter while they explained to you what they were doing there. Every once in a while it was a preacher's son or a schoolteacher's daughter, and then you might make them get out of the car first before they got dressed. Then you got a really good look and you knew they sure as hell weren't going to go home and tell any tales.

If the couple was black, that was a different story. Catch a nigger couple diddling each other in the back seat of a rusty old Ford and you could have yourself some fun.

One night, riding with T.J., he lucked out.

After hitting them with the big light T.J. pulled his sawed-off shotgun out of the patrol car and ordered them out of the cab of the battered old pickup truck. They were teenagers, no older than the boy. She was a pretty little thing, if you liked dark meat. Both of them were scared as shit.

T.J. made them take off the rest of their clothes and then hit the dirt.

"Nah, boy, not like that. Get your ass over on top of that girl, like you was doing before."

"No, sir, Mr. T.J., we wasn't doing nothing like that," the terrified young black man whined.

"Well, you was wanting to if you wasn't, so you going to get your wish now. Do it, boy. Hump her. Now!"

T.J. hit him in the butt with the shotgun and the young man assumed the position.

Terror had weakened his ardor, however, and, as the young girl sobbed beneath him and T.J. yelled in his ear, he couldn't perform.

"You good for nothing nigger!" T.J. roared. "I promised my friend we was going to have some fun watching you niggers fuck and you're making me out a liar. What you got to say for yourself, boy?"

"I'm sorry, Mr. T. J., sir." He wiped tears and snot from his face with the back of his hand.

T.J. slapped him with the butt of the shotgun and the young man hit the ground.

"Don't you look up from there either, boy. You just lay there with your eyes closed. Do you understand me?" Then he gestured to the still naked girl sobbing on the ground as if he were the host at a party. "After you. Help yourself."

And so he did. He enjoyed himself a lot. He liked the acrid smell of fear that rolled in waves off her, which was even stronger than the odors of hair pomade, Cashmere

Bouquet powder, and Pall Malls. The smell of fear was very exciting.

But then, as she twisted and moaned beneath him—was it pain, was it fear, or did she like it—he couldn't finish. He couldn't get there.

The dispatcher's voice crackled over T.J.'s radio, and then T.J. was urging him to come on, he had a call to answer.

But he couldn't hurry, he couldn't make it happen, and he was starting to get mad.

"Fuck me, bitch," he growled into her tear-streaked face, and then he slapped her as hard as he could.

There was a small snap as her nose broke and blood gushed red across the dirt.

Then it clicked. That's what was missing.

It was the blood and the knife that got him home.

They did their magic once again.

Within two minutes, he and T.J. were back in the patrol car headed toward the interstate and a three-car accident at the Acornville Road overpass.

"Thanks, T.J.," he said.

His friend stepped on the gas and turned on the siren. "My pleasure." He grinned. He hesitated a minute. "But I guess I really didn't count on killing one."

There was a long silence as they rolled past dark fields and crossed a narrow steel bridge over the river.

"It was just a nigger."

"Right." T.J. reached over and ruffled his friend's hair, which was damp with sweat.

But after he'd dropped the boy off on the road near his house T.J. looked back for a long moment in his rearview mirror and wondered.

TWENTY-SEVEN

By five o'clock that Tuesday afternoon Annie knew she had been stood up. Would a grown man make a date on an answering machine and then not call back to confirm? Why hadn't she called him? Now it was too late. If Harry was coming, he was coming, and if he wasn't, she wasn't going to call him up and make a fool of herself.

She was on her way to the money machine at the Union Street branch of the Wells Fargo. Perry's was right next door. Harry was probably in there yakking it up with his friends and ogling the pretty young girls.

Will you stop? she said. So what if he is? He's going to take you to dinner later. In three hours. Or is he?

She was just about to cross Union to the automatic teller. The wind that always rose in the late afternoon was blowing her long blonde hair into her face. As she brushed a curl back out of her mouth, her mother's solitaire caught in one of her gold hoop earrings. Zap! The earring pulled out and was gone.

Annie wore very little jewelry. These earrings, given to her in a fit of generosity by Morose Mario, were the only pair of real gold ones she owned.

She stood frozen in that same stance she assumed when a contact lens popped. Maybe it was still on her body somewhere and if she didn't move, it wouldn't fall.

137

An elderly man walking a small white poodle stopped and asked if he could help her.

She began to tell him about the earring. As she did, it dislodged from her shoulder, where it had been resting, and flew, glinting, through the darkening cool air and landed three feet in front of her, smack on a Pacific Gas and Electric grate in the sidewalk. The earring circled, circled, slowly, slowly, and then fell. Plop. Through the slotted grate and down into a black hole.

She, the elderly man, and his dog stood staring first at one another and then down into the hole.

"Call PG and E," he suggested.

"It's after five. They probably won't come."

"Miss, is the earring real gold?"

Annie nodded.

"It's worth a try."

The PG&E lady had heard it all before. She put Annie on hold and three minutes later she was back. A service truck would be out shortly.

"How soon is shortly?"

"We try to answer all our service calls within four hours," she answered, sounding not unlike Lily Tomlin.

Four hours! It was pushing five-thirty. Annie still had to get some money out of the machine, bathe, dress, and put a fresh coat of polish on her nails before she settled down to chew them, wondering if Harry was going to show at eight.

But, on the other hand, the PG&E lady said, it might take fifteen minutes. She had to give them a chance. If she left the grate unguarded, they would come and leave and she'd never know. The man with the dog promised to watch her grate for a few minutes while she raced across the street to the bank. He'd be there, he said, unless his wife finished shopping first.

She got her money, but the man was gone. Had she missed the truck? She'd just have to wait and see. What time was it? Almost six. Had Harry called and left a confirming message on her machine? She could call Angie, who had a key to her apartment. Angie could listen to her machine and tell her.

But she had no change. The bank machine only spit out fresh twenties.

The woman in the bakery across the street from the grate was very nice about giving her $19.40 change for a croissant.

"You did what?" Angie yelled, but she dutifully went across the hall to Annie's apartment and listened to her tape.

"No, no message from Harry."

It was 6:50 as Annie placed a second call to the utility company. She couldn't wait any longer. She'd just have to start over tomorrow. She could see the writing on the wall. This was going to be just like the time one of her contact lenses lay in the dirty water in her lavatory trap for three days while she waited for the maintenance man to come back from vacation.

The dispatcher was trying to radio the closest service unit when a familiar beige-and-brown truck stopped in front of the arcade where she was using the phone. Her heroes had arrived.

One hero was short, old, and fat, chomping on a cigar. Annie thought he was beautiful. The other hero looked like a young George Peppard, with a healthy shock of prematurely silver hair. This was a PG&E man?

They were both very jolly about her predicament.

"Never had a call like this before," said the Peppard look-alike. "But we're always glad to help."

She couldn't believe it. This was a big grate and there

were thousands of them all over the city. Surely other people dropped thousands of dollars' worth of personal items down them daily. Maybe they just didn't have a nice elderly gentleman nearby to urge them to call when they did. There was probably a whole treasure trove down there.

They lifted the grate and, while the younger man stood guard, the older man climbed down a ladder inside. Annie peered over the edge and almost fainted. The bottom was twenty feet below. This wasn't just a hole, it was a subterranean passage painted battleship-gray, linking God knows what throughout the city. It reminded her of a tunnel in a James Bond movie. What did PG&E have going on down there?

Up lumbered her short, fat hero.

He was peering into his right hand.

"Two quarters, four pennies, and . . ."

He dangled her in suspense.

"One gold earring."

There it was! She kissed him on the cheek and, before she could properly thank them, their radio crackled and they were off to a real emergency.

It was 7:10.

Annie looked great when Harry arrived, ten minutes late.

His Mercedes was parked on the sidewalk in front of her building. At the restaurant he left the car in front of a fire hydrant. He said he never got a ticket. She wondered if a Mercedes had diplomatic immunity.

His choice of restaurants was Fanny's, a pretty little place in the Castro.

Harry wasn't exactly rude, but he was peremptory. He didn't ask her if she wanted a drink before dinner. He simply ordered a bottle of wine. He was impatient with the slow service on a slow night. He corrected the waiter, who attempted to remove his salad plate while she was still nibbling on her endive.

He was saying, "Then Xerox wanted to transfer me to Houston. That's when I decided to strike out on my own. Couldn't live without the bright lights of San Francisco."

Harry was a mortgage banker who brought together brokers, buyers, sellers, and cash for real-estate deals. Annie's idea of a real-estate deal was paying her rent on time.

Over some excellent salmon and sole they talked about movies, France, restaurants, what they'd been doing for the past thirty-odd years. They laughed a lot. Between the excellent Stag's Leap chardonnay and the laughter, Annie began to relax.

As Harry pushed his dinner plate aside, Annie noticed a pile of rice on the tablecloth. He noticed her notice and reached over and shoveled rice off her plate too. When the waiter came to clear the table Harry apologized to him for his messy date.

They shared a piece of chocolate fudge cake, brandishing forks for the larger portion. Annie couldn't remember the last time she'd even approached a food fight.

As they stood to leave, he walked toward her. He backed her into the wall behind her chair, put his hands on her shoulders.

"You have beautiful ankles. Size twelve shoes? Wonderful eyes. Size six blouse?"

Before she could figure out whether to thank him for the compliments or slap him for the presumption, he cupped her face in his hands and kissed her thoroughly, softly, slowly.

"I've wanted to do that for the last hour," he said.

The man was funny. And charming. Could he hear her heart thumping? Close your mouth, Annie, she warned herself. Do not tell him you think he's the greatest thing since sliced bread.

Before she had time to tell him anything, he picked her up, threw her over his shoulder in a fireman's lift, and carried her past the amused staff out of the restaurant. Depositing her neatly on the sidewalk, he kissed her forehead, took her hand, and led her to the car without a word.

It takes a tall woman, a woman one doesn't throw over one's shoulder casually, to really appreciate that kind of move. How did he know that? Was he funny, a great kisser, charming, and clairvoyant too? Or did he just have a whole bag of tricks he pulled out at random?

Where did she want to have a drink? He didn't blink when she suggested the upstairs bar of Café San Marcos just a few blocks down the street. It was a beautiful mirrored room, very sleek, very New York, but it was also very gay. He parked the car in a bus zone.

They were the only straight patrons in a sea of pretty male faces, but the bartender made them welcome as he poured Martell cognac into warmed snifters. Harry stood and she sat on a tall stool. They were crowded very close together. Even if the bar had been empty, she would have wanted to be this close to him, to smell the leather of his dark brown Italian jacket, the slight hint of a woodsy cologne. She felt very pretty and a little flustered, the way she always did when with a man who reminded her that she was a woman.

Before she even thought about it she had asked him to accompany her to Sam's benefit ball the following week.

"I'd love to," he said, "but I lost the pants to my tux. I can't imagine where."

Did that mean yes or no?

"I can't dance, don't ask me," he hummed in her ear.

No or yes?

142

"Sure, toots. I'll be there with bells on."

Yes.

Mostly they sipped their cognac and touched. Was she getting tipsy? She was running her hands up and down the front of his red cashmere sweater.

She caught herself.

"What am I doing?"

"Feeling up my tummy," he said and kissed her. They were thirty-seven and forty-one, necking in a gay bar. It felt wonderful.

He started to say something and then stopped himself.

"Nope, can't tell you that."

"No fair. You can't start and not finish unless you give a reason."

"Reason is—I don't know you that well."

It was one of her least favorite reasons for anything.

But as he said it he dropped his eyes. Annie followed his glance and understood. He didn't know her that well, indeed, as he stood at the bar with her, an erection pushing against his nicely tailored charcoal corduroy slacks.

"I've been like this for the past half hour," he muttered into her ear. "Let's blow this popstand." He took her jacket, her hand, and led her down the stairs. The car was still there, unticketed.

As they drove back across town, they talked very little. Harry dialed in a late-night station playing honky-tonk blues. He was driving like in high school, with one arm around her. He parked illegally in the alleyway across from her building.

"You might get a ticket here."

"Just as long as I don't get one upstairs."

For one brief moment Annie worried about the tiny rosebud buttons on her peach silk blouse as Harry fumbled with them, seeking her flesh. But buttons could be resewn.

The loving was sweet and simple. No pyrotechnics or gymnastics. No games. Just a boldly shy, big, gentle stranger whom she'd invited to ride in for the evening and steal her heart.

He slept funny. Cold at night, he'd pulled back on his red sweater. He huddled under what was plenty of cover for her, a cold-natured woman. He clutched an extra pillow to his stomach like a teddy bear. He didn't snore, but he didn't sleep very well either.

They patted each other in the night, that kind of pat-pat, pat-pat-pat that means, "I'm here. It's okay."

About four in the morning she patted him beneath the teddy-bear pillow and they fell into one another once more.

Six A.M. was grim, dark, and cold. Harry stumbled into the kitchen in his baggy Brooks Brothers shorts and sweater and peered into her refrigerator with a frown. He had wrinkles from the pillow on his forehead.

"I dreamed that you were feeding me chicken. There's no chicken in here," he grumbled.

Quickly he dressed and, refusing her offers of coffee, he swatted her on the fanny, gave her a fast hug, and was gone out the door.

He was halfway down the hall to the elevator when Annie was stricken with panic.

"Harry," she called and then slapped her hand over her mouth.

He smiled. "I'll give you a jingle." The elevator came and he was gone.

Sam couldn't wait to hear all the details.

It was great to have someone to share both the good and bad times with, but sometimes their kaffeeklatsching troubled Annie.

144

First there was the superstition, a leftover from childhood. If you really wanted something, you shouldn't talk about it.

Second was the question of loyalty to the man involved. She had learned that men don't talk about women nearly as much as women talked about men and that the degree of their locker-room specificity is highly exaggerated. However, women talking about men could get pretty specific.

Third, maybe she and Sam simply talked about men too much. But all single women of a certain age did. "He said, I said, do you think he?" Or more common, the never ending strategizing of where to meet them. Did well-educated professional women have nothing better to talk about? Or was the ticking of the biological clock turning their minds to mush?

Annie realized that Sam was grinning at her across their shared sashimi. She hadn't been listening.

"Sorry."

"I just think that it's so great that Harry's coming to the dance. I'm sure he and Sean will like each other. Does he have a tux?"

"I'm not sure. He said he lost the pants."

Sam laughed. "That sounds like Harry. And it's going to be a fantastic evening."

Annie snorted in reply.

"Annie, Annie, you always get this way at the beginning of a love affair. Just like I do. Sad and fatalistic. But look how much I'm enjoying Sean, now that I've decided to relax. I promise you. You're going to live happily ever after. You'll see."

Harry and Annie were not to live happily ever after. He didn't send her flowers. He stood her up for the ball. And she never heard from him again.

TWENTY-EIGHT

He followed her home from the Safeway carrying a bag of groceries in his arms just as she did.

He was out of his neighborhood here. She was out of his league, too, with her fancy clothes, gold jewelry, alligator shoes. The heels click-clicking on the pavement ahead of him made her look a little taller, but she couldn't have been much over five feet. You could tell by the way she walked, with her groceries in one arm and her leather brief-case in the other, that she thought she was somebody.

A briefcase! Why would a little nigger gal need a brief-case? To carry her shoplifting home in? Or had they made her some kind of boss, the way they did here these days? With a big desk she would perch behind and a phone she would use to order men like him around.

"Do this by four o'clock."

"I said I wanted it by three, do you understand?"

He understood okay. He understood that women like her were too big for their britches. And her especially, talking in that voice that reminded him of home.

That's why he'd noticed her. He'd been in the store to pick up a couple of things, might as well since he was in the neighborhood dropping something off. Some beer, chips, and, while he was in line, leafing through an *Enquirer,* he heard her just ahead of him.

146

It had been a long time since he'd heard a nigger girl talk like that. Some of the softness was gone. She'd probably been away from home a long time. But so had he.

He'd liked listening to her talking with the woman at the checkout, who was telling her a story about people trying to buy liquor with their food stamps.

He caught up with her just as she walked out of the parking lot. She must live close by. He was careful to stay a few yards behind and then to cross over to the other side of the street. The buildings were all two or three stories. There were very few trees and bushes. He was going to have to be very cool because there was no place to hide.

But that was okay. He was just following her because he liked her voice. This was different. He wasn't going to . . . or was he?

As he thought about it, the warmth began to grow in his groin. Yes . . . well . . . maybe he was. He looked at her again across the street, tapping so efficiently toward home.

She was light, gold-colored. But look at the hair, the nose, the lips. With little brittle bones like a bird. But not too skinny. There would be softness there too. Softness that she didn't even know she had.

He'd help her find it, point it out to her.

Shit. She turned the corner. Would she notice him if he did too?

No, it was cool. She was home. She'd put the groceries down on the step and was unlocking the front door. He kept walking.

He walked all the way around the block and when he came back past her house he was on her side. As he passed her door he slowed down just long enough to memorize her address and the name she had printed on a little card on her mailbox. It was like the cards that had names on them in graduation invitations.

147

She would see her name on another little card like that, almost the same size, when he came back another day to bring her the flowers.

TWENTY-NINE

The ringing phone cut through Annie's sleep like a knife.

She bolted up and grabbed her alarm, squinting at it without her glasses in the darkness. Two A.M. Was her father dead? Her mother?

"Annie, I'm sorry, but . . ."

"Are you all right?" Annie interrupted, her heart pounding. Sam's voice on the other end was tight.

"Yes, I am. I'm okay. But I wanted to call you before you read it in the paper. She'll be on the front page. . . . This makes four."

"Sammie, you're not making any sense. Who's number four? What are you talking about?"

"He hit again. They just found her body. Sean called me when the report came in. I've got to go down to the office."

Sam's voice broke. She took a deep breath and then began to speak in simple sentences, as if the simplicity of the facts would relieve the horror.

"He said there was lots of blood. On everything. Everywhere."

"Sam . . ."

"I'm trying. He killed her, Annie. He strangled her,

choked her." Sam took a deep, deep breath. "And then he took a knife, and he . . ."

"Who, Sam, who?" Annie was yelling into the dark apartment.

Finally the words plopped from Sam's mouth like drops of blood.

"He took a knife and when he finished, in the hole where her heart had been, where Lola Davis's heart had been, he left a single, perfect white rose."

PART
TWO

THIRTY

Fifteen minutes later Annie stood in front of the well-stocked liquor cabinet Sam kept for guests. Her mind was blank as her eyes scanned one label after another.

Finally, her hand shaking, she pulled down a bottle of Amaretto.

"Honey, you don't want that in the middle of the night." Sam's voice came from behind her. "Here's what you need." She handed Annie a tumbler of Jack Daniel's and ice, threw an arm around her shoulder, and pulled her into the living room.

The lights of Sam's Christmas tree twinkled in a corner.

Annie finished off the tumbler before she started to talk. She looked at the mounds of gaily wrapped packages.

"I bought Lola an exercise mat for Christmas." Tears welled in her eyes, and then she was leaning on Sam's bosom. "I hate this. I want to go back to sleep and start over."

Sam patted her back, smoothed her hair.

"Why Lola?"

"Hey, hey, you know there's no answer to that. This isn't something you can make sense out of. Come on. Sit down."

Annie leaned back on the sofa, lighted a cigarette, exhaled a long plume of smoke. She stared at the end of the cigarette.

"You know, Sammie, it was like this with the kids, when I was teaching. Every year there was at least one who died. It was never a rotten one. It was always a great kid who got it."

"It always seems that way, doesn't it?" Sam's voice was low. She splashed more whiskey into Annie's glass.

Annie continued. Past pain was easier than present.

"Like that little kid Danny Johnson on his bike the semi ran over. Great kid." Annie took a gulp of her drink and shuddered. "Such a sweetie. A loner just beginning to peep out of his shell. Then smack. The last thing he saw was a Peterbilt grill in his face."

"Hey, come on." Sam squeezed her hand.

"No, it's okay. I want to talk about it. You know," she said, sitting up and setting her glass on the coffee table, "you know, it was really ironic about Danny Johnson. The driver who killed him was killed himself a few weeks later. A car ran a stop sign and killed him in a pickup truck. Isn't that funny?"

"Not funny ha-ha."

"But you have to admit there's poetic justice there. It doesn't make Danny's death okay, but it makes it better."

Sam could tell that Annie was getting a little drunk, which was what she wanted her to be.

Annie gestured with her almost-empty glass. "Like I'm going to make Lola's dying better!" She raised her voice. "I'm going to find that son of a bitch and kill him!"

Sam grabbed her arm in midflight. "Right, love. But now I'm tucking you into the guest bedroom. You get some sleep and we'll talk about this tomorrow." She looked at her watch. "I mean later today."

Annie protested faintly and then began to fold. The shock, fatigue, and bourbon were taking over. She followed Sam to bed.

154

"Besides which," Sam said as she pulled a pale yellow down comforter up over Annie and handed her a glass of water and two aspirin, "you're not the sleuth in this twosome anyway. I am."

"I know." Annie smiled up her. "That's what I'm counting on." And then she was asleep.

Bright sunshine creeping around the edge of the green chintz shade startled Annie into consciousness. The orange-and-white clock on the bedside table said two o'clock. How could that be? It was two the last time she woke up. Besides, it wasn't light at two. Slowly it registered. Two in the afternoon. Preposterous. The only time she slept like that was when she had the flu.

Then she remembered and slumped back under the covers.

Lola was dead.

"Sam," she called. There was no answer.

"Samantha," she yelled. The flat was quiet.

There was a note taped to the top of the coffee maker where half a pot of French roast was warming.

"Hope you slept late. I'm having lunch with Sean. Okay, I'll see what I can find out." It was signed with her familiar *X*s and *O*s.

When Annie arrived back at her apartment there was another note. Taped to her door, it was an invitation from Angie to come across the hall to dinner.

She didn't want to, but she knew she ought to eat. And she didn't really want to be alone. Once seated at Angie's table, she usually found that everything looked a lot better.

Nibbling on salami and peppers, she told Angie and Frank about Lola's murder. They'd both wanted to meet her. Too late for that now.

"It's terrible—all this violence that's out there." Angie gestured with one hand while pushing up her glasses with the other. She was a small tornado when riled. "That's all you read in the paper these days. A gang killing here. A murder there. And what about all these damned Klan meetings? Where the hell are we living, anyway, southern Mississippi?"

"Angie, you're getting paranoid. You didn't want to talk with the insurance man last week when he mentioned that he lives in Pinole. Just because you read that there's a lot of Klan activity there. That doesn't mean the whole town is rotten." Frank laughed in his soft, slow way. "I'm the one who's black, baby. And I'm not worried."

"Yeah, well, that's not exactly true, is it? What did you tell me just the other night?"

"Awwwh, Angie." Frank gestured with hands that could hold a basketball like a grapefruit. "That's just because it was real late at night."

"What?" asked Annie.

"It was nothing. I was just telling Angie that when I had to go in to work at night last week I felt a little scared waiting for a bus on the corner at midnight. But who wouldn't?"

"Why should you have to be scared? Isn't this supposed to be a safe neighborhood? If not, what are we paying all this rent for? And if *you* feel scared, Frank, what about women like me?"

"You mean midgets?"

Angie slapped at him. "Come on, this is no time for jokes." But she couldn't stop her grin. Frank could always make her laugh.

Then she got serious again. "Well, it has to stop. This isn't Mississippi, Tennessee"—she waved at Frank when she mentioned his home—"the South Bronx. Didn't we leave those places and come here to get away from all that crap?"

"That's the same thing I said to Sam."

"Come on." Frank put a hand on Annie's shoulder. "You and I know those people we grew up with back home. You can't change those people's minds."

"I don't want to change his mind. I want to make him stop."

"Who's he?" Angie asked, looking at Annie strangely. "Who are you talking about?"

"The bastard who killed Lola."

"What are you going to do? Go after him with a shotgun? Why do you think we have cops?" Frank said. "Anyway, how are you going to find him?"

"I know who he is," Annie answered.

"What!" Angie choked.

The little hairs on the back of Annie's neck began to prickle. It wasn't until she'd said the words that she realized that she felt them somewhere deep down inside her gut.

She paused, lighting a cigarette. "I don't mean I really know . . . exactly . . . who he is. I can't explain it. I just have this funny feeling."

Frank started to interrupt her.

"I know. Don't say it. You're going to start about psychic bullshit. This is not in the same category as Angie's astrologer."

"What *about* my astrologer?"

"It's something else. And whatever it is, I'm going to follow it. I'm going to get that bastard cold."

She said the same words to Sam an hour later on the phone. Then, "Go ahead and tell me I'm crazy. I know that's what you're thinking."

There was a long silence on the other end of the line.

"Sam, are you there?"

Sam was very serious. "I talked with Sean today . . ." She paused.

"And?"

"Hush. Now, this goes no further."

"Right."

"The rose they found with Lola . . ."

"Yes." Annie squeezed her eyes tight. She wanted to block the mental picture she had of that scene.

"There wasn't just one. There were more in the kitchen in a florist's box. And a vase was out, as if she were about to arrange them when . . ." Sam let the thought trail off.

"Sean says they've been there, the roses, at all four murders."

"Roses. White roses. Are you thinking what I'm thinking?" The adrenaline started pumping. Annie was pacing back and forth with the phone in her foyer.

"It's awfully coincidental, isn't it? John Sharder in his Porsche with those roses. And the one he brought to my doorstep. I told Sean about him."

"What did he say?"

"He thought it was strange enough to have him checked out. Sean says he looks clean. He's having second thoughts now. But he's having second thoughts about lots of people.

"When there's a maniac loose like this there are all the prior offenders to track, all the phone tips. People come out of the woodwork—turning in their brother-in-law because they're pissed about a bad debt or their upstairs neighbor who's been giving them a hard time.

"It's time-consuming and maddening. Especially when you come up empty and the guy's still out there."

"So they just keep looking."

"Sean does want to talk with us. He wants us both to go over everything we remember about John Sharder and he wants to talk with you about Lola. They found the letters from the *Guardian* ad in her apartment and they have some questions about them.

"They think maybe there's some connection between the ads and the murders."

Just exactly what Annie didn't want to hear.

THIRTY-ONE

Everything had gone along great for the boy that year, his senior year, the year he'd found the place he belonged. Until the night with Missy Cartwright. Then it fell to pieces. It was all her fault.

It had been a cold evening, a cold snap like they often had after a spell of warm spring weather that would bring all the flowers into bloom.

There was a Friday-night basketball game at school. He had wheedled Pa's grudging permission, doubled up on chores, swapping two for one with Lem, who would always be known for driving a hard bargain, so he could stay in town for the game.

That morning, after carefully dressing in his best blue shirt and jeans, he'd clipped a bouquet of roses from his mother's side garden and left the house. Yellow, white, red, and pink, tight and covered with dew, they'd be good

159

till evening wrapped in wet newspaper and carefully propped in the corner of his locker.

Two days before, after almost six months of following Missy, late to his classes as he'd trailed her to hers, the break he had been waiting for finally happened. Right beside him, she'd dropped her books.

"Damn!" she said and then looked around with those big blue eyes to see if anyone had heard her.

And he had been right there.

"Oh, thank you." She'd smiled as he handed her the books. Then she winked at him and turned into her classroom as the bell rang.

He hadn't cared that he would be late again, that old Mrs. Hedgepath would yell at him.

Missy had winked at him! He was smiling like a fool as he bounced up the stairs.

Sitting in Hedgepath's class, he'd come up with the plan.

Now, clutching the roses in their newspaper as he sat in the bleachers alone, he wasn't so sure it was going to work. Even if it didn't, it was great to watch Missy as she and the other cheerleaders twirled and twisted in formation on the gym floor before him.

He couldn't take his eyes off her. That sweet mouth opened wide to shout, dimpling now as she stomped her foot in a routine. That body, round in the right places, with that tiny little waist. How could girls be so little in the middle? he wondered. How do they eat or breathe?

Just as he'd feared, at the end of the game there was no chance to give her the flowers. He'd seen on TV how sometimes when performers were really good someone came out and gave them flowers. He'd thought how impressed Missy would be, how proud, to get flowers like the ladies on TV. But there was no chance; she was surrounded by the other girls, whirling and twirling as the game ended, their team winning by twelve points.

160

He hadn't paid much attention to the game. It was his school too. But he didn't care anything about basketball, not the way the city boys from the north side of town played it, anyway. A bunch of candy asses running up and down the court patting each other on the behind.

When he and his brothers played one-on-one they didn't have any hardwood floors to run up and down, no pretty girls yelling their names, no fancy jockstraps, but they didn't pat each other on the behind either.

So Missy had disappeared before he could give her the flowers, swept up in a blur of pom-poms and smiles and big sweaty boys in blue and gray satin.

But he had another trick up his sleeve.

He stood across the street from her house, watching in the dark, waiting for her to get home from the game.

But the day had been such a long one, starting with the chores, that finally even the cold couldn't keep him awake. He didn't know how long he'd been asleep when he was awakened by the sound of Missy's voice.

"Okay, Ma, I'll be in in just a few minutes."

Her voice had come from the dark of the front porch, and then, as the moonlight shot from behind a passing cloud, he could see the gleam of her blonde hair.

How did she know? he marveled. It was like a dream. She was waiting out on her porch for him to come calling, to give her her prize.

He'd trotted out of the shadows, across the street, and straight up her front steps, his path as clean and pure as the love for her that flowed from his heart.

"Missy, I brought these for you."

There was giggling and shuffling and only then, as he extended his hand and his heart, did he realize that Missy wasn't sitting on the porch swing alone.

Bo Hendricks, the captain of the basketball team, was

161

there, too, with one big hand resting on Missy's shoulder and the other covering the letter on her chest.

Then he realized with a stab of humiliation that he was handing Missy flowers while Bo Hendricks was diddling her boobs.

As he dropped the roses and turned, Bo challenged, "Hey, Bubba, what you got there? You come calling on Missy?"

"Hush, Bo," Missy had hissed as she struggled her sweater free from his hand.

"Who are you?" she'd called to his retreating back. "I can't see you in the dark. Who's there?"

"Nobody," he'd yelled back over his shoulder as he ran the first block of his ten-mile trip back home. "Nobody, nobody, that's who."

THIRTY-TWO

They met Sean for lunch downtown at John's Grill, the perfect spot to talk about murder. The dark, men's-club atmosphere was infused with the spirit of Dashiell Hammett. There was a Maltese falcon on display, as well as first editions and manuscripts from the writer whose detectives had tracked some of their most hard-boiled murderers on the back streets of San Francisco.

Annie could see why Sam found Sean attractive. Tall, well-built, with thick auburn hair, he had a gentle, understated manner that ran at odds with the stereotype of a third-generation Irish cop.

"I put a good man on him and he checked out clean," he was saying as he cut into a lamb chop. "This roses business is screwy, but John Sharder has no monopoly on roses and weird behavior with women. I'd like to hear what you can tell me about him, though."

Annie and Sam ran through it. Sam's encounter with him on the freeway. His standing her up at the Square. (Sean smiled. Lucky for him.) His appearance at Sam's door with the rose. Halloween. And the phone calls since then.

"Just calls, as I told you," Sam said. "I've refused to see him. But I know he's been following me."

"He knows what she's been doing," Annie added. "And a couple of times when we've been together I've thought I've caught a glimpse of his car. There aren't *that* many cars exactly like his in the city." She hesitated a minute. "He does live in the city, doesn't he?"

She hoped the question sounded casual. She had checked all the local directories for Sharder with no luck. The scores of suburban communities in the Bay Area, all with their separate listings, defeated her. Information operators couldn't help her if she didn't know the name of the town.

"East Bay," Sean answered. Annie hoped he couldn't hear the sound of her mind snapping at the fact. And he was going on. But then, how should he know that she thought she could do his job for him?

"He's a pretty ordinary guy, holds down a decent job, enough to afford the Porsche. Nothing spectacular about him. You could file a complaint, Sam, if he's really harassing you, but it really doesn't go very far. We can't arrest him because he likes to pick up women on the freeway and give them white roses."

163

He smiled at Sam. Annie rather liked the smile, friendly rather than indulgent.

"I'll give him another run-through and see if anything pops. But I really don't think he's our man. Don't think he's the type."

"What's the type?" Sam asked.

"Come on, dear, you've nosed around the blood and guts business enough to know the answer to that."

"I haven't." Annie didn't want him to drop the subject. "Go on."

"You going into mystery writing next?" Sean asked.

"You never can tell."

"Okay. If we were talking about an ordinary rapist, garden variety, he could be anybody. He could be the guy at the next table."

They turned and looked at a rather distinguished gentleman in a gray suit eating his steak alone while studying a thick sheaf of papers. He felt their glances and looked up, startled.

"But a real fruitcake like this man's got to be . . . Yes, there's a type. I can't tell you what he had for breakfast or how many times his father beat him while he was growing up, but he usually has some history of aberrant childhood behavior. He's probably a loner. A paranoid. He may have delusions that he's killing because some high power wants him to, that it's a form of homage. He's not fond of women, though he may appear to be drawn to them. Women are very complicated for him. Love. Hate. Rejection. His mother. A jumble. His problems have probably manifested themselves before. He's crazy, you know."

"Would you be able to spot him as a weirdo just by looking at him? Is that what you mean?" Annie asked.

"He's not going to wear a T-shirt that announces 'I love to Murder Women.' But, yes, I'd say there's something about him that would make both of you uncomfortable if you met him in a bar. A vibration that I think you're street-wise enough to pick up. He'd spook you." He hesitated. "I hope."

"Not always, huh?" Sam asked.

"No, I can tell you all this and then there's the exception to the rule. The perfectly ordinary-looking guy in a blue suit your mother would love to have you bring home to dinner, who in his spare time rips people's guts out." He looked down at his plate. "I'm sorry."

They ordered coffee. Annie studied Sean.

He wore a gray chalk-striped suit with a gold watch chain across the vest, white shirt, paisley tie. He looked more like a successful lawyer than a detective. According to Sam, he had been known to speak of art, music, the ballet. And he didn't wear his gun to bed, where Sam said he was a generous and enthusiastic lover.

Of course, he was a bit rabid on the subject of criminals and capital punishment. Annie suspected his politics might be a little to the right of Torquemada, but she occasionally heard statements indicating a creeping over-thirty con-servatism coming out of her own mouth.

Hadn't she been talking about doing away with Lola's killer?

Sean was looking at her.

"Tell me more about Lola. Why would a woman like that run an ad in the personals?"

"What do you mean, 'a woman like that'?"

"Whoa. Hold on," Sean said. "Lola Davis was beautiful, intelligent. She had a lovely home, a great practice. She seemed to have everything going for her. *That's* what I meant. So why would she be looking for love in the pa-per?"

Sam and Annie exchanged a look, shook their heads. Why indeed?

"Let us tell you about reality for a single woman in this city, my friend," Annie began. They were on a third cup of coffee when they finished.

Sean shrugged his shoulders. The look on his face was skeptical.

"Well, I hear this from other people, but I don't know what to believe. Do you really think that a woman like Lola, a woman like either of you"—he looked at both of them—"could expect to meet someone she'd like through a personal?"

They both laughed.

Annie apologized. "An in-joke, Sean. I'm sorry. But I sure as hell hope so.

"Maybe not Prince Charming, maybe not the love of her life, but not someone who's going to kill her either. Look, I've answered ads and I've placed one, and the guys I've met may be boring, or ugly, or plastic, but none of them has ever been a murderer."

"That you know of. I think you're taking an awful gamble, Annie. In the best of circumstances you can't be too careful and I think this ad business is foolhardy."

"Why is it more dangerous than meeting someone in a bar or a restaurant?" Sam asked him pointedly.

"You'd already met me. Through work."

"I'm not talking about us. I'm talking about the millions of casual ways that people meet. We can't always wait for our Aunt Penny to introduce us to nice men who are the sons of their oldest friends, you know. And what's to say even some of *those* aren't psychos?"

Sean pushed back from the table. "Okay, okay, you win. I just think it pays to be as careful as you can, that's all. Now, I do think this ad business is worth a look. We'll check into all the letters Lola received."

"And Sharder too?" Sam asked.

"Yes, him too. Again."

Sean caught the look that passed between the two women.

"Okay, what's going on here?"

"Nothing." They were all wide-eyed innocence.

"Never try to con a con man." He smiled grimly at both of them. "Listen, dear things. I know that Lola's death hit close to home. And I know that you think you're on to something with John Sharder, but believe me, your men in blue get paid to do this job and we will do it by ourselves, thank you. Stay out of it, ladies. You could get in our way and, more important, you could get hurt. I wouldn't like to see something happen to either one of you."

"Yes, Sean." They nodded gravely as they both crossed their fingers under the white tablecloth.

After lunch they headed toward Sam's office.

"We've got to sit down and talk about what we're doing," Sam had said.

The going was slow through the midtown Christmas shopping, with sidewalks that were packed.

They stopped for a minute before the florist Podesta Baldocchi's windows. This year, as always, they were filled with a forest of magnificently decorated trees.

"Oh, let's go in for just a minute."

Annie was easily tempted.

Sam stood before a tree that was a fantasy of pink and gold. Angels flew, bugles blew, palest pink angel hair floated in a soft veil over it all. The tree took her back to her childhood. She felt six years old again, standing with her nose pressed to the window of F.A.O. Schwarz.

Attached to a lower branch was a neatly lettered sign that read ALL ITEMS ON THIS TREE FOR SALE.

"I really want it."

"The whole tree? That's a little extravagant, Sammie, even for you."

"No, silly, the sign. Wouldn't it be funny to put on my tree at home?"

Despite her engaging manner, the salesman steadfastly refused to sell Sam the sign.

"But the sign says everything on the tree is for sale and the sign is on the tree. Therefore, it must be for sale too." Annie tried a little deductive reasoning with him.

The man couldn't be budged.

"I'm sorry, madam, the sign is not for sale."

"Is that the silliest thing you've ever heard?" Sam sputtered as they fought their way back out onto the sidewalk.

"You really want the sign?"

"Of course! What are you going to do? Go back in and break his arm?"

"Nope, no need. Close your eyes and hold out your hand."

"Annie . . ."

"Uh-uh, guess you don't want it."

Sam did as she was told. Annie laid the little lettered card in her hand.

"What?!"

"Remember I told you once that I belonged to a gang of shoplifters when I was a kid? A lift a day at the dime store or you were out? I like to keep my hand in now and then."

"Annie, that's just ter . . . wonderful!" And she gave her best friend a big hug. "Let's don't tell Sean, okay?"

"Fine by me. I don't want him to call my mother."

A few doors down, Sam stopped and bought them chocolate truffles in the Candy Jar.

"I really shouldn't be rewarding such heinous behavior," she said. They crossed Union Square, where the Christmas lights, the bums, and the pigeons vied for space with the shoppers headed for Macy's across the street.

They arrived at Sam's office red-cheeked and ready to get to work. They both squeezed into the cubicle that bore Sam's name, barely large enough for more than herself, her computer terminal, and a cup of coffee.

"He said East Bay, didn't he?" Sam said, knowing full well he had, handing Annie a stack of telephone books she'd scavenged from a pile in the center of the bullpen. "Let's start digging."

Their fingers flashed past the towns: San Pablo, El Cerrito, Pleasanton, Walnut Creek. They didn't know how far north or south to go. The western boundary of the area was the Bay, but east could go as far as Livermore.

Sharder. Scharder. Schaerder.

There was one.

No answer.

No John.

No Jack.

No luck.

They ended up with a small list of maybe's, which they divided up to work on at home.

"Have you thought about what we're going to do when we find him?" asked Sam.

"Sure," Annie answered, tucking her list into her bag and pulling on a bright purple beret. "We're going to be very civilized about it. We'll ask him for tea."

THIRTY-THREE

The boy had run with the searing pain in his head until he almost couldn't see for the agony. The old headaches came back when he was upset, blood pounding with no release.

He didn't know how many miles he'd run and walked, oblivious to everything but the shame and the pain, when he looked up and found himself in front of a nigger house on the far edge of the Quarters. Parked in front of it, between two old tires planted with petunias, was a dark green Volkswagen with New York plates. Yankee do-gooders, like the ones run off from New Blessings, for sure.

He'd waited, crouched, for only a minute, pictures of Missy on that front porch replaying in his mind, when the Yankee bitch had come out to her car, calling good nights behind her.

She hadn't gotten very far, but far enough, on the tire he'd punctured with his knife, when she had to get out on the dark road alone.

She was by herself for only a moment and then she was dead.

He felt a lot better. Now he could only faintly hear the echoes of Missy's laughter ringing in his ears.

It was very late. He should have been home hours ago. He sneaked up on his back porch, his boots in his hand, when suddenly his pa reached out of the shadows and slapped him upside his head. In his hand Pa was holding the broken ax handle.

"Let me be, Pa. You ain't going to whip me tonight," he growled, trying to push his father away.

His father didn't say anything, but just kept shoving at him, pushing him back into the yard, away from the house and the hearing of his mother.

"You ain't going to do this, Pa," he warned him again. But his pa wouldn't listen and the ax handle was poised above his head, ready to strike the first blow.

It was his last. The boy grabbed the handle as it struck home and turned it against his father. He hit him again and again until he was still and there was no sound but that of his own breathing. When he looked down at his feet he couldn't recognize the face in what was left.

He'd run then. Run the two miles to the Reverend Jones's house. He didn't know what else to do.

The preacher listened gravely to what the boy told him, loaded him in the back of his old station wagon under some blankets, gave his wife instructions not to answer the phone until he got back, and drove southward, straight through the night.

When they got to Darcy decisions would be made.

Just after dawn they were welcomed into a warm kitchen where they were fed thick, hot, French coffee and sweet sticky buns. Then the boy was asked to sit in the living room, where he watched pictures on the television with no sound while the men talked. There was a calendar from a gas station on the wall. He looked at it and wondered about the next month and the one after that.

"Son." The man who had sworn him in months before in the pasture just outside, who had given him a reason for being, called him in and put an arm around his shoulder.

171

"As much as I hate to lose you, 'cause you been doing a hell of a job, we've got to get you out of here. We're going to help you, but you've got to disappear."

He couldn't believe what he was hearing. They were going to send him away? But he'd done everything they ever asked of him—and more.

He tried to argue, but there was no appeal in this court. After another cup of coffee Reverend Jones stood, shook his hand, and wished him luck. He had to get on back before he was missed.

A stranger said, "This way, son. We might as well get started."

Reverend Jones and the other men nodded somberly at the car as it pulled out of the driveway.

Jones looked to the man who made the final decisions. "You're right, we had to get rid of him."

"Yep, bring us nothing but trouble. He's crazy, you know."

The first man drove him to Lake Charles. There he'd been passed to another, who took him to Austin. It went on like that, one large, faceless, nameless man after another who just drove, taking the boy to the next stop along the way. Until five days and 2500 miles later, he was alone with $500 in his pocket in California.

That had been a long time ago. He'd been alone ever since, except for the times his particular appetites had gotten him into trouble and he'd shared space with lots of other men in jailhouse orange. Hard times, they were, very hard times, locked away without his knife to find even an occasional moment of release. But eventually he'd always made it through.

Eventually they'd always let him out.

THIRTY-FOUR

They found John Sharder in Port Costa.

The phone was listed in his mother's name. When Sam called Mrs. Sharder was very helpful. She said John would be home at six o'clock in time for his supper.

Port Costa is a minuscule one-street town perched on the shores of the Carquinez Strait a few miles northeast of the city. Its populace is a loose coalition of independent souls who preserve the best of the spirit of the Old West. They are most famous for telling the federal government to take a hike during a dispute over the town's water-treatment system.

Annie and Sam arrived well before six and decided to kill time at the bar in Matilda's Restaurant. The decor was fun-house kitsch. Dusty Christmas decorations hung permanently. A ticket booth trimmed with garlands of plastic flowers and signs sat in the middle of the room. Mason jars served as glasses. The silver didn't match. The portions of home cooking were legendary. But the real attraction of Matilda's was the lady herself.

As they sat at the bar, they could hear her from the kitchen.

"Hustle your ass up here, sonny, the potatoes are getting cold."

They grinned. This was nothing. They had seen Matilda in action before.

She stormed through the kitchen's swinging doors, waving a spoon. Matilda was a very wide, short woman of late middle age. Her graying hair was twisted up in a knot. Her enormous breasts heaved beneath a gaily flowered muumuu.

As she headed toward the bar, a young couple at a table for two caught her eye.

"Hey there, son." Her voice was first cousin to a buzz saw. "Getting enough . . ." She paused to watch the blood rise up the young man's neck. "To eat?"

He smiled nervously first at his date, then at Matilda, who was circling behind him. She leaned over and pressed her mammoth breasts against the back of his head, which slipped into her canyonlike cleavage. He was surrounded.

When he was sufficiently scarlet and gasping for breath, the crowd at the bar roaring with laughter, Matilda heaved herself off him, cackling, and began to yell at the bartender about a late delivery.

Satisfied that it had been taken care of, the lady of the house waggled toward another mission, brushing past Annie and Sam.

Annie would never know what came over her.

"Excuse me," she addressed Matilda. "Do you happen to know a man named John Sharder?"

Sam leaned onto the bar, covering her eyes with one hand. She couldn't believe it.

Matilda's eyes narrowed behind her cat glasses.

"Of course I do. There ain't but a hundred or so sons-abitches who live in this town."

"Could I talk with you about him for a minute?"

"What do you want to know? You writing a book? I'll tell you what you'd better do."

174

Sam had already figured it out. She dropped several dollars on the bar and grabbed her bag and Annie's arm.

"That's right. Pay up and clear out," Matilda trumpeted. Her voice followed them out the revolving door. "And don't come back."

Sam softly socked Annie on the side of the head. "Nice going, Sherlock."

Then they collapsed with laughter, Annie leaning against the side of the building.

"That wasn't exactly the most subtle exchange I've ever heard," gasped Sam, wiping her eyes.

"We'll chalk it up as practice. I'm going to get better at this private-eye stuff as we go along."

The Sharder house was small, neat, and old—well kept, though the front porch was sagging. Blue shutters were freshly painted. Smoke curled from a red-brick chimney into the early dark. Low bushes snuggled up close to the front steps.

The aroma of home cooking drifted toward them as they approached the front door. Pot roast for dinner.

John Sharder's white Porsche was parked in the driveway.

"Ready when you are, C.B.," Annie said.

"Okay, this is it." Sam knocked on the front door.

John Sharder opened it, beaming. They had thought there was both safety and advantage in surprising him in his own lair. If he were their man, surely he wouldn't murder them in front of his own mother. But they hadn't figured on his welcoming them with open arms.

"Samantha! How wonderful to see you. Please come in out of the cold."

John looked as if he had just arrived home and removed his jacket and tie. He was still in the trousers of a navy-blue

175

suit and a blue-and-white striped shirt. He smelled of soap. His hair was dark with water and freshly combed.

"Who is it, dear?" Mrs. Sharder caroled from the kitchen. She came into the living room wiping her hands on her flowered apron. She was a tiny, white-haired, pink-cheeked, little old lady with blue eyes and a merry smile. John introduced them.

"How nice of you girls to drop by," Mrs. Sharder said. "Samantha, I've heard so much about you from John. And I follow your writing in the paper. I feel as if I know you."

Annie and Sam exchanged a look. Sam hadn't identified herself when she'd called looking for John. Had Mrs. Sharder guessed who she was? Or was she just as loony tunes as her son?

"I'm so glad you're here in time for dinner," she continued.

"Oh, no, we couldn't possibly."

"Nonsense. Of course you can. I won't take no for an answer. Now, you girls just settle yourselves down here with John for a few minutes while I finish up in the kitchen. It's pot roast, John's favorite," she said, twinkling. "John, give the girls a sip of sherry. I won't be but a minute."

Annie wondered if this little old lady could be the Wolf in disguise. Like Little Red Riding-Hood, were they going to be eaten up?

This certainly could be Grandmamma's cottage. The living-room floor was covered with a highly waxed linoleum patterned in squares of pink, green, and brown, spotted with braided rag rugs. The rocking chair in which Annie sat was draped with a dusty-rose afghan. Sam was sitting on a pale green sofa embossed with flowers. It reminded Annie of hot summer days during her childhood when a similar sofa at her aunt's house had prickled the backs of her skinny, bare legs. Heavy swag curtains at the little windows blossomed with pink and crimson cabbage roses. The room was a little too warm and stuffy.

"It's been such a long time since I've seen you, Samantha," Sharder said, smiling widely at both of them. "Halloween. And it's getting on toward Christmas. That's much too long. We must get together more often."

Annie studied him carefully as he handed them each a beautifully engraved glass half filled with sherry. He seemed perfectly at ease.

"Well, it's not as if we've had much of a chance to talk together," Sam replied warmly. She had decided to just play it on through and see where his fantasies took them.

"I know, I know," he said. "That's my fault. I've been quite negligent and I apologize. I hope you'll forgive me."

For what? Annie wondered. For not tracking her down in the street? Killing her? Smothering her with roses?

"Come and get it, children. Your supper's getting cold," Mrs. Sharder called from inside.

John ushered them into the large, square kitchen and seated them at a round table covered with dishes. There was the roast, gravy, mashed potatoes, green beans, corn, a green salad, a quivering, rosy-red gelatin salad, homemade biscuits, and plum jam.

"And chocolate cake and banana pudding for dessert." Mrs. Sharder beamed.

"This is just lovely." Annie smiled at John's mother. "It's like Sunday dinner back home in Atlanta. But," she wondered, "were you expecting company?"

"Atlanta!" the older woman exclaimed. "How charming. I thought I heard a bit of the South in you." She passed the butter to Annie. "No, I always cook like this. Just can't break the habit of so many years. Even if there are just the three of us."

John looked at his mother sharply, the first negative

emotion either of them had ever seen on his face. His mother felt it too.

"Oh, I'm sorry. I meant the two of us. I always speak as if John's father were with us still."

"He's been dead for twenty years, Mother." John's voice was cold.

"I know, dear. I'm not that dotty." She turned to the two women. "John's father was such a dear man and such a strong personality that I still feel his presence. But I *know* he's gone."

"I'm sorry about Mr. Sharder," Annie said with her best southern manners. "But," she added, "this would be a generous dinner even for three of you."

"Oh, yes, dear. I know. You see, I used to run a boardinghouse back in Kansas. I'd cook two meals a day and make box lunches for ten or fifteen hungry men, mostly farm laborers and railroad men, though sometimes we had a maiden lady schoolteacher or two.

"Lord, I loved those days." Mrs. Sharder's eyes grew wistful with remembrance. "All those people living in my house. Filling up all the nooks and crannies with their lives and their dreams. It was like having the huge family I always wanted."

"I'm an only child," John said, looking down at his plate.

"Yes, he's my darling only angel." Mrs. Sharder beamed at her son. "John was a late blessing in our lives. I wanted a dozen children, but it looked like we weren't even going to have one. John's father and I had given up on little ones. I had my boarders and my flowers, and was resigned to it, when God blessed us with John."

She began lifting their empty plates from the table. Despite their protestations, they had both eaten a helping of everything, plus a bit of both desserts. It was wonderful, comforting food, but they groaned like stuffed Strasbourg geese.

"Speaking of my flowers"—Mrs. Sharder gestured toward a low vase of white mums on the table—"would you girls like to come out to the greenhouse and see them? John, do you mind cleaning up while I show the girls my babies?"

The small greenhouse had the warm, fecund odor of pampered vegetation. Flowers bloomed aggressively with no regard for season. Ruffly orchids pushed their way in among red, pink, and violet cyclamen. Annie caught the unmistakable sweetness of roses. There they were—tall, long-stemmed, white.

"Aren't they pretty?" Mrs. Sharder caught Annie's glance. "They're my favorites. I grow only the white ones. Here." She reached out with a pair of shears. "Let me cut you some."

"No," Annie recoiled, the final scene at Lola's flashing in her imagination.

"You have to excuse my friend." Sam frowned at Annie. "I'd love to have some roses, Mrs. Sharder."

"Oh, I'm sorry." Annie blushed. "I didn't mean to be rude. It's just that white roses remind me of . . . of an old boyfriend. I'm afraid it's not a very pleasant association."

"That's all right, dear. I know what you mean. Flowers are like colors and scents and songs. They're tied to memories, both good and bad. Here"—she looked around the greenhouse and reached toward another plant—"take this spray of cymbidium instead."

She cut a branch of the tiny green orchids before Annie could protest and pressed them into her hand.

Mrs. Sharder continued her tour, chatting on about her flowers and the vegetables she grew year-round. Onions, potatoes, beans, squash, plus herbs to flavor the vegetables before she served them up on her round kitchen table. She talked about how much easier it was to grow things in California than in Kansas, how quickly she had adjusted to her

179

new home when Mr. Sharder had moved them, though she'd been reluctant to leave old friends. And all the time she was patting a plant here, pinching a bud there, pruning and pampering as she talked.

Then she stopped for a moment, suddenly hesitant. There was something she wanted to say, but was afraid to.

"You have to forgive my John." The words came slowly and tears began to well in her eyes.

They stopped and listened to her, somber-faced, stock-still, as if fearful that movement would stay her words.

"He's a loving, well-meaning boy. I hope he hasn't been pestering you too much. Or frightening you. There's really nothing to be frightened of."

They both nodded.

"He's a good boy. A good son. He works hard. He takes good care of me. But he's always had this . . . this"—she searched for the exact words—"*oddness* with women, pretty women."

They both tried to keep their faces expressionless.

Mrs. Sharder shook her head. "Oh, I know. I know what you're thinking. But there really isn't anything wrong with him." She paused and dabbed at her eyes. "He's never hurt anyone. But he stopped somewhere when he was growing up. It's as if he were so enchanted by the land of fairy tales that part of him went there and never came back." Her fingers started to work at the dark soil on a potting table.

"He still believes in fairy tales. In knights. White horses. Shining armor. And, most of all, in chivalry, heroic deeds done for ladies worshiped from afar."

Sam took a sharp breath. It was, eerily enough, exactly how they'd joked about him.

"I don't know exactly what John has said to you," his mother continued. "I'm sure you found him strange. That's why you're here, isn't it?"

180

They both nodded. That certainly was part of it.

"I've taken him to scores of doctors, and they all say he's harmless. And he is. He's never hurt anyone. I'm sure he never will. He'll always be just a little odd. My odd little boy."

Annie was skeptical. She wasn't so sure he was harmless. Also, he couldn't always be his momma's little boy, because Mrs. Sharder was easily pushing seventy. What would happen when she was gone?

But she wasn't going to argue with a little old lady who had welcomed her into her home, fed her a wonderful dinner, and given her orchids.

They drove in silence for about twenty minutes until they were on the Bay Bridge, with the lights of the city before them. That familiar downtown skyline—the Transamerica building standing out like an Egyptian pyramid in a nest of tall cracker boxes.

"So what do you think?" Annie asked.

"I'm not sure. You?"

"I think I believed her. He's crazy, but harmless crazy. I'd like to believe her, anyway."

"Me too. I liked her. And John, too, actually. At least we can have the roses examined and see if they're the same."

"I never thought of that." They drove in silence for a few more moments. "But you know, Sam, that really doesn't tell us anything. If they're different, maybe he simply didn't take the flowers from his mother's garden. And if they're alike—can a lab tell if they're from the same plant?"

"I don't know. Maybe plants have fingerprints, like people."

"Somehow I don't think it's going to be that easy to determine if John Sharder delivers those funeral flowers or not."

But it was. That part of it was. Because while they were sitting at Mrs. Sharder's table eating pot roast with her and her little boy, John, back in the city, South of Market, a young woman named Paula Eisenberg was cooking her last supper.

THIRTY-FIVE

Paula stood, humming to herself, as a duck sputtered in the oven. It was going to be a wonderful meal. She hoped Brad would like it.

She loved to cook. She often thought that if she had to choose between food and sex, food would win. It had a lot more variety and you could buy it whenever you wanted it at the grocery store. But tonight with Brad, maybe she wouldn't have to choose; maybe she could have both.

She'd seen him only a couple of times, if she counted the day she'd met him on the bus. She hugged the memory to her breast, and took it out and looked at it as she had many times in the past few days.

He'd gotten on the bus a couple of stops after she had. He was carrying a box of carpenter's tools. Paula had looked up his tall, lean Levi-covered legs, past a gray sweater, into his smiling blue eyes, and had been unable to tear her glance away until he had passed and taken the seat directly behind her.

He had stared at the back of her head so intently that she had to turn around. They'd chatted, exchanging the kind of conversation that first passes between a man and a woman. It could be a discussion of U.S./Middle Eastern relations or they could just say words "Hamburger, hamburger" over and over. What they were really saying was "I like the way you look."

When she arose at her stop he did too. He continued talking as they got off the bus. They walked for half a block before she asked, "Do you live in this neighborhood?"

"No." He laughed, a little flustered. "But I knew if I didn't get off when you did, I'd maybe never see you again. I didn't want that to happen."

She had laughed, complimented, but a little flustered too.

"Would you like to stop and have a drink?" she asked shyly in front of a neighborhood pub.

He was a cabinetmaker and lived with a vile-tempered, twenty-two-pound cat named Bertram in the Haight, the onetime bastion of the city's flower children. Paula had watched him as he talked. She liked his smile and his long, square-tipped fingers. She was glad he'd gotten on and off her bus.

They'd met for dinner a week later and had drunk enough wine to grow warm and giggly together. Then they'd walked up to the Buena Vista area, which towered above a good portion of the city, and stood on a street corner looking at the twinkling lights of the East Bay. They'd brushed fingertips and then held hands on the walk up. When they arrived at the top Brad had held her head in his hands and brushed his face through her short dark curls.

He'd kissed her softly, his lips like butterflies exploring a dark, secret room.

"That's all we get for now," he'd whispered as he ended the kiss with a big hug. Then they'd run back down the hill to her door, where he'd left her.

Paula had lain awake for an hour that night, open-eyed, with the moonlight pouring across the foot of her bed. She hadn't felt like this in a decade—since high school. When finally she slept she dreamed of white lace curtains floating in the wind and a dark chesnut horse blowing as he cantered riderless down a lane.

And tonight. Tonight she was giddy with anticipation. Tonight she knew they would make love and she'd . . . *Brrrrr.* Her fantasy was interrupted by the ringing of her kitchen timer.

No, it couldn't be. She frowned for a minute, puzzled. If it wasn't the timer . . . Oh, it was the buzzer from the door downstairs.

That was funny. It was only six-thirty. Brad wasn't due yet for another hour. He wouldn't come early, would he? Surely not *that* early. She still had to bathe and get pretty. But she wasn't expecting anyone else.

Brrrr. It rang again.

Paula zipped around the corner into her hallway and had her finger halfway to the buzzer to release the lock of the street-level door when she paused. She remembered the agreement that the four tenants of the building had recently made after a flurry of robberies in the neighborhood. Even though it was a drag, because there was no speaker system, none of them would let anyone in without checking to see who it was.

Leaving her apartment door ajar behind her, she ran down the two flights of stairs.

184

Through the beveled panes of the heavy front door, she could see a man holding a long, white box.

"Hello?" She opened the door.

"Paula Eisenberg?"

"Yes."

"Flowers for you." He pressed the box into her hands.

"For me?" Paula's voice was full of excitement. "Who would send me flowers? Is there a card?"

"Uh, I think so. Probably inside. Could you sign for me, please?" He laid a small clipboard with a delivery receipt atop the box.

Paula looked at him expectantly. She had no pen or pencil.

"Oh, just a minute," he said, slapping his T-shirt pocket. "Damn, I guess the lady at the last delivery kept my pen. Do you have one? If I don't get the receipt signed, I get hell back at the shop."

"Sure," she said. "Come on up."

Paula raced up the stairs, carrying the box. She couldn't wait to open it. Were they roses? From Brad? Who else? God, this man had to be the answer to her mother's prayers.

"Come on in," she said to the deliveryman when they reached her door. He was a few yards behind her.

"Whew!" he exclaimed. "You must be in good shape, running up and down those stairs all the time." He pushed his sandy-blond hair back off his forehead.

"Well, you're not in bad shape," Paula responded, noting his muscular arms and sturdy build.

"Yeah, I work out." He looked around the kitchen Paula had led him into. She put the box down on a yellow-and-white-tiled cabinet. "Smells good in here," he said.

"Yes. Thanks, it's a duck. I'm cooking dinner for a friend." She was struggling with the stiff, green, florist's

185

ribbon that encircled the box. Then she realized he was standing there watching her. Waiting. "Oh, I shouldn't be doing this now. I'm keeping you. I'm sorry, let me find a pen."

"No, that's okay. Here, can I help you with that?" He brushed her body slightly as he took the box away from her.

"There," he said, having deftly loosened the knotted ribbon. He'd pulled it off and held it loosely in one hand.

"Thanks!" Paula could stand the anticipation no longer. She lifted the box's lid. There, cushioned in green tissue, were a dozen long-stemmed white roses.

"Ohhhh," she sighed. "Aren't they lovely!" She had never seen anything so beautiful in her life.

Tucked into the side of the box was a small white envelope.

She fumbled opening it, tearing it a little in her excitement.

Brad, Brad, what a wonderful man.

But, no, what was this? These words weren't Brad's.

You BITCH.

She stared at the letters. Her mouth fell open. Tears were bright in her eyes. What did this mean?

Paula stared down at the roses.

Her eyes were unfocused with shock, so she didn't see it coming. She just felt it, the bright pain encircling her throat. She dropped the hateful card as her hands flew upward. The pain grew tighter, stopping her breath. Her fingertips scrabbled at the pain and then she felt it—the smooth ribbon, its edges cutting into her skin. It was going to leave ugly bruises, she thought.

She struggled to push her fingers under it, under the pain. The room started to move, to buzz with light. Familiar objects, her refrigerator, her stove, where the duck

186

cozily sizzled, were outlined with halos of light. She had to get a handle on what was happening here. Things were out of control.

Control . . . control . . . the word turned around and around in her mind as if it were stuck on a turntable. Who's in control? He is. *He is!* The man with the flowers—choking you to death.

Suddenly she was aware of him behind her. Before there had only been her throat and the ribbon and the pain, the pain that made things flash with strange lights in the growing darkness of her kitchen.

Now he was there, too, cupping her body with his, pressing against her as if he were a lover taking her from behind. The motion of her hips echoed those of love as she tried to shove him away with her body. He pushed back, harder and harder. He pushed his erect penis against her backside.

"That's right, baby. Do it, do it to me," he whispered into her hair. His mouth was hot and wet. "Soft, soft ass," he hissed as he jerked the ribbon tighter.

Paula scratched at her throat again, leaving dark red scratches with her nails. Blood was beginning to well at the edges of the ribbon where it cut into her tender flesh.

Her fingertips were starting to feel numb. Her forearms.

Someone was whispering in her ear.

"Choking you to death . . . to death. You are going to die . . . to die."

The words seemed to echo through a tunnel. Was he saying those words? Were voices talking to one another in her mind?

"NO!" she gasped. A burst of energy coursed through her. She flailed at the man behind her holding her life by a green thread.

"Yeah, fight me, you bitch. You show me. I like that." He ground into her with his pelvis. His mouth was obscene with spit.

In the battle between the blackness and the lights flashing and haloed in her mind, the dark was gaining. Here and there was a pinpoint of light, but it was growing very, very dark.

The last thing she felt before all the lights went out was his tongue, hot and wet, very wet, sliding in and out of her ear.

He grinned. Just as he'd hoped. He cut through the crotch of her jeans with his razor-sharp knife. She was wearing lacy white bikini panties. Pretty. Just like in the movies.

But the white was blotched with red. Was she on her period?

No, he'd cut her. Just a little too deep with his knife.

He carefully slipped out of his jeans and T-shirt, holding them in his rubber-gloved hand. He didn't want to get them stained. Much easier to wash the blood off his body in her shower before he left.

He propped her knees up, her feet flat on the kitchen tiles, as he pushed himself into her. Her legs fell apart and her unconscious body flailed loosely from side to side.

She was wet. He knew she would be. They all were. They all wanted it, just pretended that they didn't. It never occurred to him that blood is just as wet as passion.

He began to laugh as he pumped, and then he could feel the tingling beginning. He moaned aloud. But she was groaning, too, under him.

He pumped faster, faster, watching her face. He wanted to see her smile. Her eyes opened. And then she started to scream.

She was going to ruin it. Bitch. He slapped her hard. Once. Twice. Again. She couldn't stop him now, not now. Blood began to trickle from her nose.

The tingling grew and concentrated and grew, and there

it was. There. There. There. He spurted, staring into her open, screaming mouth.

Why was she still screaming? It was over. Didn't she understand? She had to stop screaming now.

The knife stopped her. It took fifteen or twenty times, but finally she was quiet. They knife made little red roses all over her gauzy white blouse. They were almost pretty, strewn across her breast.

But then, when he slit her blouse open, her chest was a mess. There was no white space left at all.

He would have to turn her over and use her backside.

Carefully this time, so as not to spoil her, he slit her blouse and jeans down the back and peeled them open to her snowy-white flesh.

The Buck knife was very, very sharp. It did good work.

He pulled a comb out of his pants pocket and combed his hair, damp from his shower. Then he checked to make sure he had everything. The gloves. His knife. All of his clothes were back on.

He looked back into the kitchen before he opened the apartment door.

It was a nice job. You could read the letters from here, the letters he had carved so neatly across her back.

He smiled and closed the door behind him.

Fifteen minutes later Brad pushed the downstairs buzzer for the third time. Maybe she was still in the shower.

The possibility that she had stood him up crossed his mind, but he rejected it. He was crazy about her and he knew she liked him too. This was going to be the night.

He clutched the bouquet he had brought Paula tighter in his left hand as he rang the buzzer once more.

Maybe it was broken.

He walked to the corner grocery store to find a pay phone to call her.

The call rang and rang and rang through the silent apartment, where a duck overcooked and grew dry in an unwatched oven.

THIRTY-SIX

Sean called the next morning. "Annie, I just spoke to Samantha." The words were clipped. Uh-oh. She knew he was angry. "Didn't you both promise to stay out of this?"

Annie mumbled an affirmative.

"I don't understand it. Sam should have better sense. And I don't know what *you* think you're doing."

"We told you before. Lola was a friend."

"I don't care if she was your mother!" he exploded. "I just won't have you butting into police business."

Annie decided to ignore that. "Did she tell you we think Sharder's harmless?"

"Harmless, huh?" His voice reeked of sarcasm. "I love your methodology, Annie. I really do. Very scientific police work. Is that how you think we solve crimes, with intuition, on hunches?"

"Maybe . . . sometimes."

There was silence on the other end of the line. Annie could hear him sucking on his pipe.

"Well," he admitted, "there *is* some intuition involved.

190

But it's informed intuition, goddammit, on the part of professionals. Not amateurs muddying the waters, taking chances on getting themselves killed."

"Sean . . . we just . . ."

"You just thought you'd help, right? We don't need your help." Then his voice softened. He sighed heavily. "Well, I hate to even tell you this. It's just going to encourage you. But your seeing Sharder last night did accomplish one thing."

"What?"

"It proved he's not our man."

"See . . ."

"But," he hastened to interrupt her, "not in the way you think—unfortunately. While you were with him in Port Costa, the killer claimed his fifth victim here in the city."

"Oh, God!" The news hit Annie like a slug in the stomach.

"Good news, bad news joke, isn't it? Good news, Sharder couldn't have done it. Bad news, we don't know who the fuck did. And he's still out there." He heard himself. "Excuse my language, Annie. This is really eating at me."

She knew that was a gross understatement of how he really felt about the murders he couldn't stop. But what a gentlemanly homicide detective he was. She used much worse language than that herself on occasion.

Sean continued. This killing was definitely the handiwork of the same maniac. For what it was worth, they were able to pinpoint the time very closely. A neighbor had heard her come in from shopping and then had heard her let somebody in. She hadn't heard him leave. Her boyfriend had arrived about an hour later and had called the police when she didn't answer.

He wouldn't tell her anymore. "You don't want to know.

191

This guy's very sick, a vicious SOB. One of my men tossed his lunch when he saw the body.

"He really is a maniac. I want you to stay away from this, do you understand? You don't want to find this man."

Annie digested what he was saying. Then she asked, "Sean, did you find letters in her apartment? You know, letters from men from the ads, like at Lola's?"

Sean whistled in exasperation. "You're a terrier, aren't you?"

"Well?"

"No, we haven't, not yet. It certainly did occur to us. But we're still examining the apartment. It'll be days before the reports are all in."

"But it won't be that long before you know if there are letters or not. Will you tell me if there are?"

"No."

"But, look, maybe there's a connection. I still have all my letters, and you have Lola's. What if you took all of them and cross-checked them? They all fall within the same period of time, I mean, since the murders have been happening. If Paula has letters, too, maybe he's there. What about the other three? Did they do the personals?"

"Annie, I'm not discussing this with you."

She was silent, waiting him out.

"Look, even if all of the victims and you got a letter from the same man, so what? Haven't you answered more than one ad at a time? There's no law against that. And he didn't, thank God, come after you."

"Yes, but that's because I'm not black." She knew as she spoke that it didn't compute.

"What do you mean? Do you think Paula Eisenberg was black? Or Marcia Cohen or Sondra Weinberg?"

"Oh, my God."

"I thought you would have gotten that before, smart

192

lady. There's a pattern here, all right, but you've just focused on Lola." He didn't tell her about the swastikas and the letter *K* repeated three times that he'd carved on his victims' bodies. No one knew outside the department. And they hadn't found letters in the other apartments. But then, they hadn't especially been looking for them. You didn't know what the hell to look for with a crazy.

"Listen, I would like to see your letters. Bring them down and I'll buy you a drink."

"Does that mean . . ."

"It means nothing. But if we find some matches with yours and Lola's, I'll let you know. And then we can talk about them."

"Are you sure you'll want to? You won't think I'm just butting in?"

"Will she never stop busting my chops?" he asked under his breath. "Why don't you act like a schoolteacher?" he asked her. "Twist your hair up on your head, wear Dr. Scholl's, and keep your nose out of my business."

"Because I'm a writer," she answered him crisply. "Besides, you don't even know what a schoolteacher looks like. You think they all wear habits and are named Sister Rosalie."

Writer. Some writer. She'd better get to it, she thought. The deadline for the outline and first three chapters of the book was growing uncomfortably near. And the stories increasingly crazier. The problem with truth was that it was indeed stranger than fiction and she wasn't sure if her editor was going to buy some of these tales.

Who would believe Powell, for example, the bisexual painter who'd answered her query ad? Who'd had his honeymoon with his lesbian girl friend ruined by a red-tick hound named Harold who was afraid of linoleum.

Annie tossed Powell's interview notes aside. She'd never

get away with this one; her editor had never been to San Francisco.

Nothing was making her happy today. She was worried about the book. Sean was bitching at her about minding her own business. And Lola's murderer was still out there. It was that awful week between Christmas and New Year's when nothing got done and everyone was tentative. And it was raining.

She felt antsy. She hadn't talked with David in months, by choice, but sometimes she wondered if half a loaf wasn't what her hunger needed. The thought of Harry still ached sometimes like a bad tooth. She'd called Tom Albano to say hello, and he'd told her about a nurse he'd met who'd invited him to a New Year's Eve party. He sounded happy and excited. She didn't want to hear it.

What was wrong with her? Just the holiday blahs? Then she tuned into the dull throb in her forehead that was growing sharper and the pain behind her knees. That was the giveaway. It was more than cranky; it was the flu. A reason to retreat.

She checked her cupboard for soup and tea. Ice cream in the freezer. Lemons, tissues. She'd call Sam to bring her a pile of fashion magazines and she'd be set. She could tuck in and take care of herself and let New Year's Eve just slide on by.

A week later she and Sam were celebrating the return of her good health and appetite at the Little Italy with a dinner of spiedini, linguine with fresh clams, and veal and peppers.

"And I had Dungeness crab with Sean at lunch today. I should be ashamed," Annie said.

Sam just stared at her. She had never known Annie to be regretful of a forkful in her entire life.

"So what did my darling have to say?"

"First, he reminded me to mind my own business, but he always does that. I don't take it personally. He said there were no personals letters in Paula Eisenberg's apartment.

"But they did find some correlations between mine and Lola's. Remember the crazy therapist who went on and on about love and food?"

"Right! The hungry one."

"He wrote to Lola too. But he's safely tucked away in Napa State Hospital, where's he's been crazy for all these years.

"The other was Stan Levine, the man who looks like Gene Wilder."

"The one who wanted to take you to the hot tubs?"

"Yes. He has alibis for the nights of all five murders."

"Did Sean say they inquired about all of Lola's letters?"

"Yes. All twelve. Four were from prisoners. That leaves eight. Levine and the Napa loony leave six. The rest all check out, except one who's away on a cruise, which lets him out. And none of them was David. So I guess that's that with our ad theory. No connection."

"So we're back at ground zero. Did Sean say *anything* else?"

"No fingerprints. He must wear gloves. A partial bloody shoeprint from Lola's that matches one from Sondra Weinberg's. They're questioning all the neighbors over and over in hopes that someone will remember something."

"Jesus H. Christ! I can't believe you got all that out of him. What'd you ply him with, eight-year-old cognac at lunch?"

"Nope." Annie grinned. "I promised I'd buy you a copy of the *Kama Sutra*."

Sam laughed at Annie's joke, but later she worried about it. She knew Annie well enough to know that she joked when things were bothering her, and the absence of a man in her life was giving those jokes a hard edge that made Sam feel a little uncomfortable and a little guilty about her happiness with Sean. Something had to break soon.

THIRTY-SEVEN

Annie watched Samantha hurrying away to meet Sean at his apartment.

Annie was going home alone.

Always a bridesmaid, never a bride, she thought.

You're feeling sorry for yourself, Annie. You were too a bride. And you will be again. Someday.

In the meantime, she had tomorrow night to look forward to with her friend Tom, who was always fun.

But maybe not this time. She wondered what was on his mind. They'd planned to try yet another new Chinese place out near Quan's, but he had called and asked if she would mind cooking if he brought wine and dessert.

"I think I need a home-cooked chicken," he'd said. That was about as close as he ever came to saying he needed some mothering, and she was happy to accommodate. She'd certainly cried on his shoulder before.

He'd listened to her on the subjects of Bert and Mario. He'd disapproved of David. Had wanted to punch out Harry.

He was one of the strongest supporters of her writing, had encouraged her in the move from teaching. Of course,

196

she hadn't bothered to tell him of her latest sideline, amateur sleuthing. He knew that Lola had been her friend, and had been shocked and sympathetic at the news of her death. But he knew nothing of Sharder, Port Costa, their nudging Sean for news. If he did, he would have locked her in her apartment and thrown away the key.

Tom arrived right on time, beeping a quick shave-and-a-haircut-six-bits on the downstairs buzzer. As she opened the apartment door, she could hear him pounding up the last flight of stairs. He never used the elevator. It was part of his schizophrenic fitness routine, which consisted of major athleticism tempered by cartons of cigarettes.

His curly head poked around her kitchen door and he wheezed hello as he leaned down to kiss her.

She frowned at him.

"Unless you've stopped smoking I don't want to hear a word about my wheezing," he said. "Besides, is a frown any way to greet a man with a bottle of champagne?"

Annie turned from the sink and really looked at him for the first time.

She was stunned. It was a totally new Tom Albano.

"Holy Thomas Aquinas! You're absolutely gorgeous. Is the champagne to celebrate the union between you and Elizabeth Arden?"

He gave her a bear hug to cover his embarrassment.

"Shut up, Annie."

"No, really." She pulled away to look at him. "What happened?"

Tom turned to rummage in her cabinet for wineglasses, pretending to ignore her.

"Hold still." She stepped back and appraised him. "The beard is gone. The mustache and sideburns are shorter. New glasses! They must have given you a wonderful trade-in for your old ones, especially for the Scotch tape."

Tom pressed a glass of champagne upon her.

"Go ahead, let's hear it all."

"Well, I don't know where to begin. New loafers. Oh, wait, turn around."

He did. She could almost see the grin through the back of his head.

"Your pants fit! And congratulations, you do, indeed, have a perfectly lovely fanny."

They drank to it. Tom continued to grin at her.

"So," she said, "what brought all this on? The nurse's handiwork?"

He nodded. She was surprised. No one else had ever been able to effect any changes in Tom's appearance. A man with a beautiful eye for design who never seemed to look at himself in the mirror. Must be *some* woman.

"I finally gave in, and Sandy and I spent two weeks on this," he gestured. "The new me. I've got suits, too, ties, shirts, sweaters, the whole works."

"Well, Sandy should be very proud of herself. She has excellent taste in more than men."

"She does," he agreed. "In clothes, I mean, but . . . well . . . I'm not seeing her anymore."

Why did that secretly please her?

"I just wasn't the right man. Or she wasn't the right woman. Actually, I think we bored one another once we got through shopping. But," he leaned past her and opened a pot on the stove, "I didn't come over here to bore you too. I came to eat dinner."

"I think I can take a hint."

As she finished in the kitchen, he set the table. The roast chicken, his favorite, was done to perfection. While doing the dishes, they talked about his latest project.

"They really don't care how much money it costs, these electronics people. They've got it to burn." In the plant's recreation area he was doing an Olympic-size pool, four tennis courts, a weight room. "They're all workaholics, never go home. So the company's more than willing to provide a total environment for them. And I'm proud to carry their money to the bank."

She turned with soapy gloves to look at him. It was amazing, the difference. Not that he hadn't always been an attractive man. But those little things. They really did change him.

They settled in the living room with cognac. He lit cigarettes for them both.

"You ever miss teaching, Annie? Ever want to go back?"

She shook her head. "Not that way. I like the classes at State, but when I'm asked I don't say I'm a teacher anymore. Nope, I'm a writer. I get in much more interesting conversations that way, instead of the same old dreary one."

"What do you mean?"

"At parties if you tell people you teach they always want to tell you how horrible the system is, how their kids can't read and write. When *they* haven't seen or spoken to them in the last six months except to yell at them to turn down the television."

"I guess that could get pretty old."

Annie warmed to the subject. "Or they think all teachers are like Kotter—or Diane Keaton."

"Pardon?"

"Diane Keaton. Remember in *The Godfather* when Corleone comes looking for her after she's gone back to teaching? She's in a park with all these little kindergarten kids and Corleone drives up and crooks his finger, and she jumps in his limo and drives off—just leaves those little boogers in the park."

He laughed. "I'd forgotten that."

"The woman has single-handedly ruined the rep of teachers in this country. Let us not forget Mr. Goodbar. Not only is she a slut, but an irresponsible slut. She teaches these special kids, and one day she can't make it to school because she spent the whole night screwing her brains out. So when they flash to her classroom the next day, the little kids are running all around the room, throwing things. There's no substitute teacher, no one."

"And the lesson is?"

"Good teachers have no sex life. Didn't you know that?"

"Well, do you want to spend the rest of the evening writing a letter of protest to Diane Keaton, or would you rather play gin rummy?"

She reached for the cards.

"Good," he said. "I've got to pay for these new threads somehow."

Fat chance. As if she ever intended to pay off her gin debt.

She watched him as they played. She still couldn't get over the change in his appearance. He really did look wonderful.

She picked up her cards, brushing his hand.

What was that?

That was Tom, stupid. Comfortable old Tom. Old-shoe Tom. Sitting on your sofa, beating your fanny at gin rummy, drinking your cognac. As always.

What was she thinking about?

About screwing up one of the best friendships she'd ever had?

"Hey, hey, hey. Where's your mind tonight? I like taking your money, but this is ridiculous."

"Sorry."

She smiled. He smiled back. Their gaze held.

What did that mean?

What was *he* thinking about?

"My mind's on the book. Sorry, I guess I am a little distracted," she said.

"Do I get to read some more tonight?"

"Sure. Let's play a few more hands and give me a chance to get even."

"Honey, we don't have enough years for you to get even."

He leaned over and kissed her on the cheek.

Her face burned.

He never did things like that. Or if he did, they didn't feel like this. Was she crazy, or was he different? And what was she feeling? What was going on here?

Three more hands. Tom poured more cognac for them both. They were drinking a little more than usual.

Annie ginned on the third hand, put down her cards, and yawned. But she wasn't tired. Actually, she was very nervous. Was he bluffing? Was she?

"It's getting late," she said, stretching elaborately. Was she showing him she was sleepy or was she showing off?

"You're right." He watched her long arms, her body in full extension. Then he looked at his watch. "What time is it?"

"It's midnight. Awfully late for you to drive all that way."

What if she had misread this? Was he going to laugh at her? Would it become part of the mythology of their friendship—the night Annie put the make on him?

"Do you want to spend the night?"

"Sure." Tom nodded. He didn't look her in the eye, but stood and headed for the john.

Maybe he thinks I mean for him to sleep on the sofa, she thought as she poured him another cognac. Had he ever done that before? She couldn't remember.

201

He read the chapter she had waiting for him on the coffee table in two minutes flat.

"I love it."

"Do you want to read some more?"

"Not now, Annie." He turned and cupped her face in his hands and looked her straight in the eye. "Right now I want to go to bed with you."

Well, of course. Didn't they do this every night?

She led him by the hand into her bedroom, chattering away about nothing. She started unbuttoning casually, trying to hide her nervousness, still talking all the while.

"Stop," he said, taking her hand away from her blouse. ' And shut up."

Oh, Jesus, this is going to be awful, she thought. I've always loved this man, but he never made my blood sing. He's my friend, not my lover.

For a big man, Tom's touch was like a baby's breath as he gathered her to him.

"Relax," he whispered into her hair. "I know what I'm doing, lady."

"Ladies don't do this." She giggled.

"They most certainly do," he said, slowly running his tongue down the side of her neck.

She felt the long, strong muscles in his shoulders, his back.

He slipped her blouse off her shoulders.

"How do you know they're ladies?"

She unbuckled his belt.

"They leave a tip."

They fell laughing to her bed, half dressed, half drunk.

Tom was right, as he was right about most things. He did, indeed, know what he was doing.

Sometimes when she made love, when it was very, very good, as this was, Annie saw visions. It was as if she had a little videotape machine in her head, flashing pictures.

This time it was a rerun of her dreams. She was running down a hill in a sheer dress, carrying a big, floppy hat. He was beside her, the faceless, big-shouldered man, laughing as they tumbled down, down through the grass. But this time she could see his face. The face of her beloved. She'd known him all along.

Afterward Tom slept soundly, but she was too excited to close her eyes, running and rerunning the lovemaking in her mind. Then the gremlins crept in.

It will be different in the morning. It always is. He'll wake up and wonder what the hell that was all about, if he remembers it at all, and then he'll pull on his clothes and go home.

She kissed his shoulder, savoring the sweetness while she had it. He stirred and rolled over.

"Annie," he murmured, "you're still here."

He gathered her to him, into his warm, snuggly cave in the bed, as if he were trying to squeeze them both into the borders of one cookie cutter. He kissed her fingertips and nose.

"Didn't you know that I've always loved you?" His voice was middle-of-the-night hoarse.

"Yes, but . . ."

"But not this way, right? Well, now you know."

"I'm . . ." She hesitated. Was it stupid to admit it?

"What?"

"I'm scared."

"I know you are. But don't be. Trust me."

With that, he pounced on her and they rolled and giggled and wrestled, eventually falling off the bed. Finally Bunny, on the other side of the wall, got her chance to bang with righteous indignation.

Annie laughed and shushed Tom. It was about time.

THIRTY-EIGHT

Sam frantically punched the story into her terminal. She'd never get used to the thing glowing at her and breaking down. Her old Smith-Corona never failed her, especially at times like this.

Another light flashed—her phone.

"Samantha Storey here. Lunch? Christ, Annie, didn't you read the paper this morning? No, nothing major. Headlines and most of page one, that's all. The real Mt. Diablo killer, that's what. The genuine article. Yes, sure, but I can't talk now. Is it important? Okay, meet me at John's at noon and we'll grab a bite. I'm going to be here all night. Good. Great. In the meantime, Annie, read the paper. It's the all-time Samantha Storey special."

It was big, all right. The headlines screamed at her. Big and grisly, terrifying, shocking, sad. And depressing. Annie slumped onto her elbows on the dining-room table.

The killer's whole story was there. His lonely childhood, his problems in connecting with people, his frustration, and then the release that he found—in rape and murder. The pattern, over and over. Twice convicted and jailed for rape, attempted murder. She looked closely at the photos. She wanted him to look like a monster. He looked like a nerd.

204

These guys never looked the way they did in movies or in nightmares. They didn't breathe fire or sprout bristles out of their noses and ears. They didn't shout in hideous voices or wave machetes. Most of them were quiet, sad, little men. Wimps. Nerds.

Annie threw down the paper in disgust. She hated to think she was becoming an over-thirty law-and-order fanatic. But when it came to violence maybe she was. How many women does a nerd have to rape, ravage, kill, before they throw away the key?

How many women like Lola? She stopped for a minute, picked up the paper again. Was there any connection? She scanned the pages. There was a sidebar quoting Sean, spokesman for the department. The official word was no. No connection. One down, one to go. He was still out there.

Samantha ordered coffee for them both.

"I wonder how many cups I'm going to drink before this story's finished?" she asked Annie, who had pumped her all through lunch for every detail. "But I'm up to here"— she gestured at her brow—"with murder. Your turn. Give me the good news. Tell me a love story."

"I'm not sure that it is good news," Annie said.

"Are you kidding? You sit there looking like Hudson with cream on his whiskers and say this isn't good news?"

"Yeah, but . . ."

"Yeah, but you're scared. We're all scared. So what?"

"God, Sam. You sound more and more like my Aunt Essie every day."

But she told it, from the top. When she finished she added, "He called me this morning from the office. Between meetings, crazy, rushed like he always is. Out of breath."

"What did he say?" Sam raised her voice with the frustration of waiting for Annie to get to the punch line. Heads turned. She blushed.

Annie almost whispered. "He said, 'I know that it seems like a dream today. But it's not. It was real and it is real and I love you.' And then he had to run."

Samantha sighed. "Just like in the movies."

"There's more. An hour later the buzzer rang and it was a delivery boy with . . . Sam! What is it?" Annie started at Sam's sudden gasp.

And then it dawned on her. "Oh, God, I didn't even think about that. Jesus! And they were in a long white box. But it's okay." Annie smiled across the table at Samantha. "They were from Tom, bushels of Peruvian lilies."

They both took a deep breath.

"So why isn't this good news?" Sam asked.

Annie wrinkled her nose. "Why should this time be different from any other, this man different from any other man?"

"He is different. He's Tom. He's not some bozo you flirted with at the post office. He's your friend."

"Yeah. But I never knew him this way before. And it's this way that I always screw up. If I don't get bored in two weeks, he gets bored. Or I get scared or he gets scared. Or I don't like the way he chews. Aaaaargh. Anyway, I always end up alone eating heart sandwiches."

"Your pessimism at the outcome of your romances is only exceeded by your optimism that there will be another one around the next corner."

"Like my mammy always said, 'Men are like streetcars. If you wait long enough, there'll always be another one coming along.'"

"But what about the one who's at your door right this very minute? He's perfectly fine, Annie. Tom is a wonderful man. There's absolutely nothing wrong with him. At least nothing I've ever seen. So why not just enjoy?"

"Because I'm scared."

"Scared that it won't work out or scared that it will?"

"Both."

"It's okay. You're just a little crazy—it's called being happy. You'll get used to it. I've got to run. Now remember that you're going to call Sean to see if there's anything new on the Strangler. He seems to be telling you more than me these days."

They hugged good-bye at the restaurant door. "By the way," Annie added, "I'm going to the flower market in the morning. Going to fill my whole apartment with tulips. Can I get you anything?"

"Sure. Grab me two dozen of anything pretty. And wholesale."

Annie called Sean.

"No, thanks but no thanks, we're doing just fine without you two."

"There's nothing we can do?"

"Well," he hesitated.

"What? Tell me."

"You could take Samantha to the movies for me."

She slammed down the receiver. One of these days she was going to slap that man.

And then she thought about it. She hated to admit that he was right, even a little right. Maybe she and Sam were on to something, and maybe with a lot of luck they'd have found it. But maybe they wouldn't have wanted to when they did.

Was this what having a new/old lover was doing for her? Turning her into a chicken?

She jumped at the ring of the phone. Was it Tom?

No. It was Slim. She'd almost forgotten him.

"Hey, Miss Annie. What's happening, baby?"

How could she forget that snaky dark voice trying to slither into her ear?

"Everything's happening, Slim. Everything's cool."

"Why that's great, baby. Just great." She could hear the drugs on his tongue.

"That's right, I've found a man."

"You getting married?"

"Just might. If I do, I'll send you an invitation to the wedding."

"Right on. You do that, y'hear. You be happy. Just keep on being happy. I'll catch you later."

And then he was gone. How easy that was. She'd done it before. . . . "Sorry, I'd love to, but I've become engaged since the last time I spoke to you. Yes"—meaningful pause—"he *is* a lucky man."

So why hadn't she thought of it before now? Maybe she'd gotten religion. Maybe the lie had to have a kernel of truth in it for her to pull it off. Did this one?

Did it, old jump-the-gun Annie? Out of the gate before the shot has sounded? Why will your heart not be still? Because the man made you feel loved in bed? That's an easy trick. Because he said he loved you? You've heard that before. Because you love him? Yes, you love him. You've always loved him. But *love* him?

She carried Tom's lilies and the phone into her bedroom. He had said something about a meeting with his partner. This late?

Annie, Annie, she caught herself. What are you doing? Already you're making yourself crazy. You are crazy. First you go to bed with an old friend. He calls you the next morning and tells you he loves you. He sends you flowers. And now you're anxious because he hasn't called in eight hours. Nuts, absolutely nuts.

* * *

"Hi, it's me." Tom sounded as if he had smoked two packs of cigarettes since noon. "Can I come over?"

"You're forty minutes away. You have to go to work in the morning. But I'd love to see you."

"I'm not forty minutes away. I jumped in the car as soon as I was finished and just drove. I'd parked when it dawned on me that this might not be cool."

"Where *are* you?"

"A block away, on Fillmore. Outside the liquor store. Shall I bring some Jack Daniel's? Or Southern Comfort?"

Southern Comfort. She'd forgotten how much she loved it.

She ordered the Southern Comfort. "And step on it."

"Consider me there."

Five minutes later she did consider him. There as he untied the little bows of the straps of her thin, white, cotton nightgown, touched with tucks and lace. She'd quickly slipped it over her head after his call. He slipped it off again.

"What about my drink? My Southern Comfort?" she murmured, teasing.

"You're it, dear. My long-legged southern belle." He kissed the tender places behind her knees as he slowly turned her over.

"Do you think it's just sex?"

"Well, it certainly is sex." He laughed. "But if you think I'm simply after your body, I can stop." His tongue was in the spaces where her fingers met.

"No," she said, reaching up for him. "I'll take your word for it." She closed his mouth with hers and mumbled, "Now, hush."

209

When she awoke he was sitting on the edge of her bed, smelling of shaving cream and soap. He was holding her blue mug.

"Ready for some coffee?"

She smiled, stretched, yawned, and reached for his hand. I am going to go blind or get hit by a truck, she thought. God is not going to let me be this happy.

"I've got to go play architect," he said. "And you need to get up, lazybones. Your typewriter is waiting for you."

She glanced at the clock: six-thirty. Why wasn't she tired?

"I'll get to it, when I get back from exercise."

He smiled down at her body, and her eyes followed and then met his. She could read in them the memory of their communion a few hours before. There was that electric message that says: I know you naked. I know your secret places. I remember the things you whispered in my ear.

She had to look away.

"I'm going while I can," he said. "Dinner tonight?"

She nodded.

"I'll be here at seven. Work well."

He was gone.

But he was coming back.

She found a note taped to her coffeepot.

"I've always loved you. I always will."

Now *that's* the way to start a day, she thought. Damned sight better than a garbage truck.

THIRTY-NINE

She bounded through exercise class. Her teacher Mimi raised an eyebrow.

"New vitamins or a new man?"

"Old man. New love." Annie grinned. "Let's have lunch this week and I'll tell you all about him."

Throwing her bright yellow sweat shirt and pants over her pink leotard, she ran across the street to the Marina Safeway. Shopping went a lot faster when she was concentrating on it, rather than on the other customers. Marina Safeway post-Tom, no cruising—would anything ever be the same?

She drove Agatha southward and made a left on Golden Gate, across Market, where bums were still asleep on the sidewalk.

Did bums ever get flowers? Don't think about it. Anybody who can't enjoy the circus because she feels sorry for the elephants shouldn't think about bums on her way to buy tulips. She'd think about Tom, and remember to buy something for Sam and a surprise for Quynh and Hudson. Hudson loved tulips. After pig they were his favorite breakfast food.

The California Flower Market was wholesale, not open to the public. Unless, like Annie, the public had found a friendly dealer named Nick. Every time she went to his shop, one of a number of single-story shops bursting with blooms, he asked her her resale number and wrote something down on her order when she looked at him blankly. He seemed to take as much delight as she did in the mountains of tulips, dahlias, lilacs, and sweetpeas she carried away in her arms.

Today his tulips were seven dollars for ten dozen. Even sharing them with Sam, Quynh, and Hudson, they were enough to fill her entire apartment. Tom would think he'd walked into a bower tonight.

She smiled, remembering him a few years earlier as a grandly foolish Bottom in a little theater production of *Midsummer Night's Dream*. He had talked her into it and she had a two-minute role: Snout and the Wall. They had all become celebrants of the moonlit magic of nosegays, cowslips, and love-in-idleness, that purple flower whose juice made its subject dote madly on the next live creature he or she saw.

Just as Titania wakened from her flowery bed smitten by Bottom, so was she, so was she.

Her reverie was interrupted by a wolf whistle that split the sunny, morning, market air.

Eddie Simms, loading the back of a delivery truck with pink azaleas, turned from his task to look.

Great ass, he thought. Look at that. Even in that jogging suit. He wondered why women wore those sloppy things. But this one clung tightly to the woman's rear.

How old was she? Long blonde hair in a ponytail with a bow. She might be a schoolkid. But then why isn't she in school? Kids don't come down here anyway without their mothers.

Now, if she'd just turn around.

There you go, honey. Turn around and wave at Nick, the

nice man who sells flowers wholesale to all the pretty girls. Turn just a little more.

Wait a minute! he thought. With the sunglasses it was hard to tell, but that tall, skinny body . . .

It was! It was that Tannenbaum bitch from school—from that stupid English class he took to get his PO off his back. That bitch who asked him all those dumb questions, trying to cut him down, trying to embarrass him in front of everybody. Sucking up to that tall nigger kid and that old Jew lady. Like they were something special, with their stupid stories.

He could write her some stories. Stories that would *really* give her a thrill. A bigger thrill than the Halloween story she didn't like.

Was that her? He couldn't be sure; it had been a long time since he'd dropped out. Right after that night he'd spooked her in the parking lot. He'd been real busy since then.

But maybe he could make some time for her. Walk over there and grab those flowers out of her arms. Throw her down on them and do it to her right here, in front of her friend Nick, like she did it to him at school. That would show her.

Look at her, prissing away. Stopping to smell the flowers. He could show her what's what. Sure could. Wouldn't be hard at all.

She likes flowers, doesn't she?

"Holy Christ! Did someone die?" Tom looked around her apartment in amazement.

"For a man who sends posies himself, you have no romance in your soul."

He kissed her forehead. "You're right, my dear. And it could just as well be a wedding as a funeral, couldn't it?"

213

There was that word, wedding.

"We can play with the posies when we get back, but right now let's go eat. I'm starved!"

"What do you want to eat?" He winked at her.

"Calamari salad. Spaghetti with meat sauce."

"I give. Once your mind's on food, there's no fooling around. Soundsa lika we're onna our way to mya relatives inna North Beach."

Once in the elevator, Tom waited patiently for the exterior door to close before he pushed the button so the message would register.

"You're learning," she teased him.

"About your buttons? It's taken me long enough, hasn't it?" As the elevator began its descent, he reached over and touched the panel, extinguishing the elevator light.

It was like falling into a well.

She gasped.

Tom folded his arms around her from behind.

"Relax. I didn't mean to scare you."

He hugged her tight.

"I didn't know you were afraid of the dark."

"I'm not." She turned to kiss him, searching for his face with her mouth. "It's just a funny feeling."

In the lobby they ran into the super, who leered and winked at Annie behind Tom's back.

"Why isn't a nice girl like you . . ." he was always asking.

She made a face at him as the door shut behind her.

"We should have gone through the garage and taken my car so you won't lose your parking place," she said to Tom, ahead of her.

He agreed, and waited for Annie to drive out so he could close the garage door behind her. He slammed it, checking it twice to make sure it was locked.

214

*   *   *

Across the street, leaning against the side of a building in the alleyway, Eddie Simms waited. He had been there for an hour, smoking and watching and waiting.

He hadn't known where she lived, but that was easy enough. She was listed in the phone book. Didn't even use her initials like most single women did. Once he'd found the address her name was by the buzzer outside the front door.

He watched the tall, curly-headed man as he waited for her to drive the old Volkswagen out of the garage. He watched him slam the door and check the lock. As if locks ever kept anybody out.

"Did you make a reservation?" the man asked.

Eddie couldn't hear her reply as the tall man got in on the passenger side and they drove away.

That meant dinner. Plenty of time for him to look around.

The restaurant didn't take reservations and, as usual, was crowded. They waited at the bar.

She played with the stirrer in her Campari and soda.

"Okay," Tom said after a few quiet moments. "What's on your mind?"

"Nothing."

"Yes, something." He kissed her fingertips. "What's wrong? You don't believe it, right?"

Annie nodded her head reluctantly. "Right." She turned on the bar stool to face him. "Look, I'm going to be honest with you about this."

"Good."

He sipped his drink, smiling through his new horn-rims at her. The clothes were different, but he was still the same. Could she be serious about a man who drank Seven and Seven?

"You know, two nights ago this was not exactly what I had in mind," she opened.

"I know."

"What do you mean, you know?"

"I mean, when it comes to men you are sometimes very dumb. Why would I not know that? It's not as if you were head-over-heels in love with me as we headed toward the bedroom. Bed, *that's* what you had in mind."

"Right. I mean, I loved you, but like I've always loved you."

"Like a brother."

"Yes. Sort of. But I thought that the sex would be simple. That it would be a good time had by all. Separate from our friendship. It would be—I'm not explaining this very well."

"I know what you thought. But it didn't turn out that way because there was always more to it than that for me. Because I've always felt both with you—love and in love. I was just waiting for an opening."

"What took you so long?"

"I tried once."

"You mean that time in my old apartment? I was never sure what that meant."

"I know. And I didn't know how to tell you. But it wouldn't have worked then, Annie. I had to wait until I'd finished with Clara. And then I needed some time to get my head straightened out."

"You were taking a chance, mister. I haven't exactly been sitting home alone every night since Bert. I could have gotten married again while you were waiting around."

"But you didn't, did you? I knew you'd get around to me when the time was right."

216

Annie shook her head in wonder. She was such an impatient person. Impatient with everything in life. How could Tom do that? Acting on faith? It was incredible.

"Do the Jesuits teach you that kind of perseverance?"

He laughed and ordered them another round of drinks.

"Maybe. Maybe I've just taken the virtues of patience and faith and applied them to you."

"You've got to know I'm not a good risk."

"Why? Because you're afraid if you commit yourself to someone, the very next guy walking through the door might be Prince Charming? Or are you just afraid you'll get bored?"

She couldn't look him in the eye. How could he know her so well?

"Don't worry about it, babe. I'm not rushing you. You don't have to move out of your apartment or marry me." He paused. "Tonight."

Then she did look at him—straight on, with a question in her eyes.

"No, not tonight, sweetheart. But someday you will. And you can put that in the bank."

"How do you know?"

He grinned. "Because I'm a gambling man. I know me and I know you, and I can figure the odds. Plus I have a winning hand."

"If this is a proposal, it's the funniest proposal I've ever heard."

"Sweetheart, I proposed to you years ago. You were just too busy talking to hear."

By the time they had returned from dinner full of pasta and a little too much wine, Simms was back in the alley smoking. Getting in the building had been easy. Now he had everything he needed to know. Except her schedule, and that was just a matter of time.

217

He waited until he saw the light in her bedroom go on and then off a few minutes later.

He stepped on his peculiar-smelling Picayune and walked toward the bus stop on Fillmore. He liked the plan. It had some funny angles to it. But then she was different, this one. Tannenbaum. Different from the others because he knew her.

And he hated her guts.

Annie flipped on the kitchen light briefly while she fixed a tall glass of ice water for them to share in bed. She glanced through the dining-room window out at the corner, where the man from the blue Victorian was walking his Labrador. There was no reason for her to check the lock on the window itself, the one that led onto the fire escape. She hardly ever did.

Tom was already naked under her white cotton sheets with the dimmer on her bedside lamp turned very low.

"Are you smoking dope?" she asked.

"Not without you, toots. Why?"

"Don't you smell something funny?" She sniffed.

"Nope. But between the asthma and the cigarettes, I'm not the one to ask."

"It's not dope." She was thinking aloud. "But it's something kind of like that. It's something I've smelled before, a long time ago. You know how smells stay with you—like the perfume your mother wore when you were a kid? But I can't put my finger on it."

"What about your nose?"

Annie flicked ice water on his naked chest in response.

"Hey!" He reached for her.

"Wait a minute. I don't know what the smell is. But why is it here?" She sat up in alarm. "Tom, do you think somebody's been here?"

"No," he said, groaning, but getting up. "Let's look and you'll feel better."

They quickly checked the obvious. Her television, typewriter, stereo, money, jewelry, camera were all in place.

Annie headed for the chest of drawers in her bedroom with a funny expression on her face.

She opened the second drawer and closed it with a sigh of relief.

"What was that all about?"

"Don't you remember when I was living in San Jose after I left Bert? And some bozo took off my doorknob with a pipe wrench and stole all my underwear?"

"I always thought you made that story up."

She swatted at him. "It was true. Didn't touch a single other thing, but completely wiped out my lingerie."

"And nothing else?"

"Well, he did something I don't like to think about in my dirty clothes."

Tom laughed.

"Did I double-bolt the door when we left?" she asked. "Was it on when we came back?"

"I don't remember." He grabbed her naked bottom. "Come on, babe. It's nothing. Maybe you're just smelling the butts of my new, low-tar cigarettes."

She sighed and took one last look around.

"Okay. You're right. It's probably nothing. Now," she leered at him, "what was I thinking about before the lights came on?"

As the #22 Fillmore bus threaded its way south from Annie's apartment through rougher and tougher neighborhoods, two men sitting in the back of the bus took one another's measure.

"Honky motherfucker," thought Slim as his cop's cool

eye totted up the evidence. The boots, the greasy Levis, the dirty blond hair, scabbard at his belt. What are you up to, you sucking piece of white trash? he thought and stood up.

"Hey, bro, sit down, man," called the driver from the front. He knew Slim, of course, knew he was an undercover MUNI cop. Cops and robbers—he liked to play the game.

Eddie Simms listened to the driver. He spat in disgust. Bro. Brother. That shit. What did these jigaboos know about brotherhood?

Slim lurched toward Eddie, then caught himself just in time, grabbing for the bar above his head. He got a good look at the tattoos on Eddie's arms.

They glowed bright blue on the white skin, tinged with green by the bleak bus lights above. The four backward 7s in a cross that spelled out hate. The three *K*s. The skull and crossbones further up his arm. Poison. Not just his arms, thought Slim. This *man* is poison.

Yes, this trashy son of a bitch is *sick*. And Dr. Slim has got just the medicine to fix him up. To cure what ails him.

Slim turned for a moment and caught the eye of the driver in the rearview mirror, giving him the high sign. The driver had seen Slim in action before. He laughed and got his foot ready for the brake.

Eddie glared up at Slim. Welfare titsucker, he thought. Nigger bum. Let me get away from him.

Just as Eddie half stood, Slim started making gagging noises. Eddie tried to get out of the way, but Slim, carefully positioned, blocked him.

Slim gagged, he drooled, and then just before Eddie was clear, he wheeled, stuck three fingers down his throat, and vomited full in Eddie's face.

The driver hit the brakes and pumped the back door open and then closed.

220

Slim vanished into the black night, wiping his grinning mouth on his sleeve.

The bus driver raised a right fist into the darkness in silent salute to Slim. Then he revved up the bus again and headed toward Market Street.

In his mirror he saw the white man crouched, his head down, as his own vomit followed Slim's. Everyone else had moved far away, giving him plenty of room.

The driver chuckled to himself. "Spooks sure are pussies these days. Just ain't got no heart for the game."

FORTY

The next day dawned ridiculously gorgeous, even for San Francisco.

"'We're off to see the Wizard,'" Annie crowed through Sam's sun roof as they rolled north across the Golden Gate Bridge.

"Sit down and buckle your seat belt, my friend, unless you want to lose your head," warned Sean.

"I've already lost my head, Mr. Policeman, sir," she answered as she plopped down into Tom's arms. "But you're right. This is a terrible example for Quynh."

Snuggled next to Tom, Quynh and Hudson both looked owlishly at Annie. You wouldn't catch either one of them sticking their heads out of a car.

"God, would you look?" Sam gestured toward the Bay below them. It was dotted with hundreds of sails, white against the deep turquoise water mirroring the clouds in the lapis sky above. Near the St. Francis Yacht Club the yellow, red, and purple of spinnakers billowed as a regatta chased toward Alcatraz.

"An absolute pisser of a day!" Annie exclaimed.

Quynh frowned her disapproval at Annie's choice of words, but broke into giggles when Annie goosed her.

"Come on, sourpuss, lighten up. We're playing hooky, remember? No school today."

No school. No work. Today they were all children on holiday. Their yellow brick road wound past Sausalito, Mill Valley, the foot of Mt. Tam, heading north on up through Marin County.

"What's in the bag, Miss Anne?" Sam asked.

"Maps. Zinfandel, Brie. A little pâté. And the cow guide."

"I understand the food," said Tom. "In case we have a flat and might starve to death. But what's a cow guide?"

"Hudson doesn't eat beef," Quynh said.

"This isn't a cookbook, silly. Look, it's drawings of the cows you see along the road. So you can tell them apart. Herefords, Holsteins, Guernseys, Angus. Wouldn't you rather say, 'Look at the Ayrshires' instead of 'Look at the cows'?"

"I'd rather say 'Look at that beautiful New York steak,'" Tom offered.

"Yuk!" said Quynh.

"Meat and potatoes. That's what I've got on my hands here," said Annie.

"Have you never traveled with this one before?" Sam turned to ask Tom. "We spent an hour on the phone planning our itinerary. I'm talking about redwoods, little towns, the ocean. Annie's talking about lunch."

"That's okay, guys. There's always room for both.

222

Here." She passed bread and cheese and the bottle of wine into the front seat. Quynh sipped on apple juice while Hudson nuzzled her, slobbering a little, ever hopeful of an egg.

"Hey," Sean protested. "You want to get me arrested for an open container?"

"Oh, hush," said Sam. "You know you'll just flash your badge at them and they'll go away, bowing and scraping, 'Yes sir, boss.'"

"Does that go for speeding tickets too?" asked Tom, who had had a fair share in his time.

Sean began to explain the intricacies of professional courtesy in law enforcement. Annie and Sam smiled at one another and leaned back, listening to the men getting to know one another.

They had often talked about bringing their various beaux together. But it never seemed to work. A radiologist and a baker. A rarely employed actor and a gallery owner. These two, however, were getting along just fine.

"Puerto Vallarta," Sam murmured.

"Venice," was Annie's vote.

They had traveled together, had had good times, but also had talked about how much fun trips would be as a foursome.

As they drove past Mt. Tam, the men's conversation turned to the Mt. Diablo case.

"Here's your expert," Sean demurred to Sam.

"Oh, let's don't talk about it today. I want to forget about all that and just enjoy the scenery. It's such a great day to be alive."

A shadow fell across Annie's face. She thought how much Lola would have enjoyed being here.

She said so and added, "We can't forget her. And all those other women. We can't just walk away."

Sean turned and gave her a sharp look. "Nobody's walking away from this, Annie."

She was embarrassed. "I'm sorry. I know you're doing all you can."

"Yes," he agreed, mollified. Then added, "But it's never enough until we stop him. He could be at it right now."

"What?" Quynh asked.

"Nothing, baby," Annie answered.

Quynh shot her a disbelieving look. You couldn't hide horror from a child who had been weaned on it.

Tom had a question too.

"Who are you talking about? The Mt. Diablo killer? Or that strangler?"

"The Strangler," said Annie. "The one in the city. We keep running into dead ends."

"We!" Tom exclaimed. "What do you mean we? What do you have to do with this?"

"You're in for it now, Sherlock," Sam said, then looked out the window, trying to pretend she wasn't there.

And in for it Annie was. Tom wouldn't be put off with excuses and demurrals. He wanted the whole story—and he wanted it right then.

Driving toward the little town of Sonoma, Annie and Sam told it all.

Tom was even less pleased than Sean had been with their snooping.

"Goddammit! I can't believe this. Skulking around. Following people. You're poking your noses into some very serious stuff here, ladies. This man is a murderer. This isn't the amateur hour."

He huffed. "If I'd known, I'd have locked you in your apartment and thrown away the key."

That's exactly what I thought he would do, Annie reminded herself. I was right not to tell him. And, thank God, here they were in Sonoma. A reprieve.

224

Situated at the foot of the wine-rich Valley of the Moon, little Sonoma was rich with history. They poked around for a bit, Sam searching for the ghost of the nineteenth-century fief lord, General Vallejo, whom she fantasized she was related to in a previous life.

Annie led them to a French bakery, a sausage factory, two cheese makers, and a hot dog shop that understood about chili dogs with mustard and onions. Quynh had two and saved a bite for Hudson, slavering in the car. They ended with a stop at an old-fashioned drugstore soda fountain that served up real chocolate malts.

Not bad for a town of six thousand, Annie thought. Might be a pleasant place to retire to. But not today. "On to Nick's Cove!" she announced.

Sam groaned. Nick's meant barbecued oysters and beer.

They took it easy, meandering through the backroads toward the coast. They all ganged up on Annie when she tried for one more detour to the Rouge et Noir cheese factory.

Her cries of "I need to do a story on this place" fell on deaf ears.

It was a lovely drive. The winter rains had kissed the rolling hills. Sheep, goats, and cows munched on grass green as shamrocks. In summer and fall the hills were golden but dry, and fire was a constant worry. But not today.

Today was hill and dale from Petaluma, the chicken capital of the world, to Marshall, a couple of stores and cafés holding on by their toenails to the rocky cliff above the cold blue Pacific. A couple of miles north of Marshall was Nick's, where they would while away the afternoon on a sunny oceanside deck with barbecued oysters, French fries, and beer.

Neither Sean nor Tom had been to Nick's before. It didn't take long for its magic to capture them. Quynh con-

225

sidered the oysters gravely. Hudson, secured by a leash, sat on the railing overlooking the water and dared sea gulls to come his way.

Sam and Annie had been here together and with other men, other times.

Annie was reaching for the catsup when a voice from one of those other times sneaked up behind her.

She turned, and there in the blaze of white that was his smile stood Harry. She hadn't seen him since before he had stood her up for Sam's party. But there he was, smiling as if he had just taken her for a soda yesterday. His arm was thrown casually over the shoulder of a milk-skinned red-head, as casual and studied as the blue cashmere sweater about his neck.

"Hey, author," he boomed.

How long had it been since she'd heard him call her that? Him, whom she'd obsessed over for weeks, months?

He enveloped her in his huge hug and assessed Tom over her shoulder. He murmured into her ear, "Looks like your ship came in."

"Not tied up, but at the dock," she answered.

He released her and there was a flurry of introductions and handshakes. Then, as quickly as the squall of activity had begun, it blew over. Harry and his redhead were on their way, then gone.

Annie was flustered. She couldn't look Tom in the eye. As she leaned toward the catsup, he stopped her hand and raised it to his mouth.

He knew. He remembered about Harry.

"It's okay, sweetie," he said.

He was right. It was okay. Harry was then and Tom was now. She answered him with a kiss.

Quynh rolled her eyes and Hudson yowled at a rude bird.

*　　*　　*

Much later, on the drive back home, with the sun roof snugly shut against the cold evening air, Annie began to sing.

> This is number one, and the fun has just begun,
> Pull me down, roll me over, and do it again.

"Where did you learn that," asked Tom, "in Girl Scout camp?"

"Exactly. My counselor, who was about seventeen, brought it from Pat O'Brien's. She'd been sent to New Orleans to 'get away from a young man,' if you know what I mean. I was about twelve, a little older than Quynh." She smiled down at the sleeping little girl, her cat blissed-out belly up atop her.

By the time the toll taker had reached out his hand at the San Francisco end of the Golden Gate, it was dark, the moon high, and they had learned twenty-seven verses with twenty-seven choruses of "Roll me Over in the Clover."

So had Quynh, who had been faking slumber all along.

Before they fell asleep that night, Tom turned to Annie and asked her once again, "Promise?"

"Promise," she said. "I'm leaving it to the cops. I'm out of it, completely."

Eddie Simms began that same Saturday morning by rolling over and frowning at his alarm. He didn't work on weekends. Why was he awake so early?

Then he remembered. This was the day to begin.

He lay in bed for a few minutes thinking about her face, her ass, idly scratching himself.

How would *Miss* Tannenbaum look as his cock slipped

into her? Would she moan? Would she smile? Gasp with pleasure? Pain? She was his new favorite fantasy. He tightened his grasp on his penis.

And then he remembered last night. And the nigger on the bus.

"Motherfucker!" he cursed in the empty apartment. Rage made his head buzz. He could smell the hot vomit again and he retched.

He stumbled out of bed toward the sink, but there was nothing left in his stomach.

Then he rested, naked, on a kitchen chair for a few minutes before he got up to fill the coffeepot with cold water.

The night before replayed in his mind.

After he got off the bus the bastard had disappeared. Eddie had hailed a taxi and tipped the cabbie to put up with his stink. Once home, he had stripped outside his door and dumped his clothes in the garbage. He'd showered in water as hot as he could stand and then smoked a joint. Slowly—after a little target practice into the bull's-eye he nailed against one wall—he'd calmed down and was able to sleep.

If it hadn't been for her. It was all the bitch's fault.

That was okay. Her time was coming. He'd get her back for this one. He reached for his knife and a honing stone.

FORTY-ONE

There was no better way to spend a Sunday. After the big pot of coffee Tom had made while she was still asleep they devoured bagels, lox, and cream cheese in bed. Then they turned to one another, and it was noon before Tom pulled on his pants to walk over to Fillmore for *The New York Times* and four in the afternoon before they got around to the *Examiner-Chronicle*.

Tom was deep in the sports section, plotting strategy against his father in the basketball betting wars. Annie was reading a competitor's food column with a very critical eye. Tom rubbed absently on her thigh. Then a little higher.

"Come here," he said as he leaned down and started blowing softly on her toes.

"I swear." She laughed as a sudden flush of blood turned her fair skin to rosy red.

The phone rang and rang and rang. Annie and Tom couldn't hear it because the night before, looking forward to a long, lazy, uninterrupted Sunday in bed, she had unplugged it.

To Eddie Simms, on the other end of the line, it rang as if the apartment were empty.

He was just checking. But it didn't really matter where she was this weekend. Her last weekend.

He smiled.

It was weekdays she had to watch out for. That was when he did his best work.

FORTY-TWO

A truck is going to run over me. My teeth are going to fall out. I am going to die, Annie thought. God didn't let you get away clean with this much happiness.

Millie, her agent in New York, had called shortly after she had kissed Tom good-bye and wished him a happy Monday morning. He looked as if he might even have one, a big smirk hovering on his face.

And her Monday? She couldn't believe it. Millie loved the first three chapters and outline of her book, and so did two editors. There might even be the tiniest of bidding wars. But the book was a go!

"I told you this topic was hot!" Millie had said. "We'll do 'Today,' we'll do 'Donahue.'"

Was Millie crazy? She'd only written three chapters and now TV! She had nothing to wear.

Millie had chattered on with the cheerleading and motherly clucking that made her so valuable as an agent and long-distance friend.

"Just go sit at the typewriter," she had signed off. "I'll take you shopping when you get to New York."

Annie couldn't contain herself. She called her parents,

Sam, Tom, Quynh, Angie and Frank. She called almost everyone she'd ever known. By the time she was done her long-distance bill would be bigger than her advance.

When she finished the calls nobody was available to play and she couldn't just stay home. So she took herself downtown and bought something short, black, and slinky. In Magnin's she ran into her writing student, Eve Gold, and flung herself on Eve's bosom with the good news.

Mrs. Gold grabbed her hand and marched her straight into a cab, over to Nob Hill and Fournou's Ovens at the Stanford Court Hotel.

"My friend, the famous author, needs a snack," she said to the waiter. "A bottle of your best champagne and four ounces of Beluga caviar—for now."

Annie was happily drunk by the time she arrived home. A message from Tom awaited her.

"Sorry about this damned meeting tonight. I'd love to be with you. But tomorrow night we'll celebrate. Get dressed up pretty, and be hungry and ready to go at eight."

That was easy. She held up the new, slinky black dress against herself in the mirror.

And then she gave in to the champagne whirlies. It was time for a nap. A well-deserved, very long nap.

"Toot-toot!" The raspy bleats of children's party horns heralded the arrival of the three musketeers at her door. Along with a shower of confetti and a bouquet of balloons.

Sean poured a round of champagne and, after toasts to the book, to friendship, to love, they were ready to step out for the evening.

Almost.

"Not quite so fast there, little lady," Tom said. "Close

your eyes. This is *really* going to be a surpise!" And with that he slipped a blindfold over her eyes.

"Trust me," he said, "you're in good hands."

It was thrilling, this fantasy of abduction, even if she did know she was in the back seat of a sedan with Sean, a policeman, at the wheel. Her other senses heightened, she was aware of her slip of a black satin dress sliding against the leather seat. Samantha's laughter from the front seat was silvery. Tom's after-shave, cigarette smoke, the zing of a breath mint. The tires whooshed on the pavement and she leaned heavily into the hard, woolly warmth of Tom's body.

They drove for maybe ten minutes. Then she heard brakes, the voice of a valet attendant. Hands helped her out. A burst of laughter, a few steps, and they were inside a space crowded with noise and people.

"Surprise!" The blindfold came off and she was awash in the sparkles of revolving ballroom lights.

"I'm your lifeguard. May I help you to your seat?" asked a tall man in red swim trunks and T-shirt.

It was her favorite cabaret—*Beach Blanket Babylon.* She'd seen many versions in its seven-year run, but not this latest: *BBB Goes to the Stars . . . and the Beach!*

She clapped her hands with delight. Tom, Sam, and Sean smiled. It was the right choice for her celebration. With food flown in from New York: Sabrett hot dogs, knishes, egg creams, and the famous Madison Avenue Greenberg's brownies. Who could ask for anything more?

The cabaret was loonier and tunier than ever. It was the quintessential San Francisco show—funny, camp, magical, fantastic. A dancing box of Tide rushed in and kissed the shore. An Academy Awards envelope belted "There's No Business Like Show Business." The headdresses of Cuckoo

Racha, the matchmaker, grew more bangled and bananaed with each costume change as she tried to help the innocent Snow White in her search for Prince Charming.

There were razzmatazz, fancy hoofing, and ridiculous puns that had them pounding on one another with helpless laughter.

In among all the silliness, the lyrics spelled out the show's theme.

Someday he'll come along, the man I love.

On stage, Snow White burst out of her shell, opened her heart, strutted her stuff, and discovered the man she loved in "a very pretty little city without pity" San Francisco, right in her own backyard. Annie's eyes filled with tears.

Her book, her friends, Tom—it was too much. She thought her heart would burst.

FORTY-THREE

Across from Annie's apartment, Eddie Simms watched and waited. He'd been following her routine for three days now. A pile of stubbed-out Picayunes grew at his feet as he watched Annie Tannenbaum come and go, her apartment lights flick on and off.

It had been difficult at first. She had no regular pattern: no nine to five, exercise classes at odd times of the day, her boyfriend in and out and overnight. Eddie's hours at the flower market were three to eleven in the morning. He couldn't afford to miss a day of work.

But then it dawned on him. The one constant in her schedule. Of course. He had known it all along. Her Monday- and Wednesday-night classes. He had dropped out, but she had always been there. He could depend on that.

So it would be a little different from the rest of them, maybe a little harder. But the prize would be worth it.

"And then," Eve Gold was saying, "I add a little allspice, my secret ingredient." She was sharing her recipe for chili with Annie as they walked toward their cars in the parking lot after class.

"Sounds great. I'll have to try it for Tom. He's mad about chili."

"Looks like that's not the only thing he's mad about." Eve beamed at her. "You're simply glowing."

"Does it show that much?"

"My dear, love always shows in a woman's face. Just like pregnancy. Five minutes later, I can tell."

"Five minutes? You under the bed?"

Mrs. Gold waggled a finger at her. "You know what I mean. Anyway, I'm so happy for you. I was beginning to worry."

"About me?"

"Of course about you. A smart, nice-looking girl like you, you should be married."

"Eve, you sound like my Aunt Essie."

"Obviously your Aunt Essie is a smart lady. She knows what's good for you too."

Annie laughed and buttoned her blazer. It was cold out here near the ocean. She should have worn a heavier sweater.

234

"Did it ever occur to you that I might not want to get married again? That I like living alone? Just the other day I read something Katharine Hepburn said about marriage being overrated. Maybe I agree with her."

"Katharine Hepburn is an old lady. Besides, Spencer Tracy was already married."

"That doesn't mean she was wrong."

"Doesn't mean she was right either. And she's a movie star. You're not."

At Eve's car, they continued to talk.

"Take my advice. If this nice man who makes you look so happy asks you to marry him, do it. I look around me in this city. I know what's going on. It's not as if most men I see are even interested in women. You're not going to get an offer every day.

"Now," she reached in her bag for her keys, "you want to go for a drink?"

"I'd love to, but I'm a little tired after last night. Have to get my beauty sleep if I'm going to look pretty for my . . . beau."

"That's the spirit! Maybe next Monday. And," she shot Annie a cautionary look, "you keep thinking about what I said. A hard man is good to find."

Annie laughed. "You mean a good man is hard to find."

Eve Gold winked. "That too, dear, that too."

FORTY-FOUR

Driving home from class, Annie tuned in KFAT, her favorite country and western station. It broadcast from Gilroy, garlic capital of the world.

The DJ was playing one of her all-time top ten—the name of which she could never seem to remember. Nor did she ever get to it in time to tape it. It started like an ordinary C&W song, but broke in the middle with a verse that tried to wrap up the entire C&W experience:

I was drunk the day my ma got out of prison
And I went to pick her up in the rain
Before I got to the station in a pickup truck
She got runned over by a danged old train

One of these days she was going to have to call the station and find out the name of that tune.

She passed Petrini's Market a block from home. What was she going to make Tom for dinner tomorrow night?

Chicken? She'd done that too recently.

Angie's mother's spaghetti sauce? Maybe he wouldn't like it as well as his own mom's. Anyway, she'd need to start it tonight and it was much too late.

She stopped the car in her driveway and got out to unlock and open the garage door.

236

Maybe a rack of lamb. She hadn't done that in ages. With lots of garlic and French rosemary.

She flipped on the light switch beside the garage door and climbed back in the car.

Lamb and broiled tomatoes with fresh basil. Could she find basil this time of year?

She parked Agatha in her spot in the back of the garage and locked her. She'd like to think she could trust her new radio and tape player to the people she shared a garage with, but common sense told her she couldn't be too careful.

Rice? No, buttered noodles. Or roasted potatoes. That would be good. And a green salad.

She pulled the garage door down by its rope on the inside. It crashed with a satisfying *ka-boom* on the concrete floor. She was getting so strong in exercise class. One hand!

Maybe fresh asparagus if she could find it. She'd look for it along with the basil. It would be worth calling around for.

She turned and walked toward the door to the lobby, keys in hand.

And for dessert . . . apples and cheese would be fine. Maybe a Stilton, a double Gloucester. Or even a Gorgonzola.

Suddenly the garage went black.

Profoundly black. It was like the elevator ride when Tom had turned off the light.

The bulb must have blown, she thought. But there were several. Would they all have gone at once? She'd have to find the other switch, the one beside the lobby door. Now how far ahead of her was it? She couldn't see a thing.

Eddie Simms had closed his eyes against the garage light when he'd slipped in after her and crouched behind the first

237

car. Eyes squeezed tight, he'd listened to her park, to her footsteps as she approached the garage door and as she'd walked away. Then he counted to five, reached up, and doused the light. He'd planned it carefully, knew how many steps it would take her. Now he must be quick.

He opened his eyes. Just as he'd planned. He had cat's eyes, and in the dark she was blind.

Goddamn Tony, she said to herself. Why couldn't he replace the light bulbs once in a while? *Before* they blew.

She groped toward the door, bumped into a car, dropped a book.

But what was that sound? The falling book, or was that something else? Before she had time to finish the thought Eddie Simms crooked his left arm around her neck.

"Gotcha," he rasped into her ear.

Her blood stopped. In her mind's eye she saw it, dark red, like a pool of Cabernet, deep and still in a wide-mouthed glass.

Her fear thrummed like a wave across the tension of the ruby-red liquid and then skittered away as it hit the edges.

Visions flashed in milliseconds on the screen inside her head. She saw her ex-husband Bert lifting the back of a pickup truck out of the mud on a lonely back road, his back straining with the force born of necessity.

Herself, one cold night in Atlanta, carrying a friend who had slit her wrists over a love turned sour into the college infirmary at midnight. Carrying her as easily as if she were a bag of groceries.

Then steel replaced the blood in her veins, coiled steel. But she'd have to be patient, to wait until the right time to unleash it. While she waited, time crawled, the black creeping in. The dark of the grave.

238

"Yes, bitch, I've got you now," he whispered in her ear. His voice was the one that desperate men use in the middle of the night on the telephone, to terrify women they can't see. The voice that arouses women from a deep sleep they're afraid to return to.

Eddie tightened his hold on her neck, flexing his biceps. If there had been any light, he could have seen the blue lettering of his tattoos jump above the coiling muscles. He liked that.

The muscles in his groin quickened too. He felt himself jump up against her hips. Not as high as he'd have liked. He had heard her heels tapping against the concrete floor. She was taller than he'd expected. But he'd get her down soon. Down where he wanted her. It was just a matter of time.

He smelled the perfume radiating off the warm neck he cradled in the crook of his arm. And her hair, those masses of blonde hair fresh with shampoo, enveloped him, billowing into his face, creeping into his open mouth as his breathing grew faster, harder.

Where had she heard that voice before? It pinged around the edges of her memory, a pixilated phantom, diving like a mosquito in heavy summer air, drunk on her blood. But just out of reach. She couldn't quite find it with the fingers of her mind to slap it down.

His right hand grasped her skirt and inched it upward. What soft thighs the teacher lady had. Smooth, like the silky slip twisting around them. Twisting up, up, and then, as she strained, trying to push away, he felt the whipcords beneath their downy surface. Long, strong legs he'd love to feel around his body. Well . . . maybe he could. Maybe he

239

could get her to do that, with a little persuasion pointed at her throat.

She felt him against her hips. She thought of Tom, Harry, David, Mario, Bert, but could visualize none of their faces. Faceless lovers, taking her in love from behind. Her mind floated, her heart disconnected when there was no face to stroke and love.

And this, this stranger in the dark, thrusting himself against her. Faceless as the man on a crowded bus who had once hunched and pushed against her and left his nameless, fatherless children wet against the back of her skirt.

Her flesh was warm, soft, smooth as he shoved his fingers inside the elastic of her panties.

He felt her tears sliding down her cheeks and splashing on his arm crooked beneath her chin.

"Don't cry, Miss Tannenbaum," he whispered. "If you're a good little girl I won't hurt you."

That voice. If she could only place that voice. And a smell, the smell of his breath. It was peculiar, but recent, vaguely familiar.

The smell reminded her of something old. Something from her past.

And yet, something to do with Tom. No, Tom didn't smell like this. Was Tom there when she smelled it . . . did he say something about . . .

Yes! She had it. The smell in her apartment. This was it, the same smell, like tobacco, but sweetish, slightly sickly, strange.

It reminded her of New Orleans. Sitting in the Café Du Monde drinking café au lait, eating *beignets*. Jackson Square across the street. Pigeons squawking, wheeling, whirring. But not the smell of pigeons.

She was losing it. New Orleans faded. Everything was fading, dimming. No more pictures in her head. Her mind was almost as black inside as the garage, black and out of focus.

"That's right," the voice whispered. "Just relax. Be a good little girl and lean back against me."

It was so tempting. To just let go. She felt so tired, limp. She had kitten bones.

She felt herself sliding. Slipping farther and farther down, but just before the dark horizon in her head met the pitch black of the garage, an alarm somewhere in her gut sounded.

He'll KILL a good little girl! it rang.

He loosened his hold on her neck as he felt her relax and grabbed her by the shoulders to help her slide down onto the concrete floor. Down, baby, down, yes, I'll take good care of you.

"NO!" she screamed and every muscle and tendon in her body recoiled. She flailed wildly into the darkness and stomped her right heel into the arch of his foot, puncturing it, snapping a small bone.

"You bitch!" he shouted and lunged for her with both hands.

He couldn't see what he had grabbed. Clothes tore beneath his hands as she jerked away. And then she was coming back toward him. Something rushing toward him in the darkness like a bat.

Sharp, hot pain ripped at his face, jabbed at his cheeks, tore his nose. The pain jingled as it bit into him. It was the jingle-jingle, like small bells, of her keys.

He hit her, he didn't know where, but he felt softness

241

and then bone and heard her fall. Good. That was where he wanted her. Down.

There was blood in his mouth. She had hurt him. None of them had ever hurt him before. None. Except Missy. And that was different.

He'd show her. He'd take back his promise not to hurt her. She hadn't been a good little girl.

Why did he think she would be . . . why did he think she'd give him anything?

He had something to give her though. Eddie reached toward his right hip.

If she could just reach the door and get the key in. Maybe she could. Maybe she could reach the light. So she could watch him? Why would she want to do that?

Her right foot wasn't working. Maybe the bones popping hadn't been his. The foot didn't hurt though. Nothing hurt. Not even when he slammed her in the chest. She couldn't feel a thing.

Eddie quickly unsnapped the Buck knife scabbard. He'd had years of practice. He could open the scabbard, draw out his knife, and flip it open in a long, smooth motion, a single stroke that took only one second.

And there it was, Missy Annie, he grinned. Coming at you.

Eddie couldn't see her. But he could hear her breathing. He stabbed into the dark at the sound.

Her scream told him he'd hit home. Quick. Again. Again.

She rolled, and his knife rasped against concrete. But he knew she was still right there. She was screaming.

Suddenly there was a sound behind them, the sound of rolling metal. And headlights. The garage door had

242

opened, and then a car door opened and closed. A click, and the overhead lights flashed on.

"Go ahead and park it, Frank, I'll get the door." Angie's Bronx accent sounded to Annie like the voice of an angel.

Annie looked down at her arm where the knife had pierced. The wound didn't look very deep, wasn't bleeding too badly. But her right ankle was bent at a very strange angle.

"Frank, oh my God, Annie!" Angie was screaming. She was trying to tell Angie that she was okay.

Then Frank's hands were gathering her gently to him, his strong arms lifting her up off the cold, wet concrete floor.

Later, in the hospital, she wasn't able to tell Sean what the man had looked like. She had never seen his face.

Angie and Frank had only seen a blur as he'd flown past them out the open garage door into the dark night.

FORTY-FIVE

Annie doubted that the Queen of England had ever had a more royal convalescence. If she had ever entertained any claim to the title of Jewish American Princess, this was the time to call for her crown. She was only afraid that by the

243

time her ankle and arm healed her teeth would have fallen out, because Sam and Tom and Sean seemed to be using her housebound recuperation as an excuse for the Great Chocolate Tour.

Everyday more of it came, delivered in person or by special messenger.

There was a one-pound block of Kron's dark chocolate with macadamia nuts, packaged in pink tissue paper and a shiny purple bag. Accompanying it was a sterling-silver knife. In a large basket came chocolate and raspberry tartlets, themselves miniature baskets. A Grand Marnier cake from Cocolat, the bakery she passed everyday on the way to exercise class, though not these days. A chocolate hazelnut torte. A regular bake-off of chocolate chip cookies: from the Oakville Market, Mrs. Field's, David's. A chocolate macaroon in the shape, almost, of her own nose from the Polk Street shop Unknown Jerome's. Chocolate almond fudge ice cream. From Tassajara, the Buddhist bakery, came a very holy chocolate macaroon.

The only thing they hadn't sent her was a can of Black Magic—Hershey's chocolate syrup—which *High Times*, the drug magazine for connoisseurs, had once rated the equivalent of Grade AAA Colombian for the chocoholic.

Sam had also sent her an extra-large brown T-shirt that she wore as a bed jacket. It read GIVE ME CHOCOLATE OR GIVE ME DEATH.

She could laugh about it now from the safety of her bed, surrounded by sweet love.

In addition to the gifts and the chocolate, the flow of visitors never stopped. Tom sent Western Onion with a singing telegram of show tunes, along with a pizza. From her class, Cornell brought a pint of Jack Daniel's to tuck under her pillow "for sipping" and Eve Gold appeared with what looked like the entire contents of a New York deli.

244

Hoyt and Emmett arrived with a stack of fashion and design magazines, the *National Enquirer, People,* and a new Dick Francis mystery. Quynh came every day, carrying a wicker basket with beautifully arranged tidbits from Quan's kitchen, or a single perfect orchid.

Tom struggled in one evening with a gigantic rubber tree for her bedroom. She wasn't exactly sure what it meant, but it was a sweet idea. Sam bought into the Peruvian lily and dahlia market as heavily as if she were investing in a new commodity. Sean sent her a hot-pink azalea that looked like it might break into song if she came near it.

She was becoming fairly adept with crutches, considering the fact that her left arm wasn't fully operational. But the knife wound hadn't required a sling. She could maneuver with some difficulty, take herself to the bathroom, make coffee, but in the week since the attack she'd not ventured outside. It was just too much trouble. Besides, with all the help from her friends it was awfully comfortable at home.

No one gave candy or flowers to Eddie Simms as he recuperated from his wounds, deep lacerations in his face and neck, severe bruises on his right foot. The attendant at the clinic where he had his cuts stitched had sighed wearily when he explained he'd been in a fight with his old lady. She'd heard it all a million times before and was not dispensing cookies, tea, or sympathy.

The guys at work just gave him crap.

"Ran into a filly you couldn't handle, huh, Simms? Wouldn't mind tangling with a woman with a little spunk. Hope I'd look better than you, though."

In the emergency room where the ambulance had first taken her, Annie had undergone the standard attack-victim

245

examination. Smears and scrapings were taken, and her clothes secured in plastic bags for the police.

The next day Sean had gone over and over the details with her. But she had little to tell him. The episode had transpired in total darkness. It had taken about four minutes. He'd grabbed her, choked her, fondled her, hit her, stabbed her, and then he was gone. There was a smell that reminded her of New Orleans and a voice that was familiar but that she couldn't place.

Sean wasn't pressing her for more, though he pounced on the voice. But once he'd pushed it as far as he could and still nothing surfaced, he said, "Let it go. Don't worry at it. It'll just come, maybe in a dream."

"God, I hope not. No nightmares, please."

"I wish you nothing but the best."

Dear Sean. He was the gentlest cop in the world. He should have been a doctor with his wonderful bedside manner.

"If it doesn't float up, we could try hypnosis. It frequently does the trick."

"Great. Maybe it could cure my smoking habit at the same time."

Sean laughed. "We'll see. In the meantime, rest, relax, and we'll work on what we've got."

Eddie didn't know how long he was going to have to wait this time. Now, as he watched, the traffic in and out of her apartment was heavier than ever. But he knew where she was—all the time. He'd made sure of that as they struggled in the dark and he'd hurt her.

But she'd hurt him too.

After she'd promised to be nice to him.

That's how it always was. Bitches. Missy. Miss Anne with her nose so high in the air you'd think her shit didn't stink. Well, they'd just see about that.

246

*   *   *

Tom called her every day at noon.

"Hi, darling, how many buildings did you build today?"

"Only six so far. All I've had time for this morning. And how's your day going? How's your ankle?"

"I've done six miles and two hundred push-ups. Quynh's here, with Hudson. A school holiday. She brought me a yummy lunch from Quan."

"Great. Now what have you really been doing?"

"Really I've been reading the book you sent me, *Delta of Venus*. Such naughty stuff. What are you trying to do to a poor crippled lady?"

"Is your mouth broken?" he asked.

"My dear."

"By the way," he continued, "did you get the other package I sent you? It should be there by now."

"No, I don't think so. Nothing's come today."

As if on cue, the downstairs buzzer sounded.

"Oh, wait, babe. That must be it now. Quynh, Quynh," she called. But Quynh was in the bathroom. Hudson stared at her with big, owlish, golden eyes. "Why don't *you* get the door, worthless," she asked him.

Annie put the phone down on her bed and slid to the foot of it, where her crutches were propped against a chair, which she used to pull herself up. In a small miracle of juggling she half crouched, her right leg stuck straight out in front of her, grabbed the crutches and quickly threw them under her arms before she fell on her face.

"I'll be right there," Quynh called.

"It's okay, darling. I've got it." She crept toward the buzzer, which sounded again. "Coming, coming," she muttered.

"Annie Tannenbaum?" the voice asked, tinny through the speaker system.

"Yes," she said.

247

"Flowers," he answered. "I'll bring them right up."

"Great. I'm on the fifth floor." She pushed the button marked DOOR, buzzing him in.

"I know where you are," he said to himself as he opened the door and walked into the lobby carrying the long white box.

"Who is it, Auntie Annie?" Quynh asked as she came out of the bathroom pulling down her Michael Jackson sweat shirt.

"A deliveryman. It's flowers from Tom. He's on the phone. Do you want to say hello to him?"

"Yes! Yes!" Quynh loved Tom, who kidded her, but also let her beat him at gin rummy. She took the phone from Annie's outstretched hand and said hello excitedly. "Tom says he didn't send you flowers. Here, he wants to talk to you."

"No, no flowers today, babe. I sent you something from Saks, something pink and lacy. Must be your other lover."

"Silly, I wonder who . . ."

And then, just as Sean said it might, the voice floated back into her head. The same voice that whispered "Gotcha!" The voice that answered "Flowers." The voice that had been so insolent, so creepy in her class months ago. The voice that belonged to that blond-haired, blue-eyed (cold eyes, eyes you could die from) Eddie Simms. And now he was on his way up, to bring her flowers.

Flowers, flowers, flowers—the word spun around and around. And then she got it.

"Oh my God, Tom," she breathed into the phone as she grabbed Quynh to her, "I've just buzzed the Strangler in."

FORTY-SIX

"Annie, Annie!" Tom shouted, but she didn't answer. She stood, precariously balanced, the receiver in one hand, Quynh's hand grasped in the other, teetering, but, inside, frozen still.

This time he's going to get me, she thought. She felt the pressure of her crutches in her armpits. I can't run. There's nowhere to go. No one can save me this time. He's going to get me, like he got Lola and all the others. There's nowhere for me to hide.

But she had to hide Quynh!

"Quynh." Her voice was calm. "I don't have time to explain this to you, but it is very important that you do what I say. Do you understand?"

The little girl nodded solemnly. "What do you want me to do?"

Annie tried to think. Quickly, she must do it quickly. Quynh was very small. Where could she hide that would be safe? Where she couldn't see what was going to happen here? Annie's mind raced through all the possibilities. Under the bed. In one of the closets.

But what if he had been watching? What if he knew Quynh was here? He'd find her. No, no, he couldn't have Quynh too.

There was no other way out. Only the one door. Quynh could run out and down the hall, use the stairs. If she passed him, he wouldn't know who she was. Unless, unless he had been watching. Then he'd know. There wasn't time for that. There was no escape.

Escape! That was it! Why hadn't she thought of it before?

"I want you to go to the dining room and open the window and go out on the fire escape."

Was it safer to go to the bottom or to the roof?

"When you get to the bottom, you won't be at ground level, but just sit there. Wait and someone will come and get you down." She shoved Quynh with a crutch and whispered, "Now go!"

Quynh flew like a bird. She stopped as she pulled the window down behind her and mouthed "I love you." Then her dark head disappeared.

Quynh was safe. But Annie was still standing in her entry hall, weakly propped upon her crutches. She was dimly aware of Tom's voice floating out from her hand. She looked at the receiver as if it were a foreign object, a machine she had never seen before. A voice came from it, but the voice was of no more aid to her than the tinkling of a music box. The voice couldn't step out of the machine and help her—the voice from the speaker below was going to walk up and kill her. That was the voice that mattered, the voice of Eddie Simms. All the voice on the phone could do was listen to her die.

She let the receiver drop to the floor.

She felt so alone, so helpless, waiting.

This was what it came down to at the end, wasn't it? Funny. All her life she'd been strong, capable of taking care of herself, just as her mother had taught her, and yet when it came down to it, none of that made any difference. Because now, when it counted, she was as helpless as a bird with a broken wing.

She was so afraid. Tears welled in her eyes. I feel like an old woman, she thought. Or a frightened little girl.

But I'm not as small as Quynh. Where can I hide?

Once again the inventory. She couldn't get under the bed. There were four closets, but how could she hide herself with her cast, her right leg sticking straight out?

Perhaps the big trunk in the hall closet. She could pull the afghans over her, and the old clothes, and the baby quilt with cat faces her mother had made for her when she was an infant.

But he would find her, wouldn't he? He'd know she was in there somewhere. And he wouldn't go away. It would just be a matter of time. And could she stifle her screams through the waiting, the listening, as he opened one door after another and waved that shiny knife?

As she stood, staring at her apartment door, her only door, she heard the clunk of the elevator arrive at the fifth floor. It was only a matter of seconds. A short distance, thirty yards, and then he would be standing there.

Brrrrrr. The bell. He had arrived.

He was only six feet away on the other side. She could see his form vaguely through the ripple panes of patterned glass.

He was waiting for her to answer.

Brrrrr.

She stood, frozen. The sound was as mesmerizing as a cobra. She couldn't tear herself away. Even if she could, where would she go?

"Miss Tannenbaum," he called. Such a polite voice, the voice of a florist's deliveryman. So well mannered, as if he were hoping to earn a big tip.

Her mouth opened. Her tongue worked.

"Leave the flowers outside," it said. How clever of your tongue, she thought. Why didn't *you* think of that?

"No, ma'am, I'm sorry. I can't do that. You have to sign for them."

Now what, tongue? What's your next line?

"I can't. I'm sick and can't come to the door. Please just leave them there."

Silence from the other side. But she could see a slight movement. The cobra waved from side to side.

"Open the door." The voice had changed. The polite deliveryman was gone. He was not going to play nice-man games anymore.

Annie raised her left hand to her mouth. The freed crutch clattered to the floor.

Another flicker of movement. The cobra was ready to strike.

"Go away," she breathed in a small voice. She had used that voice with her ex-husband sometimes when his will to win had overpowered hers and she had no resources left. "Please go away."

"You'd like that, wouldn't you, Miss Tannenbaum?" And then he laughed. It was the most obscene sound she had ever heard.

"Say 'Pretty please,' Miss Anne."

Then the voice coarsened.

"Beg."

Two beats passed.

He spit the last word out.

"Bitch."

Then there was silence. She shifted her weight. It was difficult standing with one crutch, leaning on her bad leg. But then, she thought, it really didn't matter if she fell. So what if she hurt herself again? What could she do that he wasn't going to do worse?

Again a flicker against the glass panes. Then a little sound, a little scratching sound. Of something sharp on glass.

Yes, of course. A glass cutter. He was neatly snipping out the pane, the one nearest the dead bolt.

Her head snapped back. The new dead bolt! Tom had installed it after the attack in the garage. You had to have a key to open it, on either side. It could keep him out!

Except, on the inside, just beside the moving glass cutter, the key sat in the lock. In a moment the glass would fall and he would capture the castle.

Move! she willed her legs. Now! Get the key!

She lunged forward and fell against the door.

At the same instant, he shoved in the pane and glass shattered all around her.

His hand drove through the jagged space, feeling for the lock. She stretched up as far as she could. She must get it first. His hand grabbed her arm.

She could see his face through the opening where the pane had been, grinning at her from the other side. He leered at her, his eyes glistening like a madman about to skin a cat.

She stared down at the forearm crushing hers. His skin was alive with blue, tattooed squiggles like the markings of a snake. They meant the same thing, these markings: I am poison, I am death.

I'm going to faint, she thought. His face before her began to spin. He was laughing at her again. Laughing on and on. But her fingers kept working, scrabbling, grasping upward toward the key. And then she had it!

He heard her pull it out, heard her victory, and he roared.

It was a sound she had never heard a human make. There were no words, just a horrendous reverberation in her ears. Like the sound of a voracious furnace, maddened, out of control. Like the cry of Beelzebub.

The roar rushed in and out of her head, attacking all her senses, as he forced her arm back toward him. He was going to pull it through to his side. He was going to win.

253

She watched as if from a far distance as the force and the sound pulled her arm closer and closer to destruction. Darkness and terror whirled all about her.

Suddenly it was as simple as flicking on a switch.

All she had to do was let go.

She opened her fingers and the key fell behind her, safely out of his reach.

He roared again, the sound of his frustration filling her ears.

She didn't want to hear it. She closed her eyes, resting her head on the floor. Then the roaring stopped and he released her arm. She turned her head and looked. His hand had disappeared back through the gaping pane.

She heard his footsteps on the hall carpet, heading away. He was leaving.

She had won.

Her eyes flickered closed, open, closed again. She was so tired, so limp. She felt as if she could sleep right there forever.

But a sound kept disturbing her. A voice. It sounded dim, very far away. A familiar voice. Tom.

Tom! He was still on the other end of the line.

"Annie, goddammit, Annie!" He was sobbing, hysterical.

She crawled over to the receiver, cradled it like a lover to her face.

"I'm okay," she whispered. "He's gone."

On the other end, Tom struggled for speech.

"Are you really, babe?"

"Yes, oh, yes," she crooned, "I'm safe."

"Do you hear the sirens? We called the police on another line. They should be there any second."

She listened. No, not yet.

"And Quynh?" Tom was saying.

She'd forgotten about Quynh! But then she remembered. Quynh was safe. Safely outside.

254

"I'll be there right away," Tom said. "I'm leaving now."
"You don't have to. I promise—he's gone away." Then a small aftershock hit her body. She trembled all over. "Yes, do, do, I need you." She added, "Hurry."

"Get back in bed," Tom ordered. "Sam's been called too. She'll take care of Quynh. We'll take care of everything. Just get back in bed."

Now Annie could hear sirens in the distance. She didn't need them now. She had won.

"You be careful," she admonished Tom. He'd drive eighty up the freeway.

"Right, my love. I'll be careful," and then he laughed. It was so nice to hear him laugh. "You take a little nap while you're waiting for me." And he hung up.

Annie lay on the hardwood floor, her head resting on the corner of a small, pale blue Oriental rug. Shattered glass was sprinkled about. Her crutches were tangled up against the edge of the upside-down wicker basket on which her telephone and answering machine rested.

I can't get up, she thought. I can't make myself do it. Maybe I'll just take my nap right here.

She closed her eyes and began to drift. Once the adrenaline was gone, she felt the way she had once when she had fainted, out of her body, floating along just above it.

Then something soft brushed her face.

She started and looked full into Hudson's golden eyes. He was tickling her cheek with his whiskers.

"Hudsonian P. Pussycat!" She had forgotten he was still there. Where had *he* hidden during all this? He licked her face with his sandpapery tongue. Never had his kitty drool been so welcome. She hugged him to her with her good arm and he howled, but he didn't move except to better situate himself on her chest. Now he was there for the duration.

Over his purring she could hear the sirens draw closer and closer to her building. Any minute they would be here, and some nice man in blue, maybe even Sean, would come in and pick her up and put her back in bed.

Maybe when Samantha came she would make her hot chocolate. Tom would pull her comforter up and draw the curtains, and it would be all cozy inside, with her friends sitting on the edge of her bed laughing and soothing all the bad away, telling her bedtime stories until she fell asleep.

Annie floated, just like Mimi told them to do in her soft voice at the end of each exercise class, when they lay spent on the floor. "Imagine yourself on a white, fluffy cloud floating out over the Bay like a magic carpet, floating to wherever you want to be." Where did she want to be? Somewhere far away from all this for a while. Somewhere with a beach, good food, a scrumptious hotel. In Italy, in Positano, perhaps, at the Hotel Siranuse.

She could start making plans any minute now, after someone put her back to bed. Along with Hudson, who had fallen asleep and was twitching. Dreaming of bacon-and-egg sandwiches, no doubt.

She heard a noise. Ah, that must be the police now. She opened her eyes.

But the noise was coming from the wrong direction, not from down the hall. It was from the other side. She turned her head.

There, crouched on her fire escape, outside her dining room window, holding a long white box in one arm, was Eddie Simms.

He grinned at her.

Oh, no, she mouthed. This isn't really happening. I've fallen asleep here on the floor, and I just have to make myself wake up and he will be gone.

She squeezed her eyes tight, then looked again.

The tip of his silver knife winked at her as he slid it under the bottom of the window frame.

The lock will hold, she thought.

But of course it wasn't locked. Not after Quynh had gone out through it.

The window began to rise and her body went slack. Hudson jumped off her and padded into the bedroom, taking the warm spot on her chest with him. The last breath of hope flew out that open window. It was useless. What difference did it make if it were locked or not? He still had his glass cutter. Or he could just hurl himself through. No matter what, the man was going to kill her.

Look at him. He walked right in the window and across her dining-room table. Right past her typewriter. Well, somebody else would have to write about those cute meetings. She'd never know how it all would have turned out if she'd become a rich and famous author. Because Eddie Simms, jumping off the table and landing like a cat six feet from her, was going to cut off all her words.

He stood and looked down at her.

"I brought you some flowers, Miss Anne." He smiled.

He set the box down on her kitchen cabinet and undid the green-satin ribbon. Off came the lid, and there they were in his hands. The beautiful, long-stemmed white roses.

Beautiful white roses for her bier.

She looked up into his smile, his eyes. Those clear, bottomless, pale blue eyes. The eyes of a madman.

Once again her tongue seemed to work on its own, making no connection with her conscious mind. She heard her voice, honeydripping, revert back to its Atlanta home.

"Would you please put them in some water for me, Eddie?"

"Why, yes, ma'am," he answered in kind. "I'd be more

than happy to." He turned and opened a cabinet, looking for a vase.

"There. Down under the china cabinet behind the table. Open that door," she directed him.

He turned and walked back toward where he'd just come in through the window. Annie reached for the dead-bolt key still lying on the floor near her and held it tightly.

But even if I can reach the lock, she thought, I can't get away from him. I can't walk. And he's not going to gallantly hand me my crutches.

She could hear voices coming down the hall. Hushed male voices and muffled footsteps. But they were too late. They were outside and she was locked in with death.

Couldn't Eddie hear them? She looked back at him. He was standing at the sink, filling the vase with water.

She had to laugh. Her murderer couldn't hear the police standing just outside her door because the water was running.

Eddie'd set the roses down on the cabinet and crouched down with her as she lay, still on the floor.

"What's so funny?" He scowled.

"I'm not laughing at you, Eddie. Isn't it funny, though, that all this time I knew who it was. It was you."

"Did you? Did you know that it was me?" He spoke like a child proud of his accomplishments.

Keep it going. Keep it going, she thought.

"Yes, I knew all the time. You're really famous, you know."

Careful, careful, you don't know where his line is.

"Well, now." He smiled. She could smell the Picayunes on his breath. Had he sat out on her fire escape and had a smoke? She asked him.

"No," he said, "on the roof." *That* was it. He'd just walked up the stairs to the roof when he left her door and on down the fire escape.

"I think you're a very big man, Eddie," she crooned, stroking his face with her empty hand. Her fingers touched the stitches of a wound she'd made with her keys in the garage.

He drew back.

"You hurt me." The voice was petulant.

"I didn't mean to." Oh, shit, it wasn't going to work.

"But you hurt me." He pouted. And then the little-boy voice changed to ice. "Now I'm going to hurt you."

Could he see her heart pounding? About to thud out of her chest?

Now it comes. This is it. How do you like your scared-eyed little girl, Mr. Death?

He straddled her, crushing his weight down on her bruised body. The pain in her right leg was excruciating.

She looked into those gone-gone-long-gone, pale blue eyes, and then all the color in the picture disappeared. Black and white, her whole world dependent on those eyes, suddenly reduced to black and white.

Where were they? All those men in blue? Black and white. Only black and white. Were they standing right outside her door, listening to her die?

"Oh," she moaned.

Eddie put his face right down to hers, murmured, "Yes, yes."

Then he leaned back and the knife flashed before her. It waved, teased, tantalized, come to poppa, little girl, just above her throat.

This is it. Last Chanceville. Now or never. Do or die.

She flung her closed hand back and released it. The bright new brass key flew toward the space where the pane had once been.

Just as the door disappeared. Poof! Vaporized as the good guys rushed in.

It was a magic show. Puff of smoke. First you don't see them, now you do.

Blue steel pointed. Shouts. Heavy boots on hardwood floor.

"Drop it! Now! Let her go! Now, man, now!"

Then in a sleight of hand, she was levitated. Lifted. Floating. But there it was. You could see it. Not such a clever trick, supported from behind as Eddie held her, dragged her back, back into the bedroom, away from the men with the steel-blue guns.

"Shoot, shoot!" she shouted. But Sean, yes, it was Sean, she knew he would come, but what help were he and all his troops standing there watching Eddie drag her with a knife at her throat?

He inched slowly, back, back. In seconds he would be back against the wall, back against the windows. No place to run hide hide run hide there, Mr. Boogey Man. What was going to happen to her then?

Hudson watched it all from his perch atop the bureau. The men in blue frozen, like children playing Statues. Afraid to move, or they'd lose the game. Annie, in a long, white, cotton gown, clutched against the stranger. Close, as if in an embrace, dancing. In little, tiny, sliding steps, and then dancing dancing dancing a jig as Annie's cast caught in a throw rug and the rhythm got all crazy and they started to boogie-boogie, slip and slide, Annie leaning forward, the stranger back, his eyes wild, darting.

Hudson, claws unsheathed, pounced.

Eddie never saw him coming.

But it was enough. Enough to throw him finely, finally, off balance in this world where he'd always been out of kilter, out of synch.

Annie fell forward, face down. Hudson bounced free, frightened, hissing, furious.

260

Eddie fell backward and he flew through the window with the greatest of ease. He soared to freedom, the freedom of darkness, of final forgetfulness and forgiveness five long stories down.

At the bottom, beneath his head, a red, red rose of blood blossomed and then bloomed out of season. And the icy light in those pale blue eyes switched off.

FORTY-SEVEN

They were a jolly threesome sitting at a table outside in the February sunshine. Quynh was washing down a huge slice of chocolate cake with a glass of milk. Sam smiled at Annie, sunning her pale right leg, recently freed from its cast.

"What a day!" Sam exclaimed. It was, indeed. Yet another perfect blue sky, the air crisp and snappy after a couple of days of rain. Sweater weather, wintertime in San Francisco. It was high noon at Enrico's Sidewalk Café in North Beach, the street filled with shoppers carrying Chinese ducks, Italian bread, businessmen with newspapers, mothers corralling their broods.

Sam nodded at the pile of travel folders in front of Annie. "How can you leave all this?"

"I'm not leaving, goose, it's just a well-deserved vacation. A couple of weeks in Italy. Linguine. Calamari. Risotto. Great, gorgeous mushrooms. The beach at

Positano. Maybe a dash down to Sicily. Sure you don't want to join me?"

"It's awfully tempting, my friend, awfully tempting."

Sitting between them, Quynh suddenly gasped. They turned to her. Quynh's eyes were saucer wide, her mouth open.

She was staring with a gaze so intense that its object at the next table, a bald, bearded man in a crew-necked sweater and jeans, turned his head.

"Hello, small wonder," he said to Quynh. The stranger was her hero, the poet Shel Silverstein. Her dream had come true.

"Would you like some chocolate cake?" she offered.

He roared with delight and, with a nod at the two women, scooped up both the cake and Quynh, lifted her and gave her a kiss on the cheek before he plopped her into a chair at his table. Within seconds, Quynh was reciting *her* poetry to him. He smiled and nodded and frowned in all the right places.

"After this, how do you ever convince her that fairy tales don't come true?" Sam asked.

"You don't."

"Then here's to fairy tales." Sam raised her cup of cappuccino. "And to Italy."

"You're coming?"

Sam nodded.

"Can't have my best friend in the whole, wide world going off on an adventure without me, now can I?"

Their laughter floated up into the clear, bright air, circled around the pointed top of the Transamerica Pyramid, and hung a left out over the Bay.